"Now that Princess has dropped her foal, you'll have to start thinking about whose stallion services you are going to use this time. Seven days go by quickly." Rand pushed the journal aside.

"Seven days. What are you talking about?"

"A brood mare should be bred again seven days after her foal is born."

Lindsay stared at Rand. "You can't be serious!"

Rand's blue eyes danced with mischief. "Barefoot and pregnant—that's how you keep them down on the farm," he teased, changing slightly the words of the old song.

Without thinking, Lindsay quickly retorted, "I'd hate to be your wife, if that's the way you think." Her face reddened as she suddenly realized what she had said.

Rand's one eyelid dropped in a flirtatious wink. "I'm in the market, you know."

"Really." She placed the soup and sandwiches in front of him.

"Not interested?" His eyes challenged her to respond. "What a pity."

Not interested? How wrong could he be? Just the thought of being his wife caused a rush of adrenalin to pump through her veins. His face was the first thing she saw every morning when she woke and the last thing she saw before she fell asleep.

RAINBOW IN THE SNOW

Irene Crawford-Siano

A Wings ePress, Inc.

Romance Novel

Wings ePress, Inc.

Edited by: Jeanne Smith
Copy Edited by: Joan Powell
Senior Editor: Jeanne Smith
Executive Editor: Marilyn Kapp
Cover Artist: Richard Stroud

Wings ePress Books
http://www.wings-press.com

Copyright © Irene Crawford-Siano 2015
ISBN 978-1-61309-775-5

Published In the United States Of America

June 2015

Wings ePress Inc.
403 Wallace Court
Richmond, KY 40475

Dedication

To my Mom, Fern, who believed in me.

Prologue

A rainbow in the morning,
A horseman's warning,
A rainbow at night
A horseman's delight.

Lindsay Macaulay watched the wet snow pack against the window of the slow-moving train as her father's version of the little ditty played over and over in her mind. Strange that she could remember the ditty but she couldn't remember Jeff Macaulay or Trailwood, the family's ancestral home in Riverton County.

Now after twenty-six years, Lindsay was going home, her thirteen-year-old son, Lee, asleep on the seat beside her. She and Lee were fortunate this morning to get seats on the only train running north as a mid-January blizzard was bringing traffic to a dead stop all across Southern Ontario.

Lindsay wondered if the horseman's ditty was a warning against Trailwood, the one hundred-acre horse farm that she had recently inherited from her paternal grandfather, Jeb, or would it be a delight?

She didn't remember Trailwood, her horseman father or even the first ten years of her life. She remembered only the pain and the doctors at the Toronto General Hospital who were determined to save her badly injured leg.

Now, during the worst blizzard of the last half-century, she was going home—not because she wanted to, but because the city's juvenile judge had warned her "get this young man away from his so-called friends or next time..."

As the train slowed for its Riverton terminal, Lindsay couldn't help wonder if the ditty was going to prove *a horseman's delight or a horseman's warning?*

One

"Riverton. Riverton, next stop," the conductor droned as a gust of frigid air followed him through the standing-room only passenger car.

Lindsay glanced at her watch. Almost eight o'clock. She supposed she should be thankful they were getting to Riverton at all today as the roads were blocked with drifts as high as some telephone poles. She nudged Lee awake.

"Are we really there?" he asked, slowly stretching his arms above his head, exposing bone-thin wrists that had outgrown the sleeves of his sweater.

"Yes." She handed him the hooded jacket which was lying on the arm of his seat beside him. "Don't forget your backpack." She nodded toward the rack above her seat as she stepped around Lee's outstretched legs and adjusted her scarf, tossing one multi-tasseled end over her shoulder. If the weather was as bad as it appeared from the train window, snow blowing every whichaway, she could easily pull the scarf over her head like a hood.

She stopped when her scarf snagged onto something behind her. She turned. That something was a sheepskin coat with large oblong wooden buttons. Tilting her head back a little, Lindsay caught sight of a firm jaw, a straight nose, wavy cinnamon-colored hair slightly disheveled from travel and a pair of smoky grey-blue eyes that looked into hers.

"Well, hello," a deep voice, slightly laced with laughter, greeted.

Lindsay's breath caught in her throat. "I'm awfully sorry," she apologized. Her fingers suddenly became all thumbs as she tried to unhook the errant tassel from around the wooden button on the man's coat. Then, as if getting tangled up with his coat wasn't bad enough, the train lurched to a stop, pitching Lindsay against a wall of chest.

"You *are* having your difficulties." The man's chuckle was deep, throaty, as he reached to steady her.

"It would certainly seem so." An embarrassed grin spread across Lindsay's face as she glanced up, her own five-foot four inches short by comparison to his six-foot height. As those smoky eyes looked down at her, Lindsay's heart did a somersault. Working as a cashier in a Toronto supermarket, she met many men: old, young, on-the-make, but none with smoky grey eyes that sent a dart of awareness to her toes.

As she untangled the last strand of the tassel from around the wooden button, she silently berated the manufacturers. Why couldn't they have put plain ordinary buttons on the coat?

"Since we have become so entangled, and since we are getting off at the same station," the man said, his mouth curving into a broad smile, "I think it would be a good idea if we introduced ourselves. I'm Rand Dyson."

"Lindsay Macaulay." Then, turning slightly, she added, "And this is my son, Lee."

She concentrated on Lee, wanting a distraction from the disturbing feelings this man evoked, feelings that were more in tune with a teenager than a thirty-six-year-old woman.

When Lindsay was about to reach for her cases from the overhead rack, she found that Rand had already taken them down and they were in the aisle behind her. "Must be full of bricks," he joked, gesturing to the cases.

"Just Mom's precious painting supplies," Lee said. "And they're the light ones."

Moving swiftly, they exited the train, stepping onto the station platform where a gust of wind created a whiteout.

"Station is straight ahead." He nudged her forward.

Lindsay hoped the executor of her grandfather's estate was still waiting at the station. If he wasn't, she had no idea how she and Lee would get to Trailwood. She doubted if Riverton had a taxi service, even in good weather.

Her head bent, her chin tucked deep in the folds of her scarf, Lindsay labored against the whipping wind and snow. She moved ahead of Lee to open the station door as both of his hands were gripping the luggage.

The station waiting room was empty. "Do you think Honeyborne forgot we were coming today?" Lee put Lindsay's thoughts into words.

"Asher Honeyborne?" Snowflakes fluttered to the floor as Rand combed his fingers through his hair. "If I know Asher, he's probably toasting his toes in front of his fireplace. That man loves his comfort."

Lindsay turned toward the door as the sound of a motor vibrated through the old station. Then, amidst a blast of cold air, a man who looked more like he was from outer space than from Riverton, entered the station, stomping the snow from his boots. Even after he took off his helmet, all Lindsay could see were a pair of dark eyes, the tip of a rosy nose and a pair of thin lips, as the rest of the man's face was covered by a knitted balaclava.

Lindsay heaved a sigh of relief. Asher Honeyborne had arrived, but her relief vanished a moment later when the man said, "I'm sorry I'm late, Rand. The pickup got stuck in the snow and I had to go back for the snowmobile." Before handing Rand the spare helmet he carried under his arm, he pulled off his balaclava, exposing a weathered angular face, a dominant nose with a slight hump and a stubbled chin that needed a shave.

Rand acknowledged the explanation with a nod. Turning to Lindsay and Lee, he introduced the snowmobiler as Art Winston. "And these two are Jeb Macaulay's kin, his granddaughter, Lindsay, and his great-grandson, Lee."

"You certainly picked a stormy day for a visit," Winston said as he pulled his balaclava back on.

"Oh, we didn't come for a visit, Mr. Winston," Lee informed him. "We came to stay."

Rand, who already had his hand on the door handle, turned back and looked over his shoulder at Lindsay.

"Welcome to the country, City Lady." Then he was gone, Art Winston at his heels.

Lindsay acknowledged his welcome with a nod of her head and a "thank you." Then, loosening the scarf from around her auburn hair, she joined Lee by the thermostat controlled steam radiator which crackled and groaned at the onslaught of cold air. Seeing a wall telephone in the corner of the waiting room of the old station, she rummaged in her purse for coins and the telephone number of the missing Mr. Honeyborne. Oh, how she wished she had one of those modern cell phones. As she dialed Honeyborne's number, she recalled that in his last letter he had said that he had a good offer for the property. Lindsay had never met Honeyborne, although they had corresponded and talked several times on the telephone. He hadn't encouraged her to come to Riverton, nor, she had to admit, had he tried to discourage her. Her decision was made solely on the juvenile court judge's advice.

Lindsay let the telephone ring several times but there was no answer. If the storm had downed the wires, there would not have been a dial tone, so where was Honeyborne? He couldn't have forgotten he was supposed to meet their train.

"We might have to spend the night here," she told Lee.

"Without food?" he groaned. Although he was reed-thin, Lee ate enough for three kids. Morning snacks of potato chips, afternoon snacks of donuts and nightly snacks of pizzas, everything fattening and not an extra pound, while she had to watch everything she ate just to keep her weight close to one hundred and twenty pounds.

"I have a chocolate bar in my purse."

Lee had almost finished the bar when he sheepishly asked if she wanted a piece. She shook her head.

Lindsay was worried. No one knew where they were. She hadn't told anyone where she was going except her best friend Bonnie, her next-door neighbors Paul and Julia Martin and her boss at the supermarket. She didn't wanted any of Lee's so-called friends to find out where they were in case they wanted to ensnare him again into something illegal. And she made Lee solemnly promise to say nothing to anyone. She hadn't even written her mother that they were moving.

Lee's day in juvenile court had badly scared him, so moving to a farm in the country was a welcome adventure, especially if the farm had animals. Lee always wanted a dog. He also liked to play basketball. He hoped there was a gym nearby.

Lee had occupied his time on the train with his pocket-size Rubic's cube, an addictive puzzle that was all the rage. Made up of colors and moveable squares, it challenged the brain. The object was, by twisting and turning the miniature squares, to rotate each side in exactly the correct way so that each side would be one solid color. Although it sounded simple, it was very hard to do.

Restless, Lindsay moved to the station window and with her finger nail scratched a peephole in the frosted pane. Every minute seemed like an hour. She glanced at her watch. Suddenly, she heard the sound of a motor. Apparently Lee heard it too as he jumped to his feet. Asher Honeyborne hadn't forgotten them.

Two men, covered in snow, stomped into the station. Despite the helmet, the goggles, the snowsuits, Lindsay recognized Rand Dyson. Art Winston was right behind him. Both men had an extra helmet tucked under his arm.

Lindsay fought to hold back her laughter as she again recalled the words of the headless horseman... "as he came riding...riding...his head tucked under his arm." The laughter got caught in her throat as her eyes met Rand Dyson's. She got the distinct feeling that he was here, not because he wanted to be, but because he was a good 'help your neighbor' person.

"Boy, are we glad to see you!" Lee shook each man's hand. "We thought we were going to be stuck here all night, didn't we, Mom?"

"It's a bad night out there," Art Winston said, handing Lee the helmet he had under his arm. "We came back as quickly as we could."

"Wow!" Lee exclaimed, buckling the helmet strap under his chin. "We're going to ride on a snowmobile. Isn't that great, Mom?"

Although she had seen a few television programs showing people racing up and down hills on their snowmobiles, Lindsay had never had any desire to ride on one. Now it wasn't an option.

"Put this on." Rand Dyson handed her the spare helmet he carried under his arm. "And take off that scarf."

Before she could respond, he was unwinding it from around her neck. Seeing the flash of temper in her eyes, he modified his tone, "Anything loose can get caught in the suspension system of the snowmobile."

As she rammed the scarf into her purse, Lindsay was darned if she was going to ask him what a suspension system was. In fact, she wasn't going to ask him anything, but she was interested in what was causing the warring emotions in his eyes.

"You were right about Asher Honeyborne." Rand's tone softened considerably as he tightened the helmet strap under her chin. "He was coming for you...and he did get your food and supplies as he promised." At her questioning look, he added, "We stopped at your grandfather's place. Asher was stuck in the driveway."

"Did you just leave him there?" Lindsay brown eyes focused on Rand's granite ones.

"Of course not!" Rand snapped. "We waited until another team came to take him home."

"That's why we were so long, Ms. Macaulay," Art Williams added. "And Rand wanted to check your house, make sure the heat was turned on before we came to pick you up."

Feeling like a chastised kid, Lindsay managed a meek, "Thank you."

Ignoring her thank you, Rand told her that snowmobilers usually traveled in twos. "It's safer, something like the buddy system in swimming. If one gets in trouble, the other can go for help."

While he was explaining the snowmobiler's code to Lindsay, Art Winston was telling Lee that Riverton had a club for people who owned snowmobiles and loved snowmobiling.

"In emergency situations, like today's storm, they rescue people stuck in their cars on the highway, pick up prescriptions, take people needing emergency care to the hospital...suddenly a series of shadowy memories flashed across Lindsay's mind — *a little girl, a pickup truck, ear-piercing screams, an ambulance with wings, pain*...and through the shadows, Lindsay heard Lee's voice. "And pick up people from railroad stations."

It was clear that this was turning into a real adventure, but Lindsay knew the ride wouldn't be pleasant for her. Her "bad" leg reacted adversely to the cold, and with only her slacks, pantyhose and ankle-high boots to protect it, it was sure to cramp.

"Come on, the storm is getting worse." Rand took her arm, urging her toward the door. As he opened it, the force of the wind knocked them back a step.

To Lindsay, the snowmobiles parked in front of the station door looked more like something astronauts used on the moon than something people could use in a storm.

Rand held her arm while she straddled the seat. After he was settled in front, he half-turned to face her. "Put your arms around my waist...and keep your feet on that little ledge," he shouted above the roar of the motor.

Reluctantly, she did as instructed. Rand pulled her arms a little higher so the sleeves of his snowmobile suit covered her hands and lower arms, protecting them from the cold that cut through her coat and gloves.

"Ready?"

"Yes." She clutched him tighter as he revved the motor.

"Hang on. We're in for a helluva ride." They roared off through the blinding blizzard. Art Winston and Lee followed close behind them, their snowmobile towing a sled with Lindsay's and Lee's luggage aboard.

The snowmobiles sped around drifts, over drifts, between drifts. Sometimes, Lindsay wondered how Rand could see where they were going, because the blowing snow limited their visibility to twenty meters and sometimes ten or less.

The muscles in Lindsay's left leg began to cramp and she gritted her teeth to keep from crying out with the pain. She knew she had to focus on something beside the pain and the cold. And it was cold! Canada's thermometer outside the railroad station had read ten below zero.

Lindsay tried to focus on Lee. She knew he was enjoying this. He loved speed and excitement and this ride was so different from anything else so far in his young life.

Before leaving the city, Lindsay had prepared herself for the loneliness of living on a farm. She hoped that her hobby of porcelain painting would fill the hours not taken up with farm work, but she hadn't prepared herself for this world of cold and blowing snow—and pain.

"We're almost there," Rand hollered over his shoulder as he eased the snowmobile around another drift. Only it wasn't a drift. It was Asher Honeyborne's snow-covered jeep.

Just beyond a stand of tall pine trees, Lindsay saw lights—yellow peepholes in the face of the storm.

Rand cut the motor and in one fluid motion was off the machine, holding out his hand to her. As Lindsay turned, bringing her right leg over the seat, she glimpsed the outline of a frame house with a closed-in wraparound verandah. As she tried to stand, her left leg refused to bear her weight. She pitched forward. Rand caught her before she went right down. Then, swinging her up into his arms, he strode toward the steps of the verandah. Still holding her, he opened the door, strode through the verandah into the kitchen and set her on the nearest chair.

"What happened out there?" Removing his helmet, goggles and gloves, he hunkered down in front of her. "Get a cramp in your leg?"

Lindsay nodded. She had no intention of telling Rand Dyson or anyone else in Riverton about her leg. It was her problem. But, oh God, how it hurt!

Lee, however, was not so closemouthed. "Leg giving you hell again, Mom?" Carrying his backpack and a suitcase, he had followed Lindsay and Rand into the kitchen.

"Lee!" Lindsay wasn't sure whether her protest was against his language or the fact that he had revealed the problems with her leg.

Squatting there in front of her, Rand's grey-blue eyes met hers. "This has happened before," he said as he removed her boot.

"A few times."

"A lot of times," Lee corrected. Though they argued and said cross words to each other, Lee was very protective of Lindsay. She was his friend as well as his mother. They relied on each other. Cried with each other. "Ever since that accident..."

"Lee! Would you *please* open the door for Mr. Winston?" Lindsay could hear the man stomping snow off his feet, so she knew was carrying the rest of their luggage into the house.

Usually when Lindsay said "Lee" in that tone, he obeyed. Tonight he had an audience.

And he wanted to show off a bit. "Remember, the other night when you came to meet me at the gym at the Y, your leg cramped and I grabbed you..."

"Lee!" This time her sharp tone did stop him.

Much to Lindsay's chagrin, Rand removed her boot, pushed up her pant leg and began to massage the knotted muscles in the calf of her leg. She tried to push him away, but he just ignored her and went right on kneading her leg. Although the massage helped, Lindsay didn't want him to see the scars, which she was sure were visible through her panty hose.

"What kind of accident?"

"It was a long time ago," Lindsay hedged.

"Judging from these scars, it must have been a very serious accident." She knew he could feel the scar ridges around her leg, from her knee to her ankle. "Why are you so reluctant to talk about it?" When she didn't answer, he looked up. "How long?" Their eyes met. Held.

"Twenty-six years ago." Her voice, like her eyes, wavered.

"Mom had surgery again about six years ago." Lee filled in some of the blanks in the conversation. "The doctors were able to use some new type of technology. Now she doesn't limp, at least not much."

If Lindsay was expecting pity, she didn't get it from Rand. Neither did she get any platitudes. He just continued massaging her leg. "We could have stopped at my house, I suppose. It's across the road and a bit closer to the station, but I thought you would want to spend your first night in your own home."

"And he knew I wanted to check on the mares," Art Winston added. He told Lindsay that he had been looking after the Trailwood's two remaining mares ever since Old Jeb had died and even before that.

Turning to Lee, Art asked, "Do you want to go to the barn with me?" He added that because of the storm he hadn't fed the horses; they would be wondering what had happened to him. Lee didn't need a second invitation. To the boy who had never been on a farm or around animals except on school field trips, this was new and exciting.

Bending forward, a few strands of her sandy-brown hair falling about her face, Lindsay tried to stay Rand's massaging hand. "My leg is better now."

Glancing up, he teased, "Don't you like a man kneeling at your feet?" If Lindsay was surprised by his teasing tone, Rand looked just as surprised, as he rarely teased.

"To tell the truth, I've never had a man kneel at my feet." Lindsay admitted, a slight nuance in her voice as a warm flush crept into her cheeks. Oh, why couldn't she have suavely said that dozens of men had knelt at her feet? But that wouldn't have been true. And honesty was the one thing she treasured above all else.

Rand gave her leg a little pat as he stood. Although he hadn't taken off his snowmobile suit, he had unzipped it, revealing a blue cashmere sweater that would have cost Lindsay a month's wage. He stretched out his hand. Lindsay accepted it and stood, testing her leg before taking a hesitant step. It held.

Slowly, she moved about the kitchen, limping. She knew that it would be a few minutes before she would be able to walk normally. She turned, expecting to see sympathy or pity in his eyes. Neither was there. In fact he had turned away and wasn't even looking at her. He was opening a long narrow cupboard door near the kitchen entrance.

Surprised, she asked, "What are you looking for?"

"A mop." He grinned sheepishly. "We didn't take off our boots."

Lindsay glanced down at the floor. Puddles of melted snow dotted the faded linoleum. Flustered, she moved out of the way as he took an old string mop and swished it across the floor.

He had just finished when an excited Lee burst in. "Guess what, Mom? I helped Art feed the horses."

"Mr. Honeyborne didn't tell me the horses were stabled here. I thought..."

"There seem to be a lot of things Asher Honeyborne didn't tell you," Rand said. "When your grandfather died, Honeyborne asked Art to continue to look after the mares until they could be sold...or you arrived."

"That's not all, Mom, one of the mares is going to have a baby, "Lee informed her excitedly. "Any day now!"

"A foal, not a baby," Art corrected.

Lindsay's mouth dropped open. My God, what had she got them into! But before she could exclaim, Art Winston laughed. "The birth is not that imminent, Miss Macaulay. In a month or there about."

Seeing the astounded look on Lindsay's face, Rand joked, "Don't worry, Miss Macaulay, Art's never lost an owner yet."

"That's comforting." Lindsay managed a half-hearted smile. "And please call me Lindsay." As the two men prepared to leave, she extended her hand to Art and then to Rand. "Thank you both for coming to our rescue."

"Our pleasure." Rand's hand firmly gripped hers. "I put my cell phone number on that pad beside your telephone. Art's number is there too. If you need either of us, just call."

As Lindsay followed them to the door, Rand suddenly turned. His lips touched her cheek. "Take care, City-Lady."

And his words wrapped around her like a pair of invisible arms.

Two

Lindsay was awakened the next morning by the wind brushing the limbs of a giant pine back and forth against the bedroom window. Disorientated for a moment, she stared about the room. The unfamiliar walls were papered in a faded sprawling rose design with tiny spinach-colored leaves around the large clusters of flowers. A white embroidered scarf, sand-colored by time, covered the top of the walnut dresser. Despite the fact everything was from a different era, the room had an appealing ambiance.

The scuffing of the evergreen limbs against the panes drew her attention back to the window where a pair of cotton curtains drooped from a cord across the top of the window frame. In their city apartment, the shades were always drawn. Lindsay couldn't remember ever having slept in a room where the windows weren't totally covered at night. She felt naked, exposed, but this was the country. Besides, her nearest neighbor was a half mile away.

Rand Dyson. A smile curved through her mind as she thought about him. And he was something to think about. His cloud grey eyes were different than any eyes she had ever seen. Not just a different color but different in depth. She had the feeling they could look right into her soul, entrap her, if they wished. And would she really mind being entrapped by him? She wasn't sure, but she thought not.

Last night she had taken little time to inspect the house. She was tired; her leg ached and, of course, Lee was hungry. While he was inspecting the parlor cum-family-room, where a wall unit with a TV, CD player and shelves of books rested against one wall while two arm chairs had their backs to the window, Lindsay heated a can of mushroom soup from their well-stocked pantry and made both a ham sandwich. Their first meal at Trailwood finished with a glass of milk from a three-liter bag. Lindsay found in the refrigerator. Afterward, she and Lee had taken a quick tour of the house.

Honeyborne had written Lindsay that he had paid a neighbor woman to give the old house a cleaning prior to their arrival. The woman had done a good job, but the house needed a good airing. Last night Lindsay had chosen this bedroom at the top of the stairs, simply because she was so tired she couldn't go any farther. Lee had taken the smaller room across the hall.

Savoring a few unhurried moments, Lindsay wondered who else had slept in this old fashioned sleigh-back bed. It was certainly big enough for two. She doubted it had been her mother and father's room. The charm of its rolled-back head board would have been lost on her mother, Maria, who had an aversion to anything that wasn't new and perfect...like a gimpy leg.

Lindsay's thoughts regressed to graduation night—a special time in her fourteen-year-old life. She would be going to high school next year and she had asked her mother for a new pair of shoes to wear with her graduation dress. Instead of a pair of low-heeled pumps that she needed, Maria had bought a pair of higher-heeled sandals. "We can share them," she had said; their foot size was the same, but the higher heels made Lindsay's leg ache, made her limp more noticeable.

When Lindsay's date arrived, she was wearing her old shoes. Maria saw them. She was furious! How dare Lindsay go to graduation in those old things when she had sacrificed her disco night-out money to buy them for her. "You ungrateful brat," she screamed, and that was just the beginning of the tirade.

"Mom, the sandals make my leg hurt." She tried to explain but Maria just kept screaming. "Well, what do you expect? You're a damn cripple!" Maria's voice shook with rage. "You'll always be a cripple. No one is ever going to want you!"

Her date did. He took her to the graduation. He stayed by her side all evening. He took her home in a taxi. He kissed her on the cheek. He never called again.

That was the past. This was now. Lindsay pushed back the bed covers. Then, taking a deep breath, she began her morning exercise ritual: arms up, arms behind her head, body stretched, legs apart, pelvis raised, heels dug into the mattress, toes pointed downward, leg lifted, stretched, lowered, stretched, lifted and the whole process repeated again and again.

Ten minutes later, as Lindsay got out of bed, she found that the room wasn't nearly as cold as she expected. The furnace evidently worked well. The executor had told her in one of his letters that it was about five years old.

"Hey, Mom, you awake?" Lee called.

"Yes, I'm awake." She shrugged into her housecoat and headed for the bathroom tucked under the stairs on the main floor.

By the time Lindsay got to the kitchen, Lee already had two slices of bread in the old toaster and a jar of jam and another of peanut butter on the table. "I see you're having your usual breakfast," she said, pleased to see that he was temporarily adjusting to their new home.

Since there was no coffee maker anywhere to be seen, Lindsay decided she would have to make her morning "fix" in an old blue enamel pot she found on a shelf over the fridge. When Lee saw it, he chuckled. "Do you think that pot came out of Noah's ark?"

"I wouldn't be surprised, but some antique dealer would probably pay handsomely for it."

"There's a newer one in the pantry. I saw it when I found the toaster."

"Now you tell me."

"You didn't ask," he said with a grin.

"The fridge and stove are fairly new too." She continued to look around the kitchen. Although the hanging lamp above a big oak table was from another era, it had been converted from oil to electricity.

"Mom, there's a washer and dryer in the pantry—I guess it's a pantry...they're newer too," Lee said as he poured himself another glass of milk. He was familiar with washers and dryers as he often did their laundry back at the apartment.

While she waited for her coffee to boil, she peeked in the cupboard drawers of an oak cabinet which shared a wall with the fridge and stove. Tea towels, oven mitts, dish cloths, table cloths yellowed with age, were just waiting for someone to use them.

The kitchen was almost as big as their two-bedroom apartment in the city. More windows, sunlight filtering through every pane. That's when she noticed the room's color. "Oh, my God!" Bile green. Hideous, stomach turning, bile green.

Lee grinned, "Makes' you want to puke, doesn't it?"

Lindsay hadn't noticed the color last night. In fact she was so tired, she hadn't noticed much of anything, except a pair of slate-blue eyes that saw more than Lindsay would have liked.

"A gallon of white paint would make a big difference, especially if someone I know would be inclined to put it on."

Giving her an over-my-dead-body-look, Lee changed the subject. "Why did people call my great-grandfather 'Old Jeb'? He wasn't that old, was he?"

"I don't think so." Lindsay buttered her toast. "He just seemed old, I guess." Reaching for the milk jug—she liked a lot of milk in her coffee—she accidently spilled a few drops on the table.

Before she could reach for something to wipe them away, *an angry voice came galloping out of the past and the blurred image of a little girl, a table, spilled milk, screams, tears, threats....and a pair of strong arms sheltering her.*

Stunned, Lindsay sat back in her chair.

"What's the matter? Got a pain or something?" Lee asked as he put his breakfast dishes in the sink.

"No." She took a sip of coffee. "No, just..." A vague recollection of a man—an older man, not tall—stocky—slightly stooped...

Then, noticing that Lee was pulling on his boots, she asked him to wait for her. She remembered that last night. Art Winston had said something to Lee about feeding the horses. Lindsay wanted to see the horses and stable she had inherited.

Ten minutes later, dressed in a pair of old slacks, turtleneck sweater and a heavy jacket she had found hanging on a peg on the back of the kitchen door, Lindsay stepped outside into a brilliant tearing world of sun and snow. The storm had blown itself out. She breathed deeply. No exhaust fumes polluted the air. Everything was so white, so pure. The silence was broken only by the raspy caw of a crow and the distant groan of a snowplow's diesel motor.

"What the...! Lindsay suddenly exclaimed as a snowball hit her back just below her coat collar. "Why you...!" She grabbed a handful of snow, packed it into a ball, but before she could fire it back at Lee, another snowball zinged past her. Laughing, she fired the snowball in her hand and their snow-fight was on.

Lindsay couldn't believe she and Lee were playing in the snow. The freshness of the morning, their uninhibited laughter, spoke of a new beginning for both of them.

Then came Lee's exclamation. "Mom! Look at the *shape* of that barn!" She turned. Open-mouthed, Lee was staring at the octangular weather-beaten frame building standing like a sentinel on a knoll a hundred yards away. When they had arrived, the buildings were all shadowed in the darkness and even when he and Art had gone to the barn, she realized, Lee hadn't noticed its shape.

"Different, isn't it?" She, too, stared at the octangular-shaped barn as a swallow swooped from a broken pane in the cupola. "It was built in eighteen-sixty by my great-grandfather, Jeremiah Macaulay."

For a long moment, Lee just stared at her. "How come you can remember that and you can't remember living here?"

"Don't know." Lindsay shrugged slightly. Ever since their arrival, faint shadows of the past kept creeping into her memory. "I do remember that people used to come from miles away just to look at our barn."

"What about that old garage?" Lee pointed to a tilted frame building halfway between the house and the barn. "Did they look at it too?"

"Probably made bets on when it would fall down. Asher Honeyborne didn't mention anything about a vehicle in his letters."

As she headed for the garage, Lee said, "There's nothing inside. I looked." Noticing that the soft snow was above the top of Lindsay's boots, he broke a path for her to the barn where they were greeted by a squeaking door and two soft nickers. After the blinding brightness of the snow, it took a few moments for their eyes to adjust to the dimmer light inside the barn where the smells of hay, manure and horses mingled harmoniously.

Looking about the stable, Lindsay noticed that the partitions between two sets of standing stalls had been removed, making each larger for the mares, whose heads, one black and one brown, were stretched over their half-doors, which opened into the octangular feed area. Above each stall hung a narrow, polished slab of wood with "Princess" burned into one and "Queenie" burned into the other. They nickered and bobbed their heads, making sure their new owners were aware that they were impatient for their breakfast.

"I know horses eat hay and oats, but did Art Winston say anything about feeding the mares any kind of supplement?" Lindsay asked, patting Princess's long neck.

"Yeah, he did." Lee was rubbing the white blaze on Queenie's black nose. "Art said to give them a scoop of this and a scoop of that." He pointed to two barrels in the center area: one had oats scratched across the lid and bran was scrolled atop the other.

When Lindsay opened the first bin, she froze. Two beady eyes stared up at her. Before she could scream, a large rat leaped into the air, bolted over the side of the bin and darted into the hay. "Oh, my God!" Lindsay jumped back, her face screwed up in shock. Lee doubled over with laughter. "That sucker was in there last night, too."

"It's not funny!"

"He's more frightened of you than you are of him."

"And just how did you arrive at that conclusion?" Lindsay moved cautiously closer to the bin, peering over the edge.

"You're bigger."

Lindsay glared at him. "Thank you," she said as she grabbed the scoop and attacked the barrel. They were almost finished feeding the mares when the barn door squeaked open.

Recognizing Rand Dyson's "Hello," she turned to Lee. "If you say one word..."

"Oh, Mom..."

"Oh, Lee...

"Despite last night's adventure, you both seem in good spirits," Rand joked.

"We're fine," Lee answered. "We're just..."

"...getting acquainted with our horses," Lindsay finished Lee's sentence. Her pulse rate had speeded up considerably and it wasn't just a delayed reaction to her fright.

He wasn't exactly handsome; his square-cut jaw was too strong for that, but there was a charisma about him that Lindsay found attractive. Maybe it was the rugged way his jeans hugged his muscled thighs, the denim jacket that broadened his shoulders, or the wide-brimmed hat that was pushed off his forehead. Whatever it was, her femininity tingled.

Blushing slightly when she saw that Rand had caught her studying him, Lindsay moved quickly to put the scoop into the bran bin and close the lid. A mundane task, but it gave her time to get her equilibrium back in place. Meanwhile, Lee was peppering Rand with questions. How did he get here? Did he bring the snowmobile? Were the roads ploughed? Where was Art?

Rand said he had hitched a ride on the snowplow. And Art was ploughing their lane. If Lee hurried, he could get a ride on the plough. As to what was he doing here—he was checking to make sure they were all right. They were such novices when it came to country and he was just being neighborly.

"How's the leg?" He glanced downward. "No worse for last night's experience?"

"It's fine," she snapped as she turned her back toward him. Then, realizing she had done it again, overreacted, she turned back. "I'm fine, really." She answered in a softer tone. "Thank you for asking."

Ever since an insensitive gym teacher had accused Lindsay of seeking sympathy when she limped away after doing some strenuous exercises—and the class had laughed uproariously at her awkwardness—Lindsay had tried to avoid bringing any attention to her disability. Most of the time it worked and she forgot she had a slight limp, only remembering when someone made specific reference to it. Although her last operation was thirteen years ago when the doctors had reinforced the bone with tiny metal rods, it had made a big difference.

Lindsay saw Rand's mouth tighten. "I'm sorry." She touched his sleeve as he picked up a bale of hay and carried it across to the stalls. "I over reacted." Her hazel eyes momentarily met his slate grey before turning away. Then, more softly, she added, "I... I have this problem...because of a bad experience a long time ago...I'm sorry." Lindsay swallowed and casually brushed away a tiny sheen of held-back tears, which she hoped he didn't see, but it was clear he had. As she helped open a fresh bale of straw, he asked, "Has Lee ever ridden a horse?" When Lindsay shook her head, he said, "Queenie would be a good horse for Lee to learn to ride on."

"Why do you say that?" Lindsay questioned.

"She's gentle, quiet, and she has a friendly look in her eyes."

Lindsay eyebrows lifted skeptically.

"You can tell a lot about a horse by the look in their eyes." Rand raised his left hand. "Scouts' honor."

For the next minutes, Lindsay and Rand worked comfortably side by side, throwing straw in and around the mares. They talked casually about the storm and January weather in general. Too soon, the work was finished.

As Rand turned out the lights and closed the barn door, Lindsay asked if he would like a coffee. She was still feeling guilty about her curtness and she wanted to make amends. There was another reason. She liked his company.

Momentarily blinded by the bright sunlight, Lindsay missed the path through the snow that Lee had stomped earlier. "Oh, darn," she exclaimed as the snow went over the top of her boots. Rand quickly took her hand and helped her back on the foot-stomped path.

"Art will be able to plough a path right to the barn door as soon as Honeyborne gets his car out of the way." The executor's snow-covered vehicle still blocked the lane. There was no sign of the snow plough, Art or Lee. Still holding onto Lindsay's hand, Rand said, "Art's just finishing up. He and Lee will be back shortly."

As they walked toward the house, Rand said that snow-ploughing was just one of Art Winston's part-time jobs. He was really retired, but he filled the hours by doing odd jobs for the farmers. Sometimes, if a neighbor was sick or wanted a short holiday, Art would look after their animals. Art had worked around horses all his life, first as a driver, then as a trainer. He loved horses and still kept a couple of retired race horses at his small farm, just down the road from Rand's place "And he looked after Old Jeb's horses all the time your grandfather was sick."

"I assume you have horses," Lindsay mused, taking off her boots and placing them on a plastic tray just outside the kitchen door.

"Fourteen," Rand answered as he placed his barn boots beside hers. They looked nice together, hers and his. "Maybe fifteen by this time tomorrow."

Lindsay wasn't sure if he was teasing her or telling the truth. Her eyebrow raised questioning. "And what was a man with fourteen, maybe fifteen, horses doing on a slow train to Riverton?"

Rand chuckled. "My big powerful Lincoln got stuck in a snowbank along with hundreds of other cars." The laughter mirrored in his eyes told her he was enjoying the repartee. Then, seeing her skepticism, he answered in a more formal tone. "I lecture at Wolverine Agriculture College—equine management, three days a week."

Just like the night before, Lindsay noticed, Rand seemed quite at home in her kitchen, tilting his chair on its back legs, right elbow resting on the edge of the table, legs stretched out. As she poured his coffee, she noticed a small hole peeping out of the toe of his grey sock. That hole somehow made him more affable.

"Isn't February a cold month for a mare to foal?" she asked, her cold hands wrapping around her warm mug. "My grandfather always wanted his foals to be born in late May or June." Wondering how that bit of information had crept into her head, she missed noticing the lines tighten around Rand's mouth.

"Old Jeb and I had very different ideas where breeding was concerned, although I have to admit some of his methods were sound."

"Asher Honeyborne told me that at one time Trailwood Farm was considered one of the best breeding stables in the county."

"It was."

Lindsay shrugged slightly. "I'm afraid I don't know much about farming or breeding or pregnant mares."

Rand's chair went back on its four legs. "I'm sure your grandfather must have books, pamphlets, magazines that you can read, study." A grin spread across Rand's face. "Like a pregnant woman, the best thing for a pregnant mare, is tender loving care."

"You sound like an authority."

"Not on pregnant women." Rand shook his head. "My wife and I never had any children."

Lindsay's heart plummeted to her toes. He was married! So what had she expected? That he was single, eligible...eligible for what? Romance?

"My wife was a city girl. She left me for another man. That was ten years ago." A why-did-I-say-that frown crossed Rand's brow.

"I'm sorry," she whispered, instantly ashamed of the flutter of gladness in her heart. He *was* single.

"Don't be." His voice was gruff as he vehemently added, "You can be damn sure I won't make that mistake again."

That tiny sprout of hope that last night had dared peep into the light, was pushed back where it should have been in the first place, buried with her other dreams.

Lindsay had only two serious romances in her life. The first was with Derek Wilson, Lee's father. They met in the rehabilitation wing of the Toronto hospital where he was recovering from a motorcycle accident. They both spent weeks in the hospital. And time went slowly. They played cards. They listened to music. They fell in love. Both agreed that as soon as Lindsay could walk down the aisle, they would be married. Maria, Lindsay's mom, couldn't have been happier.

The day came. Lindsay arrived at the church. Then the awful news came. Derek was killed in a motorcycle accident. Lee was born seven months later.

It was a long time before Lindsay fell in love again. Martin was the assistant manager of the supermarket where she worked part-time as a cashier. He was promoted and moved to another store in the city. He didn't ask Lindsay to go with him.

Once in a while, a salesman asked her out for a coffee, but the salesmen were usually the here-today and gone-tomorrow type with a wife tucked away in the background. Having a male companion wasn't that big of a deal anymore. As long as she had Bonnie, a friend from her rehabilitation days, who had counseled, cajoled and comforted her through the bad times and good times, Lindsay was okay.

As an uneasy silence filled the room, she was glad to hear two sets of stomping feet on the veranda. Seconds later, Lee burst into the kitchen. "We're freezing!" Art Winston, who was right behind him, explained, "The heater on the snow plough conked out."

While the conversation centered around the archaic snow plough, the storm and the mares, Lindsay made sandwiches and fresh coffee. She was happy to see Lee so animated, and Rand's feelings about his city wife were pushed to the back burner of her mind.

Too soon, the men had to leave. "Don't forget our numbers are on that pad under the telephone." Art motioned to the old fashioned telephone hanging on the wall between the kitchen and the hall.

"Just remember, City Lady, if you need anything, just give us a call," Rand added, giving her hand a squeeze as he walked past her to the door. "If you can't get one of us, you'll be able to get the other."

Watching them leave, Lindsay knew which man she would call first.

Even if nothing went wrong.

Three

The next few days sped by on sprinters' feet for Lindsay. On Monday morning Art Winston took Lindsay and Lee to the Riverton Junior High school where she registered Lee. The assistant principal, Miss Ormstown, told them that as long as Lee kept up his marks, he would not be set back a grade as so often happened when a student transferred from city to the country or vice versa. The school bus would pick him up at the end of their lane.

Tuesday morning, Lindsay fed the horses so Lee could have extra time getting ready for school. Determined to look his best, he spiked his hair and made sure the natural curls in his sandy blond hair didn't show. And he wore his best baggy pants. They hung so low they barely covered the crack in his lower anatomy. He combined them with his longest, loudest, striped sweater with a hole in the sleeve. Everyone wore holes in their clothes, he told his mother when she complained about his dress. To Lindsay, holes showed they were poverty stricken. Lindsay argued that he should have dressed more conservatively. He shrugged and said, "not to worry." He wanted to make an impression. And make an impression he did, Lindsay would learn later in the day.

The school bus was just pulling away from their lane entrance when a telephone call came from the Riverton garage. The owner, Russell Taylor, told her that her grandfather had brought his pickup truck to the garage to be repaired. It was finished…in fact, it had been finished for weeks, waiting for someone to claim it. Lindsay could come and pick it up any time as long as she paid the repair bill of three hundred dollars. The garage owner said he would gladly come and get her just so he could get the truck out of his garage. Lindsay grimaced. A half ton truck and its repair bill were something else Asher Honeyborne had failed to mention. But it was a means of transportation.

Taylor brought the truck and Lindsay paid him. It almost drained her bank account. Since the Taylor garage was a one-man operation, he needed transportation back. Thank goodness she had learned to drive years ago in driver education at high school. She got behind the wheel. She turned the key. The garage owner reminded her that the old truck had a standard transmission. Her right foot pushed the gas pedal. The truck lurched forward, gears grinding. She hit the brake. The truck stopped, scant inches from the lane fence. "That was close," she whispered. They were stuck.

A grumbling Russ Taylor shoveled them out and got behind the wheel, just long enough to get the truck going forward again before turning the driving over to Lindsay. Before she got the hang of pushing in the clutch with her left foot, shifting the gear on the steering column and gently touching the gas pedal with her right foot, the truck bucked, jerked and stalled, bucked, jerked and stalled again and again until her neck felt like it had been jerked out of her body.

All the while Russ Taylor was cautioning, "Take it easy, Miss Macaulay. I want to get home alive."

Somehow, she managed to deliver him back to his garage and get herself home, parking the truck in the lane near the broken-post garage. She had barely finished a ham sandwich and a glass of milk when Asher Honeyborne called. He would arrive at one o'clock.

And he did, complete with his black-rimmed glasses, slicked-back hair, portly stomach and bulging brief case. He apologized for not having come sooner. He had been felled by a bad cold, the result of the storm and his Jeep being stuck in the snow.

After a few general remarks about the ambience of the kitchen—he didn't mention the bilious green paint—he pulled out the captain's chair at the head of the table. "Shall we get down to business?" His chair backed to the light, forcing Lindsay to take the chair facing into the light. She had read in a business feature in the newspaper that in a power struggle with a client, it was best to keep your back to the light. But this wasn't a power struggle, or was it? She gave the executor a placid little smile as moved to another chair that angled the window light for her.

Honeyborne opened his leather briefcase and took out several legal papers. The first was the deed to Trailwood Farm. All Lindsay had to do was sign the document, which he would witness, and the estate was hers. Lindsay signed.

For years she and Lee had been shuffled around from one apartment to another, one part of the city to another. Despite this place being in the country, she and Lee now had a place of their own, a place they could put down roots. Of course, Lee's name wasn't on the deed, but Lindsay felt Trailwood was as much his as it was hers.

Honeyborne pulled some more papers from his brief case. "These are the mares' registration papers."

"I didn't know horses had to be registered."

"That's how the Standardbred Association and the Canadian Trotting Association keep track of the horses' blood lines," he explained. "The better the blood lines, the better the price the owner receives when the animal is sold."

"Do Princess and Queenie have good blood lines?" Lindsay inquired.

"About average, I would say." He went on to tell her that each owner had a number which was registered at the Canadian Trotting Association office. Lindsay would use Trailwood's number. Each mare had a number as well as any stallion by whom she was bred. Foals would have to be registered once they were born. The executor said he couldn't locate any record of what stallion had been used for Princess. "Possibly an oversight. "Your grandfather was ill at the time."

Oversight? Lindsay wondered. When she and her mom and dad lived here at Trailwood before Jeff, her father, died, and long before computers, Maria, her mother had done the bookkeeping, paid the bills, deposited the cheques and did the general accounting. Lindsay's grandfather had kept the horse records, carefully recording everything in a long narrow black journal with a string of binding twine tied around it. Another recall.

She didn't have time to wonder any longer as Honeyborne was placing another paper in front of her. "This is the estate's current financial statement."

Lindsay stared at the bottom line. There was less than a hundred dollars in the account. When she had first spoken to the executor, he had said the estate was free and clear. She had assumed that the estate had money. Well, she was wrong. It was on bankruptcy row. What happened? Honeyborne hedged his explanation, saying that the whole country was in a recession and farming wasn't as profitable as it once was. And Old Jeb had been sick for several months.

As Lindsay listened to his explanation, she got a worrisome feeling that she couldn't trust this man. Working in the supermarket, she had learned to identify shady customers by their body language, especially the way they refused to make eye contact. She remembered something else...the shock on Rand Dyson's face when Lee announced that he and Lindsay had come to Riverton to stay. Did someone have a hidden agenda for Trailwood?

Honeyborne pulled more papers from his briefcase. There was a bill for furnace oil and another for hydro. The insurance on the farm was due in three weeks, and, of course, the taxes in a three-digit figure were due next month. Oh, yes, he had almost forgotten, the bill for the food that he had purchased and put into her freezer and refrigerator prior to her arrival. Lindsay hadn't even seen a freezer. It was in the basement.

Lindsay quickly calculated the amount of the bills. The sum was staggering. "Just how am I supposed to pay all these?" she asked.

"They have to be paid, Miss Macaulay." Honeyborne shrugged slightly. "Credit is like a mirror... it reflects who you are, and being a newcomer, and old Jeb's granddaughter, you want to make a favorable impression..." his words tailed off.

"I know that, Mr. Honeyborne, but I *don't* have any money," Lindsay cried. "I used the last of my savings to pay the garage for the repairs on grandfather's truck."

His only answer was a slight shrug. "The bills have to be paid."

Lindsay scanned the figures again, going over them item by item. It was clear to her inexperienced eye that over the years it was the mortgage payments that had drained Trailwood's finances. "I don't understand why my grandfather had a mortgage on his property in the first place. It was clear of debt when Dad was alive." How did she know that? She couldn't even answer her own question.

"I only began looking after Jeb Macaulay's affairs after he became ill." Honeyborne kept flicking his pen between his second and third finger. "From one of our conversations, I know that as soon as the farm was clear of debt, Mr. Macaulay had gone looking for you." A tinge of a smile caused his fat jowls to sag even more. "Possibly, he wanted to see what kind of girl you were before he left you his estate."

Lindsay stared at the executor. "I haven't seen my grandfather in twenty-six years."

"He must have seen you recently because he left you Trailwood."

"Be that as it may, I didn't see him," Lindsay answered. "And that still doesn't explain the financial distress of Trailwood."

"As I said before, farming and horse breeding aren't profit-making businesses these days and your grandfather was ill for several years before he told anyone."

There was a long strained silence while Lindsay read and reread the documents and Honeyborne shuffled papers. "There is an alternative, of course...you can sell the farm." Without a preamble, he placed an offer to purchase signed by a numbered company in front of her.

Lindsay's sixth sense told her that Honeyborne had been waiting for this moment ever since he came. She looked at the document's offer to purchase, drew it closer. The sum was staggering, staggeringly low. For some unknown reason, when she touched the document, her hand felt soiled. She pushed the document back across the table to him. "I'm *not* going to sell!"

Three weeks ago, she would have gladly signed the document, accepted the money and bought a condominium. That was before Lee's troubles...before Rand Dyson, before feeling that she had come home.

Honeyborne closed his briefcase with a snap. "Very well. But if you should change your mind, let me know, but don't leave it too long. The buyers have a deadline to meet." A few minutes later, as he shrugged into his three-quarter length, fur-collar coat, he said casually, his partially bald head turning slightly toward her. "Well, I suppose you could put another mortgage on the old place."

As Lindsay watched Honeyborne's departing Jeep from the kitchen window, she wondered where she was going to get the money to pay the bills. From the moment she had awakened that first morning, saw the drooping curtains on the window, heard the branches brushing against the windowpane, the old house had claimed her. Even that first night, in pain, cold, afraid, Trailwood reached out to her and Lee. Despite the debts, despite her inexperience, she wasn't going to sell Trailwood to some unscrupulous buyer. Even though in the beginning she hadn't wanted it, Trailwood was her birthright, her Macaulay heritage. Somehow, some way, she was going to find the money to keep it.

For the next hour, Lindsay sat at the kitchen table, the legal papers spread out before her. She added figures, subtracted figures but the final total always came out the same. She needed a job, something that would give them a cash flow. She searched the want ads in a supplement paper that had been put in their mailbox that morning. She made several calls. It was winter. Business was slow. There were no jobs available.

She went over her options again. Even if she did sell and go back to the city, that wouldn't solve Lee's problem. The judge has said the next time Lee got in trouble, he would go to jail. Lee loved the horses and he had found a friend in Art Winston. The retired horseman would make a good model for the city boy.

It wasn't only her finances that were bothering Lindsay, it was a man with dark cinnamon hair and grey-blue eyes. She could still hear Rand's voice saying, "Take care, City Lady," as he rubbed his forefinger along her cheek and she felt the gentle touch of his lips. Such a light kiss. Even light kisses had been in short supply in her life.

As long as Lindsay had Bonnie, Lindsay was okay.

Still, she couldn't help wondering about Rand. Why hadn't he come over? He had been there twice the first two days she and Lee were at Trailwood and she hadn't seen him since.

Suddenly her heart rate sped up.

Someone was stomping the snow off their boots on the veranda. Rand had come.

Instead, it was a tall man in winter-lined coveralls, a man with a broad face and a slightly receding chin whose eyes always had a twinkle. Art Winston had stopped by every day, sometimes twice a day. On his afternoon visits, he usually came to the house and shared conversation and a cup of coffee with Lindsay. She was glad of his company as she was already finding country living a little on the lonely side.

In the Toronto apartment building where they had lived, there was always someone in the corridors, going back and forth to work, saying "hello" or "how are you to-day?" There were also her co-workers and customers at the supermarket. Most were chatty and livened up her day.

She hadn't had a chance to meet her neighbors yet; that would happen, she was sure. Country people were supposed to be friendly. So far, what she lacked in quantity, she made up in quality. The first time Art had dropped in, she had offered him a coffee—he told her he had been looking after the Macaulay horses for so long, they seemed like his own as Old Jeb had been sick for almost a year before he had succumbed to the cancer that gnawed at his gut. Often Art was the only person the horses or Jeb saw during those days, and it was becoming the same for Lindsay. Although she had Lee.

When she heard Art stomping the snow off his boots on the veranda, she plugged in the coffee pot. "Just dropped in to tell you that this morning when I was here, I noticed that the oat barrel was getting low so when I was at the feed store I picked up another bag," he said, pulling out a chair at the table for himself.

"Well, you'll just have to take the oats back!" she snapped as she poured two coffees, one for him and one for her.

Art's eyebrows rose fractionally.

"I'm sorry, Art. I didn't mean to snap. I'm upset." She sat down.

"I can hear that. What's happened?"

"Asher Honeyborne was here."

"I know. I saw his Jeep when I unloaded the oats at the barn." To ease Lindsay's obvious distress and give her time to regroup, Art told her he'd cleaned out the stalls, thrown some more straw in around the mares and all Lee would have to do tonight was give them some hay and a scoop of oats.

Slowly Lindsay stood up and moved to the counter where the coffee pot was. Holding up an empty cup, she asked if he would like another. He nodded. However, it was a long moment before she began to speak.

"Honeyborne said if I can't pay the bills—and there are so many—I will have to sell."

Art pushed his peaked cap up high off his forehead with his forefinger. Removing his cap always seemed a sacrilege. "Surely there are other options."

Lindsay continued as though she hadn't heard a word Art had said. "Lee loves it here. I love it here. It's our first real home." A tear trickled down the side of her nose. "But if I can't pay the bills..."

Art reached across the table, his hand covering hers. "You have assets, girl"

"Yes, I have assets," she gulped a sob. "Two mares, one expected foal and an eight-sided barn, a house with a bile green kitchen."

"There must be money in the estate account. Old Jeb was very careful with his money."

Lindsay shook her head. "There isn't enough money in Trailwood's bank account to pay the current bills, barely enough for a month's living expenses." If only she could get a job. She had called several businesses in Riverton. No one was interested in hiring a woman with only supermarket cashier experience.

Now as she added the cost of that bag of oats to her list, she continued, "The horses are just going to have to do on hay for a while, I guess, or until I can sell."

"Surely, there are less drastic options than selling the property and going back to the city." Thoughtfully, Art stirred his coffee.

Lindsay shook her head.

"Girl, look around you. You have a lot of old things and old things are worth money. Sell them. Get some quick cash to get you over."

"Sell my grandfather's things!"

"What do you think will happen to your grandfather's things if you sell the farm? You can't take them with you. So why not use them to save the farm?" Art said as he stirred the fourth spoonful of sugar into his coffee. After a poignant pause, he added, "I once had to sell my mother's watch, the only thing I had of value, when I was hit with hard times. And it was hard."

She shrugged her shoulders. She didn't want to tell Art that these *old things* were special to her because they were her only link to a past she couldn't remember.

Unaware of Lindsay's feelings, he continued, "An old neighbor of mine had a room full of paintings, journals, letters, pictures, old records of his family and the county historical society wanted to buy them, pay him a good dollar too. He wouldn't sell. Said he was keeping everything for his family. When he died, his family pitched everything into the garbage."

A pregnant silence followed. Lindsay remembered she had seen a lot of old things in the attic yesterday. It was full of junk—everything from a feather duster to hand-carved picture frames and an old buffalo robe still in its original crate. Even the years hadn't taken away the animal smell from its long coarse hairs. And there were scads of books and magazines. She had flipped through one of the magazines and was surprised to find an article on Trailwood.

"Do you really think that old junk in the attic is worth money?" Art took his time before answering. "I know someone...lives in the city—never could stand the city myself—has a store, buys and sells old things, antiques. I'll give him a call. Maybe if he came and saw some of those old things, maybe bought some of them. That would give you some cash...buy you a little time."

"I don't know. Right now everything seems so hopeless."

As Art got up to leave, his hand rested on her shoulder for a moment. "Lindsay, you're a Macaulay and they don't give up without a fight! Find a way to make Trailwood pay its own way. Old Jeb didn't give up. You can't either..."

Hearing the veranda door close behind Art, she glanced at the clock. Lee would be home soon. She put away the papers on the table. There was no need for Lee to know about their problems. She shuddered at the thought of having to move again. Was it only yesterday that the truck had brought her kiln and the rest of their things from the city? Thank goodness the delivery was prepaid as she wouldn't have had the money to pay for the delivery.

Hearing the grinding gears of the school bus's brakes, she glanced at the clock. It was twenty after four.

The telephone rang. It was Miss Ormstown, Lee's teacher. She immediately got to the reason she was calling. The school had a dress code, a *casual rural* dress code. She suggested that from now on, Lee dress more conservatively. Lindsay told her that Lee had simply wanted to make an impression on his school mates. "He *did* that all right!" Laughter edged Miss Ormstown's words.

"But I want to tell you, through it all, Lee held his head up, took the jibes and ribald jokes on the chin. He didn't retaliate, Miss Macaulay." Miss Ormstown concluded by saying, "Despite everything, I was proud of him."

Shortly after Lindsay hung up the telephone, Lee rushed in, threw his books on the table and said he was going to the barn. Had Miss Ormstown not called, Lindsay would not have known what had happened at the school. Thank goodness for the horses. Lee could pour out his humiliation to the horses, especially Queenie, the black and white pinto with the big friendly eyes whom he had fallen in love with on first sight, at least that was what Art had told her the other day when he had dropped in for a coffee. Although he hadn't said, she thought he had a special affection for Princess, the mare in foal.

An hour later, Lee came to the house, his eyes red-rimmed. Lindsay had supper ready. She had taken special care to cook the things he liked: hamburger patties, peas and French fries with ice cream for dessert. Lee barely spoke during supper. Then as soon as he had finished eating, he stacked his dishes in the sink, said that he had to read a few pages for his science assignment and then he was going to watch a little television. As

Lindsay watched Lee go, his head down, his shoulders hunched forward, she knew how he felt—like he had the problems of the world on his shoulders.

Over the years, whenever problems overwhelmed her, Lindsay turned to her porcelain painting, a technique developed more than 2000 years earlier in ancient China. Searching for a new medium, artists had found that by grinding mineral and oxide powders together into an oil medium with paste consistency and tinted with color, it could be painted onto china. To preserve the color in the design, it then had to be fired in a very hot kiln for long periods of time. The technique, of course, had been refined over the ages, and had now developed into a new skill, designs on porcelain.

Lindsay had learned to paint porcelain when she was confined to bed for endless weeks in the hospital with nothing to do except listen to music or watch television. Often, she was too bored to even cry and the boredom became a definite detriment to her recovery.

After a painful therapy session one morning, the assistant therapist handed her an instruction book, a brush, box of paints and a white plate with a crack in it. "Something to help you put in the time." Lindsay wanted to yell, throw the book, plate and brushes after the departing woman.

After Lindsay had quieted down, she flipped through the pictures in the instruction book. She picked up the brush, wetted it, dabbled in the colors, swishing blue into yellow and pink into green. What a mess, but the mess covered the crack in the plate.

Soon other pieces of cracked porcelain found their way to her room. Could Lindsay put a leaf or something over the crack so it wouldn't show? Sometimes, Lindsay thought that Bonnie, the assistant therapist, deliberately cracked a plate, or a cup, just so she could say, "Can you hide this crack, this chip, this stain?" It became a challenge.

When Lindsay left the hospital, she continued with her craft. She found it relaxing and if she purchased porcelain from a thrift store and the paints from Goodwill, it became an inexpensive hobby. She continued to paint over the years and recently she had sold a couple of designs to a boutique store. The owner said she would take more in the spring. Now, If Lindsay could find other markets...?

As she placed her painting supplies on the kitchen table, she thought about the designs in her craft book. What would sell? What wouldn't? She finally chose a wild flower design of a buttercup. Carefully, using a hairline brush, she sketched a stem, several deeply-cut leaves and three butter-yellow flowers onto a china plate. Although she heard Lee say a goodnight, Lindsay became so engrossed in gently brushing in the yellow colors, feathering them from the center, she barely mumbled a coherent reply. Besides, there was this little saying that kept teasing her memory: "if you hold a buttercup under your chin, and your skin turns' yellow, it means you like butter." Did her skin turn yellow? It must have, because she liked butter.

It was almost midnight when she began to put her paints away, cleaned her brushes in turpentine and wiped them dry. She was just about to turn off the kitchen's hanging lamp when there was a loud pounding on the outer veranda door. Who could be calling at this time of night? She hadn't seen any headlights of a vehicle coming in the lane. Maybe she was too engrossed in her painting to notice.

Remembering horror stories of break-ins in Toronto, fear like a steel band tightened around her chest. They were going to be robbed. But robbers didn't bang on doors. A window shattered. Boots clomped on the veranda.

My God! Was this day never going to end?

Four

Seconds later Lindsay heard a window pane smash and the outer door of the veranda open. She quickly looked around for something with which to defend herself. The only thing at hand was the mop in the corner. Before she could get it, a fist was pounding on the door to the kitchen.

"Lindsay! Lindsay!"

That voice. Her heart took a somersault and she quickly opened the door. The next thing she knew she was in Rand Dyson's arms. "Are you all right?" He was crushing her against his chest. "I was on my way home. I saw the lights." He pulled back a little, searching her face. "It's past midnight and your lights were still on...and you and Lee always go to bed with the chickens," he managed a wobbly joke. "I was afraid for you." He gave her a gentle shake. "Are you really all right?"

Before she could nod, a sleepy voice from the stairs called, "What's going on, Mom? What's all that pounding?"

Her tears of fear broke into a smile of happiness. "It's all right, Lee," she assured him. "Rand saw our lights still on and wanted to make sure we were okay."

"That's nice," Lee murmured sleepily as he turned around and went back up the stairs.

Lindsay suddenly realized that she was still standing in the sheltering circle of Rand's arms; the winter cold was still clinging to his jacket. She tried to step back, but his arms held her fast. "What are you doing up so late?"

"I was painting." Her words were muffled against his chest. "Sometimes, when I'm upset, I paint."

"You should be in bed." His voice was gruff. "This isn't the city, you know." The city again—she pushed out of his arms.

"I assure you, Rand, I know exactly where I am." But she couldn't stay angry. He was concerned. Few people in the city were concerned about their neighbors. "The doors were locked and I felt completely safe." She almost added *until you broke in.*

"Yes, they were," he admitted sheepishly, as his eyes searched her face and his finger tapped the drop of yellow paint on the side of her nose. "I'll repair the window in the morning."

Searching for a way to break the tension that had suddenly sprung up between them, she moved to the table. "I had just finished this."

"It looks real," he said.

"I was hoping to send it to a store in Toronto that buys my work," she added, as a current of almost-forgotten feelings cruised through her body.

"I'm sure it will sell." Rand turned abruptly and headed for the door. "I'll repair that window in the morning." As an after-thought, he added, "Put one of those kitchen chairs under the doorknob." Then as he stepped onto the veranda, he turned slightly and said in his most charming voice, "Good night, City Lady."

City Lady. Always 'City Lady'. Lindsay wanted to throw the buttercup plate at him. Then as her temper subsided, she watched the headlights of his Lincoln backing doen the lane. Turning the car around in her yard would have been impossible in the snow.

A little smile tugged at the corner of her mouth as she wedged the back of one of the kitchen chairs under the door knob. She wasn't afraid until he had come pounding on her door. Now she had a broken veranda window, a chair pushed under a door knob and slivers of apprehension winding through her mind.

~ * ~

The next morning before she and Lee were up, the window pane was fixed and the shards of broken glass were swept away. She wished Rand had come later in the morning when Lee was at school. They could have shared a coffee and talked.

Later, as Lindsay watched the school bus pull away, she switched the radio on. The CBC reported that the Canadian Government had created a new Ministry of State and Economic Development to counter the serious recession that was gripping the country. She turned the dial to the weather station. Was it going to snow? Was the sun going to shine? Could the horses be turned out for exercise in the small corral behind the barn? Art said he had repaired it a couple of days ago.

When she lived In Toronto, Lindsay turned on the radio to drown out the clanging of a garbage demister, the honking of horns when traffic stalled, the wail of an ambulance siren. Now she turned on the radio to drown out the silence. With Lee at school, life was lonelier than she ever thought possible. Lindsay would have liked to call Bonnie, her best friend, in Toronto, tell her about the farm and Lee and Rand, but Lindsay couldn't afford the long distance telephone charges.

With a sigh, she pulled on her boots, shrugged into her grandfather's lined jacket and headed for the barn. She had two horses that needed to be fed, stalls that needed to be mucked out and if that germ of an idea that had been revolving around in her head about renting stalls to city dwellers for their horses was to materialize, she had to clean out the unused stalls. But where would she put all that junk from the stalls? She would ask Art. He had already been helpful in arranging with an antique dealer to come to the farm and see which old items in the attic were saleable.

At the barn, the horses greeted Lindsay with their usual soft neighs, snorts, and stomping. *I never got this kind of welcome at the supermarket,* she thought, just a good morning grunt or two.

She didn't bother turning on the lights. Hydro, she learned from the bills, was very expensive, so she decided to make do with the natural light from the narrow windows above each stall and the sunlight filtering downward from the cupola's narrow windows atop the barn roof.

She turned on the barn radio, a relic of the fifties. Art said the horses loved soft music. And so did Lindsay.

Then, before scooping out their bran, she carefully lifted the barrel lid and peered in—she didn't want any more rat surprises. As she threw forks of hay into the horses' mangers, she hummed to the music. Lindsay couldn't remember ever humming at the cashier register at the supermarket.

After she had finished feeding the horses and cleaning out their stalls, she decided to take inventory of what needed to be done to the stable to turn it into a "rent-a-stall for your horse" mini-business. One of the stalls had a two-wheel sulky cart with a broken shaft hanging from a rafter.

"That was your Dad's," a voice said from the entrance way. "See. One of the shafts is broken."

"Rand!"

Suddenly she wasn't lonely anymore. Rand was there.

"I was at the hardware store and since it was right next door to Tim Horton's and..." as he handed her a cup of coffee, the shadows of another time crowded out the present and suddenly *her father was standing beside her, taking her hand, placing a half of a yellow apple, face up, in it. His hand still under hers, they extended it to Woodlyn, her father's favorite racing mare. She stretched out her head, her thick blackish lips nibbled, took a bite and Lindsay laughed...*and the shadows faded into light and Lindsay was laughing as Rand was handing her a cup of coffee and a small brown bag... "And, these looked too inviting to pass up."

Not quite sure what had just happened—it had happened so quickly, she looked inside. "A honey dip! My favorite."

"Too sweet for me." There was a less sugary cruller beside it.

Instead of going to the house, they sat on an unopened bale of straw. While the horses munched on their hay, dust motes danced in the sun's golden rays to the soft country music playing on the radio and Rand and Lindsay ate and talked about nothing and everything. She even told him about the rat in the bran barrel.

Then, Lindsay got around to the question that had been at the back of her mind ever since Rand came. "Why would my grandfather keep *that* racing bike?"

"Sentimental reasons, I suppose," Rand said as he set his empty cup aside and went to inspect the cart. "My mother and I were living in Vancouver at the time, so I can't tell you for sure if it was your dad's." He lifted the two-wheeler off the wall, placed it in the alley outside the stall. "That's the only reason I can think of for your grandfather to keep a broken sulky hanging in an empty stall."

Rand spent the next ten minutes inspecting the racing cart, checking for any marks that would identify it as the one Lindsay's father was driving the night he was killed. As Lindsay watched, she recalled how the shadows in her mind had parted just for an instant and she had seen her dad and the mare Woodlyn and she wondered if her memory was beginning to come back.

"You'll have to ask Art," Rand was saying. "He's been around horse racing a lot longer than I have." He replaced the sulky on the wall. Turning back to her, he asked, "Did you know there's a picture in the Riverton Race office of your dad and his horse, "Going Too Slow" when they won the Sire Stakes."

"Going Too Slow," Lindsay repeated. "What a silly name for a horse!"

"Some have weird names, that's for sure." He again took his seat beside her on the straw bale.

"You know that Dad didn't have to race that night. It was his night off. One of the other drivers called in sick and Dad being Dad...replaced him." *How did she know that?*

Lindsay noticed that Rand's face was solemn as he tried to explain. "Racing isn't a game, Lindsay. It's a sport. And like other sports, it carries its obligation, responsibilities: not just to oneself, but to the other drivers, the other owners, the track management and the thousands of fans who come night after night to bet and be entertained.

"Racing is big business and driving was part of Jeff Macaulay's job. Perhaps not a job in the formal nine-to-five way, but it was the way he made his living. Your grandfather bred and exercised the horses; your dad trained and raced them. Trailwood was on its way to being one of the prime racing stables in Ontario."

"My mother always said that in our family horses and racing always came first." Lindsay repeated Maria's words.

"She was wrong." Rand reached for her hand. "Jeff Macaulay loved his family."

"Oh, yes," Lindsay cried. "He loved his family so much he got himself killed."

"You must have some good memories of him." Rand ignored her outburst.

Another shadow burst across her memory—a man of medium height with a broad smile, a man who used to throw her up in the air and catch her, tickle her, make her squeal with delight, and sometimes kiss her on the nose right where all the freckles were—where the freckles still were.

"But he didn't have to go that night!" Lindsay repeated. "Maria said it was his night off. Someone called in sick. And he volunteered…"

"Your Dad raced that night because racing was important to him."

Looking up, Lindsay searched the grey depths of Rand's eyes. It was as if in them she could see the crowds, feel the excitement, hear the rhythm of the horses' hooves, the whiz of the sulky wheels.

"Art told me that your father's horse was two lengths ahead at the final turn when suddenly it went down with a broken leg. Jeff was thrown from his sulky. A horse's hoof caught him on the temple and he was killed instantly." Rand tenderly massaged the back of Lindsay's hand. "No one was to blame. Not your grandfather. Not your father. Not the other drivers. Not even the horses. It was an accident."

Lindsay's tongue moved over her dry lips. It sounded so different the way Rand explained it. Maria had always made it seem so ugly, blaming Old Jeb, the farm, the horses. Sometimes, Lindsay wondered if her mom blamed her too.

"Did you know that after your dad was killed and you were hurt, Old Jeb sold his racers and concentrated solely on the breeding end of the business?" Rand asked as he helped her on with her coat and together they checked on the horses.

Lindsay shook her head. "I still don't understand why grandfather left me this place."

"You were his granddaughter. His only kin, and he loved you."

"You know I never intended to come back here," she admitted. "I was going to sell the place, use the money to buy a condominium. But Lee got into some trouble in the city."

Lindsay hadn't meant to tell anyone in Riverton about Lee, or the judge, or why they had come, but confidences just seemed to slip out—and she told Rand.

"And so you brought your son here."

As Rand reached around her to open the barn door, his lips brushed hers. "You're a good woman, Lindsay Macaulay." Then, with an arm across her shoulders, they walked side by side to the house. Lindsay felt settled. Coming here was right. And yet...

"Rand, I don't know anything about mares or foals or breeding." She gave him a lopsided grin. "As you keep telling me, I'm a farm girl at heart?"

"Well, whatever...you're a farm girl now." They had reached the house and Rand was bending over, testing the lock he had installed earlier, to see if it was sound. "Your grandfather must have dozens of books around on horses and breeding and foaling." He glanced up at her from his crouched position. "Read them."

"Oh, sure, how to deliver a foal in one easy lesson," she quipped.

He grinned as he stood. "Maybe two lessons." His head bent, his lips touched hers again, then he was striding toward his car.

And she was watching him drive away. Her fingers touched her lips. He had said she was a good woman. He had kissed her. Such a gentle kiss. When had her neighbor become more than a neighbor? Was she reading more into that kiss than was meant?

Lindsay hung her barn coat on the back of the kitchen door. She had work to do. Lee had brought his dirty clothes down this morning, flung them in a basket on the washing machine. She, too, had clothes that needed washing. At least here she had a decent washer and dryer, sitting side by side, in the pantry cum laundry room. In the apartment building, the tenants shared the laundry facilities at the end of their hall.

Although Lindsay had noticed the old dilapidated filing cabinet in the corner of the laundry room, she hadn't taken time to go through the files.

Now, while the washer was gyrating through its cycles, Lindsay flipped through some of the manila folders.

Then, right at the back of the top drawer, Lindsay found her grandfather's missing journal, although it seemed to be more a diary of Trailwood than a journal. In one section was the record of all the horses he had bought and sold over the years. There was also a breeding section: what mare had been bred to what stallion, the date and the cost of the breeding fee. The book seemed up-to-date, yet there wasn't anything about Princess or the date she was bred; no entry to say to what stallion had been used for the mare.

In the debit and credit section, her grandfather had recorded the farm's income and expenses. Lindsay was surprised to see that Trailwood had shown a profit each year, albeit a small one. She couldn't help wondering why Old Jeb had needed such a mortgage in the first place and there was no record of where the mortgage money had gone. It just seemed to disappear.

On an impulse, Lindsay decided to call Asher Honeyborne. He would know. He looked after her grandfather's estate. Honeyborne didn't answer his telephone. Didn't he have a secretary? Well, she supposed, this was the country and here executors didn't have the big offices, secretaries and receptionist, like their city cousins. Now Rand had her doing it—comparing city living and country living.

Later as Lindsay walked to the mailbox at the end of the lane, she hoped to find a letter from the shopkeeper who had bought a couple of china plates last fall. All she got was the hydro bill marked past due and a letter from an older student who said he was doing his thesis on barns and the eight-sided Macaulay's barn was one he wanted to explore. He would like to come to Trailwood for a couple of days to research the structure. He was willing to pay for accommodation and any extra expenses that his visit incurred. A return address and a telephone number were at the bottom of the letter.

Lindsay's first thought was "no way." She didn't want some unknown person staying in her house. Her second thought was money—the man said he would pay. But before she did anything, she would ask Art.

Lindsay was almost to the house when she heard the squeaky brakes of the school bus. Second later, Lee came running toward her.

"Mom! Mom! Guess what?" He was waving sheets of paper in his hand. After his first day fiasco, she was afraid to guess.

"I'm in the school play. It's only one line...just eight words."

Seeing all the sheets of paper Lee was waving, she thought he had the lead. However, anything that helped him adjust to their new life was more than welcome, even one line in a play. "And when does this great theatrical production take place?" Lindsay teased.

"Tomorrow night. At the school auditorium."

"Tomorrow night!" Surprise elevated Lindsay's voice an octave.

"Yeah, isn't it great?" Lee literally danced through the snow. "The dude that had the part got the measles. Imagine getting a kid's disease like that." He noticed Lindsay's lifted eyebrows. "Well, he did," Lee added rather sheepishly, conveniently forgetting that he had the measles eighteen months ago. "Besides, his costume wouldn't fit anyone else, so Miss Ormstown gave the part to me." A faint shadow crossed Lee's face. "You will come won't you, Mom?"

"Of course, I'll come. I wouldn't miss it for the world." She brushed the snow off her boots. Then, handing him the broom, she motioned for him to do the same.

For the next hour, in fact for the rest of the night, all Lindsay could hear was Lee repeating his line. She was sure he even practiced that line on the horses when he went to the barn to feed them.

Five

Lee was up early the next morning and waiting at the end of the long lane before the school bus came. Lindsay hoped that exuberance would still be there when he got up on the stage.

As she walked to the barn to do the morning chores, she was surprised to see her two horses out in the corral and Art hard at work cleaning out Princess's stall.

"How did you get here?" Lindsay asked. "I didn't see your truck in the yard."

"Russ Taylor gave me a ride over. My truck wouldn't start. Needs a new starter." Art leaned on his fork "Russ thinks he might have a used one in stock. If he does, I'll have my truck back later today." Art had taken off his jacket and rolled up the sleeves of his flannel shirt.

"With Princess due in a few weeks, it's best to have her stall prepared, just in case."

"Well, I'm not prepared," Lindsay replied. She had read and reread all of her grandfather's books and pamphlets on foaling, but she still didn't think she could deliver a foal.

"Girl, mares have been delivering their own foals since God created horses, and so far they've managed quite well, so quit worrying," Art told her. "Besides, if you run into trouble you have the vet's number on that pad beside your telephone...beside mine...and Rand's."

"I know," she agreed, reaching for a wide-bristle broom beside the bran box.

While Art finished putting the extra straw in Princess's stall, she swept the alley in front of the stalls. As they worked they talked about everything from the Macaulay's first days at Trailwood to Lee's role in the school play.

"Being involved in that play is good for the boy," Art said. "Makes him feel as if he belongs."

"He's only got one line."

"No matter."

Lindsay had to agree as she watched Art hang up his fork and hitch up his sagging pants. She and Lee had come to rely on this big man who favored flannel shirts, braces and a hand-tooled belt buckled under his bulging stomach.

Art had taught them so much, simple things really, like the proper way to curry and brush a horse. Lee hadn't known what a curry comb was—a long narrow plastic comb with short teeth—or the reasons for grooming a horse.

"Hold the curry comb in this hand and the brush in the other." Art had said that the comb loosened the dirt and dandruff and the brush swept it away as well as stimulated the circulation.

Art advised. He didn't criticize. He showed them what they were doing wrong, and then with a word of caution, let them find out for themselves. There was also humor in his teaching. "Just be sure you don't touch Queenie's panic button," he'd warned. "That small black spot in the middle of that white patch on her rump."

"Why not?" Lee had asked.

"You'll find out...Art hadn't completed the sentence when Lee's comb had slid over the black spot on the horse's rump. Suddenly Queenie's leg came up and Lee had gone flying.

"I told you." Art doubled over with laughter.

Lindsay, who had been grooming Princess, called out, "Lee, are you all right?"

A disgruntled "Yes" came from the adjoining stall.

Since then, Art had taught them to recognize a black spot from a panic button, a nicker from a neigh, a bite from a playful nip. He was a walking encyclopedia when it came to horses and their habits.

Now, with their chores finished, she and Art watched the two horses, their noses slightly raised, sniffing the fresh winter air as they cantered around the paddock. Frolicking like children, Princess nipped Queenie's neck. Queenie squealed and kicked out her heels. Princess galloped away.

Looking beyond the paddock, Lindsay said. "Mr. Honeyborne said our property extended just beyond the trees."

"It does, and those trees border the river...and the river borders the Riverton race track. Your father often talked of building a narrow bridge between the two properties." Art pushed the peak of his cap a little higher.

"It sure would have made it easier to get to the track, and quicker too. Instead of it taking three-quarters of an hour going around, by going across we could have been there in ten minutes or less." Before he bought his own place down the road, Art said he had stabled his three horses here at Trailwood.

"Your dad and I often worked together, exercised our horses together, and sometimes even drove in the same race."

Lindsay leaned over the stable door, her chin resting on her arms while she listened and watched several swallows swoop from the roof to a fence post, their blue backs and tawny chests glistening in the sun. "Did you know my mother too?' she asked idly.

He didn't answer for a long moment. "Yes, I knew your mother." Then, after a long thoughtful pause, he said, "Every spring Maria and I used to hunt mushrooms and puffballs in those woods." He gestured toward the trees at the back of the property.

"I don't believe it!" Lindsay exclaimed, turning to look at Art. "Maria hunted for mushrooms in the woods!"

"Maybe you don't know your mother as well as you thought," he answered.

"I know she likes mushrooms: wild, tame, cooked, raw, sauté or simmered," Lindsay said. "And I certainly know she hates being called Mom."

"Why not? Motherhood is an honorable state."

"Not for Mom." Lindsay laughed lightly. "Once in a while it was okay but those times were rare. And when Lee was born, anything other than Maria was unacceptable. Calling her Grandmother, or Gramma, even just Gram, was like waving a red flag at a bull." Lindsay turned to look back at the woods. "Maria wasn't maternal, that's for sure. I remember that Dad once kidded her about being the sexiest mother in Riverton County. She was wearing a bum-hugging pair of designer jeans and amulets that jingled on her arms. She threw a dish at him." Lindsay suddenly stopped talking. How could she remember something like that when she couldn't remember her dad's face?

Slowly, thoughtfully, Lindsay continued. "Maria never talked much about her married life, just that she and my father lived here at Trailwood with Old Jeb. After Dad was killed and I had my accident, she got an apartment in Toronto close to the hospital....and stayed in the city even after I recovered."

Art looked off towards the woods. "Maria and I had a lot in common back then. We both came from troubled families; both hung around the racetrack, looked out for each other too. Shortly after I got a job as a groom, she got a job in the racetrack coffee bar." Art smiled. "Lied about her age. She was fourteen. Told them she was sixteen."

"Didn't anyone check?" Lindsay asked.

"Regulations weren't the same back then." He shook his head. "Besides she was good-looking and everyone liked her."

"And my dad?"

"He met Maria about the same time I did." He was silent for a moment. "Your dad was my best friend. We went to school together, raced together, laughed together...and..." Lindsay barely heard his..."and cried together."

Before he could say anything more, a voice called from the other side of the stable. "Anybody around?"

Art turned, his leathery skin breaking into a wide smile. "Herb! How the hell are you?"

"Just fine, you old horse trader." The funny little man who was as wide as he was tall held out his hand as he walked toward Art. "And as usual you've got a nice looking filly beside you."

Smiling a little, Lindsay watched the two men shake hands before Art turned back to her.

"Herb is the antique dealer from the city I was telling you about." Then drawing her forward, he said, "Herb Haggitt, meet Lindsay Macaulay."

While the two men chatted about old times, Lindsay brought the horses in from the corral. Afterward, as they started for the house, Herb took a moment to stop at his white van and get a clipboard.

"Would you like a coffee, Mr. Haggitt?" Lindsay asked as she slipped off her barn boots. She knew Art was always ready for one.

"A coffee would be most welcome, Miss Macaulay."

For the next few minutes they sat around the kitchen table drinking coffee and sharing stories. The telephone rang and it was Russ Taylor. Art's truck was finished. The garage man would be there in five minutes.

Minutes later, on their way to the attic, Haggitt saw an old pine hutch in the hall outside her grandfather's bedroom and he paused to examine it. "This is a nice piece, Miss Macaulay." Lindsay told him it wasn't for sale, although the price Haggitt quoted almost made her drool. Art had told her that it belonged to her dad when he was growing up, and, for that reason, Lindsay didn't want to sell it.

The attic proved to be a hodge-podge of old and new, broken and just worn out odds and ends. Herb found a couple of oil lamps, several picture frames with their original prints browned with age, all of which he said he was sure he could sell quickly. After rummaging through some boxes, they found the old buffalo robe. Underneath was a pine cradle with rockers and a wooden hood. Looking over his list Haggitt said, "I think that's it for the day, Miss Macaulay, unless, of course, you want to sell that hutch in the hall." She shook her head.

Haggitt took his time valuing the different pieces and then handed her a cheque. The amount was enough to pay the telephone bill, buy a few groceries, and put gasoline in the truck with a few dollars over. She knew, also, that the farm would come before the hutch—need before sentimentality, she thought as she watched him drive away. Lee would be home soon. Then there were chores to do, supper to get and then it would be off to the play.

~ * ~

Lindsay's old truck looked out of place between the newer cars and pickups in the school parking lot, she thought as she headed for the auditorium. She was surprised to see Rand standing near the door.

"I didn't expect to see you here." She tried to keep the pleasure from showing in her voice.

"Why?" Rand flipped a dollar coin into the honor box for her coat check. "Because I don't have children of my own?" He pocketed the stub of her ticket. "I do have friends with children."

"Oh," she mouthed the comment with a smile as he casually took her arm, guiding her into the auditorium.

The auditorium was smaller than the one at Lee's previous school. Two large Canadian flags flanked the steps leading up to the stage which was hidden by a blue velvet curtain.

"Art told me Lee was in the play," Rand said, his hand under her elbow moving her gently out of the way of a family who was trying to find seats.

"Yes." She laughed lightly as he urged her ahead of him down the main aisle. When her steps slowed, he suggested they take seats nearer the front so they could see better.

To her chagrin, Lindsay found his *nearer the front* meant the front row. When they were seated, he said, "I forgot to ask if you were planning to sit with anyone?"

Now that was a fine time to ask, she thought as she shook her head. The only person she even recognized was the garage owner, Russell Taylor, who was sitting on the other side of the auditorium. Lindsay had intended to sit near the back of the auditorium next to the outside aisle where she could see and still be inconspicuous.

From comments Art had made that morning, Lindsay knew the arrival of Old Jeb's granddaughter and her son had generated a lot of talk and speculation. Would she sell the farm? Would country living be too tame for her and the boy? And the boy—everyone had heard about his first day at school.

While Rand and Lindsay waited for the curtain to rise, several neighbors came to speak to Rand, and of course, he introduced her. Just before the lights went down, a woman slipped into the empty seat on the aisle next to Rand.

"I hoped you would save me a seat," she said as Rand stood to greet her. Quickly, he introduced his dear friend Natalie Hunter to Lindsay Macaulay, his new neighbor. Lindsay had the uncomfortable feeling that Natalie wasn't expecting Lindsay to be sitting beside Rand. Was she more than a dear friend? Art said Rand had *someone*. But Lindsay wasn't really with him, was she? Before she could say anything, Rand was gone, the lights in the auditorium dimmed and he was on stage as master of ceremonies. He made a short "Welcome everyone" speech—coffee and muffins available at the intermission, with the money going to new equipment for the school gym. The stage lights dimmed, the curtain went up and Rand was sitting beside her again.

The Wayward Decision was a humorous play and there was plenty of laughter from the audience. The leading lady forgot her lines and had to be prompted. The leading man's pants seemed to be slipping and he had to keep pulling them up. There was no sign of Lee. Lindsay had forgotten to ask him where his entrance came in the play. Intermission came, and Rand bought Lindsay and Natalie a coffee and a muffin. Somehow, Lindsay felt drab in her corduroy pantsuit standing next to Natalie in her fuchsia pants with the white silver-threaded roll-neck sweater, chatting amicably with everyone. Thankfully, in exactly fifteen minutes, the lights flicked on and off and everyone took their seats. The curtain came up and the play continued. There was no sign of Lee and Lindsay began to worry. Had the teacher pulled him from the play? If she had, Lee would be devastated. As she worried, Rand reached for her hand, gave it a comforting squeeze. Lindsay saw Natalie tense. What was wrong? Finally Lee came on stage. In an authoritative tone, he announced, "No, my dear, this is not the way it is going to be." And the curtain came down.

The audience was on its feet. Rand was clapping. Natalie was clapping and Lindsay was clapping harder than anyone. Lindsay didn't cry, but she certainly felt moisture around her eyes.

"Need a handkerchief?" Rand's elbow edged her side as the cast took a bow. Lindsay watched Natalie ascend the four side steps to the stage and smiling accepted the last of the three bouquets of flowers which were presented to the teacher, the director and the producer. Natalie was the producer. Smiling, holding her bouquet, Lindsay noticed that Natalie's first smile went directly to Rand.

Then as the lights went on in the auditorium, Rand teased, "You Macaulays don't say much, but when you do, you say it with a punch." With the center aisle clearing quite quickly, they walked to the back of the room. Russell brought his wife Alice across the hall to meet Lindsay. They chatted for a few minutes until the lineup around the coat booth cleared. As someone else came to speak to Rand, Lindsay had to wait: he had the ticket for her coat in his pocket. Natalie joined them as Rand was helping Lindsay on with her coat.

"Where are you meeting Lee?" he asked Lindsay.

"At the truck." Lindsay tried to keep her tone light, but it was hard with Natalie glaring at her and Rand's hands lingering on her shoulders.

"If you wait a minute or two, I'll follow you home."

"That's not necessary," Lindsay said.

"Well, I don't trust that old rattletrap that you drive. It could break down any time." He turned away when someone else spoke to him.

"You really should get a new vehicle, or at least a good used one." Natalie added her concern. "Rand has enough to do without worrying about you and that old rattletrap."

"Really." Every pore in Lindsay's body went on anger alert. "That rattletrap is mine, and it is paid for, and it will get Lee...and me...home safely." Lindsay's chin notched upward two degrees as she turned and hurried out of the hall. Rattletrap indeed! Hadn't she just paid Russell Taylor more than three hundred dollars to get it out of hock?

"Lindsay, wait!" Rand called out.

"Rand, dear! Have you forgotten we have a short director's meeting backstage in a couple of minutes? And you're the chairman." Although Natalie's words were directed to Rand, they were meant for Lindsay.

As they neared the truck, Lindsay turned to face Rand. "There's no need for you to follow me. My rattletrap truck will get us home safely."

"Will it really?" Rand taunted, his blue eyes dark with anger as he grabbed her chin, tilted it upward, bent his head, his mouth sought, demanded, possessed, sending prickly currents racing through Lindsay's body. Before she could regain her equilibrium, he yanked open the door of the pickup, pushed her inside, slammed the truck door and strode back across the parking lot to Natalie.

"Wow! What was that all about?" Lee asked, climbing into the passenger seat.

"Nothing!" Lindsay snapped. "Just a misunderstanding."

Choosing to ignore Lee's, "some misunderstanding!" she maneuvered the pickup between the remaining vehicles in the parking lot and tried not to notice Natalie standing close beside Rand at the entrance of the auditorium.

Six

Sleep hadn't come until the early hours of the morning. Now, with the hands on the bedside clock pointing to nine fifteen, her eyes burning from the light, her good nature was still stalled somewhere between Lee's good performance and her old rattletrap. In between was an elegant lady, Natalie Hunter, who evidently had some kind of claim on Rand.

All through those sleepless hours, feelings warred with fact, heart warred with reason. She was a single mother who owned a debt-ridden farm. Rand was a charismatic community leader, a horse breeder, part-time college lecturer. Lindsay hadn't even finished high school. Even their education set them worlds apart. Yet, there was a chemistry between them, this feeling of rightness that Lindsay couldn't explain.

"I'm sorry I slept so late." A knowing grin spread across Lindsay's face as she smelled the coffee. Lee never made breakfast unless he wanted something.

"Mom, do you think you could afford to buy me a pair of ice skates?" he asked a few minutes later when she sat at the table.

"Ice skates?"

"There is a skating party tomorrow afternoon at Taylor's pond and I've been invited." His blue eyes imploringly searched her face. "Oh, Mom, I'd like to go and I can't go without skates."

Lindsay knew he was lonely. In the city, he'd played volleyball at the local YMCA, gone swimming at the civic center and during the summers skate-boarded at a local park. Lindsay knew he needed to feel a part of the community, needed to be wanted. Of course, there had been that trouble with the dress code at school, but Lee had weathered that storm well with Beth Taylor's help, of course. Now he had been invited to a party at her home and it was important that he go.

"How much does a pair of skates cost?" she asked.

"I don't know. Probably a hundred dollars or more. A second-hand pair would do. They wouldn't cost that much and I've got a few dollars saved."

"You have a few dollars saved?"

Glaring at her, Lee exclaimed angrily, "I promised you I would stay out of trouble and I meant it!" His voice raised an octave higher.

"Then where did you get the money?" Lindsay cried.

Lee's face muscles tightened. "I earned it."

"Earned it? How?"

Lee's chin jutted out defiantly. "Two days ago. I went over to Rand's place with Art. Rand was clearing the snow from around the barn with his tractor and blower. He said the space between the barn and his laboratory was too narrow for the snow blower and asked me to shovel it for him. When I was finished, he gave me ten bucks." Then, in a softer voice, Lee said, "I wasn't going to tell you...because your birthday is coming up..."

"Oh, Lee..." Lindsay rushed around the table to hug him. "I'm so sorry. I shouldn't have doubted you. I shouldn't have..." Tears trickled down her cheeks.

She knew Lee needed to hang out with kids his own age. So far the only people he saw outside of his school were Art, Rand and herself. Now she had shattered that fragile bond of trust between them. She should have believed him.

Where was she going to get the money for a pair of skates? She had three places for every dollar they had. Skates were more important than overdue bills. If she skimped, paid only part of each bill, she might manage to get him a pair of skates.

An hour later in Riverton's downtown area, Lindsay told Lee to keep looking for the Goodwill store on Pitt Street. "That store has to be around here somewhere."

"Look. There's the library." Two pillars flanked a 'Riverton Public Library' sign above double-glass doors. "We'll have to go there some time." Lee liked to read.

"Maybe I could find information on how to run a horse farm," Lindsay quipped, before realizing going to the library wasn't such a bad idea. She told Lee she had been thinking of converting Trailwood into a *rent-a-stall* stable for people in the city who owned horses. A how-to book would help her flush out the details. He gave her a thumbs up sign before pointing to the "Goodwill" sign just ahead. Lindsay pulled into the parking lot.

Since she and Lee had often purchased things at Goodwill stores in Toronto, they felt comfortable in this one. The store had everything from shoe laces to artificial flowers. Lee found a pair of skates which looked almost new. He tried them on. They fit. And the price fit their tight budget. Since Lee still had her birthday money and her birthday was still two months away, Lindsay suggested that he use that money to buy a sweater and toque.

"Your birthday!" Lee protested.

"You can do some extra chores around the farm for me. I would appreciate that just as much."

On a rack at the back of the store they found a heavy blue sweater and matching toque, perfect for a skating party. As they were leaving the store, Lindsay remembered that Asher Honeyborne's office was nearby. If he worked Saturday mornings and she could see him, it would save her a trip next week.

The town was divided in half by the river. Most of the municipal buildings were on the north side of the river. The Goodwill store and Honeyborne's office were both on the south.

Lindsay parked the old "rattletrap" in front of the Honeyborne building. Walking along the sidewalk, Lindsay paused to stare at the two-story brick building. "I think this used to be a bakery's livery stable."

"You're kidding." Lee's head tilted slightly to the side.

"I'm sure it was. The delivery horses were stabled on ground level, the delivery wagons were parked outside at the back and the hay was stored in the loft above the stable," Lindsay said, as frightening glimpses suddenly came to mind of a young girl *a wagon loaded with hay, a coil of rope, a huge fork jammed into the hay, an opening in the side of the loft, horses pulling, a fork of hay, swinging upward, girl's leg caught in the rope, pulling higher and higher, girl screaming and screaming, horses stopped, girl falling, grandfather crying...*Lindsay's hands covered her face.

"Mom! Mom, what's the matter with you? You look like you're going to pass out." Lee grabbed her hands trying to pull them away from her face.

"I'll be all right in a minute," she whispered softly, wiping the sweat from her brow with her sleeve. "Just shadows...of a memory."

"You're sure having a lot of those lately," Lee said. "Why do you want to see Honeyborne anyway?"

"I want to know why my grandfather needed to mortgage Trailwood. According to his journal, the farm was doing okay," Lindsay said. "And I want to know why, six years ago, when the mortgage was finally paid off, he remortgaged Trailwood."

"That's when the doctors put that rod in your leg, isn't it? " Lee asked.

"About that time, yes," Lindsay said as she followed Lee into the foyer of the building. "Maria had a friend who was involved with a benevolent foundation that provided funding for the extra money I needed, especially after the operation, to get back and forth to the rehab hospital, and, of course, wheelchair, crutches—those things that helped me finally walk without a limp."

Two suites opened off the foyer, one with Asher Honeyborne's nameplate over the door. When Lindsay asked to see him, the secretary—her name plate said Emily Pritchard—told Lindsay that if she wanted to see *Mr.* Honeyborne, she would have to make an appointment.

Lindsay abhorred people who used their position to make others feel small and insignificant. It happened occasionally at the supermarket when a customer who didn't have enough money to pay their bill challenged the *insignificant* cashier. Now, using her best sugar-sweet tone of voice, Lindsay said, "Oh, Asher didn't tell me I needed an appointment."

His secretary tensed. "He is a very busy man." She flipped through the pages of the appointment book. "What did you want to see him about?"

"Business. I'm Lindsay Macaulay."

"Oh, Miss Macaulay, I didn't recognize you." A semblance of a smile appeared. "Mr. Honeyborne does have an appointment available on Monday at two o'clock. Would that be convenient for you?"

Lindsay nodded. Then, as she turned to leave, she saw a collage of old pictures on the wall. In the center was a bread wagon and delivery man and her curiosity got the better of her. "Was this building once a livery stable?"

"Why, yes." Miss Pritchard stood and came around her desk. "The delivery horses for a bread company were stabled here. How did you know?"

"I came here once with my grandfather years ago when he was delivering hay to the stable."

"It is remarkable what can be done with an old barn, isn't it? Mr. Honeyborne bought the building about ten years ago." She pointed to several pictures hanging on the wall. "These are other buildings in and around Riverton that he has restored. He loves refurbishing old properties."

"He certainly has done a fine job on this building," Lindsay said. "I'll see you Monday afternoon."

The secretary walked with Lindsay to the door. "I'm glad to see you walking without a limp, Miss Macaulay."

Back at the truck, Lee remarked, "How did that woman know about your leg, Mom?"

"Perhaps Honeyborne told her."

"But you only met him a month ago?"

Lindsay shrugged.

That *how did she know* bothered Lindsay. Miss Pritchard worked for Honeyborne, so she would be privy to his correspondence and phone calls. But who in Riverton would know about her operation? Know that she could now walk without a limp? After Lindsay's accident twenty-six years ago, Maria had cut all ties with Riverton.

Lindsay remembered the surprise on the faces of Art Winston and Rand when Lee had said at the station that he and Lindsay had come to stay at Trailwood. They didn't know she was coming.

Something else. Asher Honeyborne had said a numbered company was interested in the property if she wanted to sell.

Yesterday Art mentioned that at one time her dad was thinking of connecting the back of Trailwood to the racetrack across the river. But that was years ago, before Lindsay's accident, and even more years before that last operation. Where was the connection?

Six years ago Lindsay had been working at the supermarket. She had come across a news feature about a ground-breaking method to repair shattered bones. To walk without a limp, without pain, would be like a ticket to heaven, Lindsay thought as she reread the feature. Could it help her? She had called the doctor who had performed the surgery on her leg years before. He recommended it. However, this type of operation would require five to seven months of rehabilitation and her sick benefit policy covered only two months' down time.

Lindsay had been rereading the article, crying, because there was no way she could afford to be off work that long and she wanted the operation so badly, when Maria had come home from her late-night hostess job at an uptown restaurant and bar. "We'll find it somehow," she had said.

Miraculously she had. There was this program—someone at work had told her about it—that helped people on low income. Maria had said she would handle the paperwork. Since she was working nights, she would arrange for someone to look after Lee and do the housework while Lindsay was in the hospital. All Lindsay had to do was agree to the operation. Maria had kept her word. She had looked after everything. Lindsay had the operation, worked through the endless hours of rehabilitation and, five months later, had been able to return to work without a limp.

Then Maria had left. While she had vowed that she loved Lindsay and Lee dearly, she wanted a life of her own and had taken a hostess job at a Whistler Mountain resort.

Shortly afterward, Lindsay and Lee had moved to a two-bedroom apartment close to his school and the mall supermarket where she worked. Within a few blocks from their apartment was a YMCA with a good teen program, a skateboard park, a theater and churches, one which Lindsay always planned to attend, and numerous senior citizens and low income housing.

Had she missed her mother? Yes, even Maria's haranguing. It had left an empty hole but Lee had made up for it. Sometimes he never stopped talking. Other times he could go for hours without saying a word.

Not today. When he saw the golden arches of McDonald's fast-food restaurant he asked hesitantly, "Can we afford a hamburger and milk shake, Mom?" Neither of them had been to a fast-food restaurant since they came to Riverton. "Can we? Please." Lee repeated. "Please."

Lindsay's usual answer was no, but the old truck seemed to have a mind of its own and turned into the drive-thru. After paying for two milk shakes, two hamburgers and fries, Lindsay had a dollar and twenty cents left in her purse.

Munching on her hamburger, Lindsay tried not to think about what she was going to do for money. She didn't want to mortgage the property again because she had no way of paying it off. She didn't want to sell the farm, even though that had been her intention when she first received Honeyborne's letter. However, Trailwood was the first real home she and Lee had ever had.

"Don't they ever fix these roads?" Lee complained later as the truck hit another pothole, spilling a bit of his milk shake.

"I'm trying to steer around them," Lindsay said. "After that quick thaw, there are holes everywhere."

They neared the intersection of their road: a small direction arrow pointed north to the main highway and to the racetrack on the other side of the river. Suddenly, the pickup's motor suddenly sputtered and died. Lee jumped out and lifted the hood. Lindsay followed. Neither knew anything about motors. They wiggled several wires, checked another to see if it was loose. Lindsay got back in the truck. Turned the key again. Nothing.

"I guess we'll have to walk the rest of the way," she said. "It's not too far. I'll call Taylor's garage from home." She was already calculating the towing bill, the repairs and the money she didn't have when they heard a car coming.

Recognizing the car, Lee waved. "It's Rand. He'll give us a ride home."

Rand. The last person Lindsay wanted to see; Natalie was with him. A minute later Rand was peering into the truck's engine.

Lindsay heard Lee telling him, "We were on our way home and the truck gave up the ghost."

"You should bury it in the cemetery," Rand quipped, nodding toward the old cemetery sign which pointed down the side road. Then over the top of the motor his blue-grey eyes met Lindsay's hostile ones. "I'm sorry, Lindsay," he apologized. "I shouldn't malign your truck. It has been a good truck. It's just old."

Even Lee sensed that more than words were being said. Natalie's, "Rand. Come on. We're already late," broke the connection.

Ignoring Natalie's command, Rand continued to fiddle with the engine. "Here's what's wrong...a wire has come off the coil." He went over to the trunk of his car rummaging around in a tool box until he found a wrench. "This will only take a couple of minutes. Then, City Lady, you can be on your way," he said.

City Lady, again! Oh, how those words rankled. Regardless, she was thankful. Ten minutes later, as Lee chattered on and on about Rand's Lincoln and how wonderful it would be to own such a car, Lindsay turned their old rattletrap into the Trailwood lane.

"Oh, will you shut up about Rand Dyson's Lincoln!" Lindsay exclaimed. Then, realizing she was taking her anger out on Lee, she softened her tone. "I *am* grateful for his help, and I did thank him. Now can we forget it?"

But Lee wasn't finished. As he jumped out of the truck, Lindsay heard, "Rand really likes you...a whole lot! Don't you know that?"

Seven

Lindsay watched Lee zig and zag around the icy puddles in the lane as he ran for the bus. He had waited on the veranda until he could hear its grinding gears slowing for their stop. Many of their rural neighbors had small wooden shelters at the end of their lane for their children. Maybe Art would build one for Lee.

When the freezing downpour had started just before breakfast, Lindsay offered to park the pickup at the end of the lane so Lee wouldn't get soaked waiting for the bus, but Lee was against it. He told her the kids made fun of their old truck, especially Ian Hardesty, who said even the junkyard wouldn't want it.

After watching Lee board the bus, Lindsay pulled on her boots, shrugged into an old hooded nylon jacket and ran to the barn. As the cold winter rain pelted against her cheeks, she thought how lucky that the Taylors had their skating party yesterday. Today the pond would be a sea of watery ice.

Yanking open the stable door, two welcoming nickers greeted her, but one sounded different. Usually both horses had their heads over the top half of their stall doors. This morning the only one she could see was Queenie's.

Shrugging out of her dripping coat, Lindsay looked into Princess's stall. "Oh, my God!"

Standing on wobbly little legs, nuzzling against Princess's underbelly was a chestnut foal, his coat wet with the film of birth. "Oh, you little beauty," Lindsay whispered, trying to remember everything she had read about newborn foals. Princess objected with a "don't touch" nicker as Lindsay grabbed an empty grain sack and wiped the shivering little foal dry and threw a blanket over Princess, not bothering to tie the straps.

What next? Call the veterinarian. She grabbed her coat and dashed back to the house. Dr. Ted Woodward wasn't in. She left a message on his answering service.

The breeder's book said the mare should be given warm mash—a mixture of bran mixed with boiling water and a dash of linseed oil. Art had left a pail half full of mash in Lindsay's pantry for a situation like this. The linseed oil was beside it.

She dialed the number on the pad above the telephone. With bated breath, she waited.

"Dyson here."

"My God, she had dialed the wrong number. Or had she?

"Hello." Exasperation hardened the timber of his voice. "Who is this?"

"I called..."

"Lindsay, is that you? Is something wrong? Are you all right?" His rapid-fire questions didn't give her a chance to answer.

Finally, "Everything's fine...Rand?" She could hardly keep the joy from her voice. "I just called to tell you Princess had her foal."

"I'll be right over."

"There's no need. I've already called the vet...at least, I put a message on his answering service. I've put iodine on the foal's umbilical cord and...I've done everything the book said." Lindsay tried to sound like a confident, experienced horse breeder. "Lee is at school...and, oh, I'm so excited I just had to tell someone!"

"I'll see you in a few minutes."

And the line went dead.

Rand was coming. Her heart skipped a beat. Was that what she was hoping for when she dialed his number supposedly in error? Had she lost her mind? She ran her fingers through her short hair. At least it was half-tidy. Grabbing the warmed mash, she returned to the barn.

After giving Princess her mash, Lindsay realized she had forgotten to feed Queenie. She pitched in a fork of hay before going back to watch the little filly wobble around the stall on her spindly legs, her stubby tail swishing back and forth like a metronome keeping time to a tune only she could hear.

"She's a real beauty," Rand said, casually slipping his arm around her shoulders. "What are you going to name her?"

Lindsay turned her head to look at him. His face was only inches away. The intoxicating freshness of the rain on his clothes, the tangy woodiness of his aftershave cologne, mixed pleasantly with the aromas of the stable. "I don't know." she stammered. "Surprise, maybe."

Lindsay heard Rand catch his breath as he tucked a stray strand of hair behind her ear.

"Congratulations, City Lady." His hand cupped her chin as an intangible thread of awareness wound around them and for one brief moment the taste of heaven was on Lindsay's lips.

She wanted to say something witty, sophisticated but all she could manage was, "Do you always congratulate people with a kiss?"

A wry smile curved Rand's lips as he touched the tip of her nose with his forefinger. "Only the ones I like."

By the time Lindsay's emotions had righted, Rand was hunkered down beside the filly. He opened her mouth, all the while talking quietly to Princess, who from her jittery movements apparently didn't like someone touching her offspring.

Next, Rand checked the filly's non solidified hooves. "They'll harden in a day or so," he told Lindsay. When she had first seen the inside of the filly's hooves, she thought they were alive with fish worms. Then she remembered reading in one of her grandfather's journals that unsealed hooves were normal for a newborn. When Rand stood to examine the mare, the little filly took off, still unsteady on her spindly legs. She had been cocooned for eleven months. Now she wanted to play.

"You know, Lindsay, I'm not religious, yet whenever I see a newborn foal, I marvel at the creation of it all."

"It is wonderful, isn't it?" Lindsay said, smiling. "I wanted to share it with someone."

"I'm glad that someone was me." Rand's eyes mirrored his pleasure.

"I also wanted to apologize." She felt the warmth creeping into her cheeks. "The other night when you fixed my truck, I was angry because..."

"....because I called your truck an old rattletrap." His long thick eyebrows lifted inquiringly.

"It was kind of you to stop." Feeling her cheeks warm with embarrassment, she grinned, "Eating humble pie isn't one of my stronger characteristics."

"That wasn't the only reason I stopped," he said softly.

Suddenly feeling out of her depth, Lindsay forced her attention back to the filly as little quivers rippled along the chestnut's back. "Rand, she's shivering. Is she cold or just afraid of her new world?"

"Both, I suspect. This is an old barn. There's a lot of cracks where the cold can seep in." Rand glanced around the stable. "Old Jeb must have run into this problem many times over the years. I'll bet he's got a heat lamp and tarpaulin around here some place."

Uncertain as to what he was going to do with a tarpaulin, Lindsay watched Rand search through a couple of old wooden chests. The first contained everything from liniment to curry combs and brushes. The second contained a heat lamp, extension cords and a tarpaulin.

With her help, Rand nailed the tarpaulin to the rafter on the inside of the outer wall of the stall, covering all the cracks and blocking out the cold when anyone opened the barn door. He hooked the extension cord to the overhead light bulb socket in Princess's stall, draped the cord to the tarpaulin corner of the stall, letting the lamp hang down about three feet. Meanwhile, Lindsay cleaned Princess's stall, covering it with fresh straw. She threw extra forksful into the corner, making a warm bed for the little foal and just as Rand was finishing anchoring his tarpaulin tent in the corner of Princess's stall, the barn door squeaked and the vet, Tom Woodward, came in.

After examining the newborn filly, he said, "You have a strong filly here. She's about as perfect as you're going to get, wouldn't you say, Rand?"

"I think so." Rand glanced over his shoulder at Lindsay. "But then I'm prejudiced." Prejudiced. Why would he be prejudiced? Before she could ask, the vet was teasing Rand about his tent building skills. Then turning to

Lindsay, he said, "I don't think you will have any problems, Miss Macaulay, but if you do, just call," he said as he gathered his medical tools and placed them back in his bag.

Lindsay thanked him and invited both men to the house for a coffee.

"Thanks, but my wife is expecting me home early and I have two more calls to make." He shook hands with Rand. "I'll probably see you later at the Hunter birthday party."

As Lindsay and Rand walked to the house, she was startled to see the school bus stopping at the end of the lane. Where had the time gone? Her appointment! She missed her one-thirty appointment with Asher Honeyborne. When Lee got near, she shouted, "We got a new filly!"

Lee's fist shot into air. "Way to go, Princess!" he yelled. "Oh, I can't wait to see her." He shrugged the knapsack off his shoulders, handed it to Lindsay and after a quick "hello" to Rand, was off to the barn, but not before Rand called out, "Be quiet, and don't touch, just look.'

As Lindsay and Rand hung their coats on the wooden pegs on the back of the kitchen door, Lindsay asked, "Are you sure you have time for coffee?" She recalled the veterinarian's reference to the Hunter birthday party.

"I'm sure," he said casually, throwing his arm across her shoulders, a casualness that seemed to be developing into a habit. "And a sandwich wouldn't come amiss. We missed lunch, you know."

While Lindsay made the coffee, heated some leftover soup and made a few sandwiches, she gave Rand Old Jeb's journal to leaf through, asking him to see if he could find to whom Princess had been bred. She listened as he read off the names of some of the stallions her grandfather had used over the years.

"Now that Princess has dropped her foal, you'll have to start thinking about whose stallion services you are going to use this time. Seven days go by quickly." Rand pushed the journal aside.

"Seven days. What are you talking about?"

"A brood mare should be bred again seven days after her foal is born."

Lindsay stared at Rand. "You can't be serious!"

Rand's blue eyes danced with mischief. "Barefoot and pregnant—that's how you keep them down on the farm," he teased, changing slightly the words of the old song.

Without thinking, Lindsay quickly retorted, "I'd hate to be your wife, if that's the way you think." Her face reddened as she suddenly realized what she had said.

Rand's one eyelid dropped in a flirtatious wink. "I'm in the market, you know."

"Really." She placed the soup and sandwiches in front of him.

"Not interested?" His eyes challenged her to respond. "What a pity."

Not interested? How wrong could he be? Just the thought of being his wife caused a rush of adrenalin to pump through her veins. His face was the first thing she saw every morning when she woke and the last thing she saw before she fell asleep.

Lee had never made a more timely entrance in his life than at that moment. "Oh, Mom, she's beautiful and her coat is so soft and silky." He held up his hand. "I just patted her once," he told Rand as he kicked off his boots and put them on the boot tray. "I nuzzled her nose, and I'm sure she nuzzled me back." He hung up his coat and then, his round face aglow, he grabbed Lindsay in a bear hug. "Oh, Mom, our first filly. Isn't it wonderful?"

Willing herself not to cry, she hugged him back. If Rand hadn't been there, her tears would have flowed like the water over Niagara Falls.

"Did you see her, Rand? Isn't she a beauty?" Lee couldn't contain his excitement. That tarp and heat lamp...where did you get all that stuff?" Not waiting to hear Rand's answer, Lee grabbed a sandwich off the plate and headed for the telephone on the hall wall off the kitchen. "I'm going to call Beth. Tell her about the foal."

Lindsay was surprised that Lee wanted to call Beth instead of Art Winston. She had forgotten that Art was looking after the horses for a breeder in the next county who was ill.

"Oh, to be that young again," Rand said, chuckling, as Lee's conversation drifted into the kitchen.

"Like you're so old," Lindsay teased, sitting across from him at the table.

"Forty-one, last count." Rand took a bite of his sandwich.

"I read once that birthdays are good for your health because studies show that those who have more birthdays live longer."

Rand laughed, reaching for her hand, giving it a gentle squeeze.

She wanted to entwine her fingers with his, but hearing Lee's, "good-bye, Beth," she moved it away.

"Beth says she's going to get her dad to bring her over after supper to see the foal." Lee grabbed another sandwich and bolted up the stairs, saying he had to change his clothes and do his homework before she arrived.

Quieter now, the ambience of the old kitchen folded around them. Rand looked so comfortable there, his elbow on the table, a few strands of hair falling across his forehead. Lindsay wondered if her grandparents had sat around this same old table, thinking, mulling over their problems.

"Rand, what am I going to do about the filly? There are no records showing to whom Princess was bred and without records, how am I supposed to register the filly with the Standardbred Association? And there's the stud fee—you know I'm obligated to pay it once the mare throws a live foal."

"First things first," Rand said. "There are only two stallions in the area that could have been used: Starmist and Clover Boy. Last fall Clover Boy was sold to White Plains in Michigan. They would have a record if Clover Boy sired your filly and they would certainly want it known that their stallion bred a golden cross." He reached for her hand again. "We'll call them in the morning."

Her question about a golden cross was overshadowed by that *we* again.

"And I own Starmist and there's no record of any dealing with Old Jeb on my books."

"Rand, I don't have the money for stud fees, not Clover Boy's and certainly not Starmist's, or anyone else's for that matter."

Lindsay knew from an advertisement she had seen in the *Trot* magazine that the stud fees for Starmist were in the five-figure range. Clover Boy's stud fees were only a shade less.

"Have you talked to your grandfather's bank manager?" Rand asked. "That's a good place to start."

"I've never met a bank manager. I wouldn't know what to say."

"Just tell him what you've told me. He's an understanding man."

"If you say so...." Lindsay managed. "I do have one little bright spot—I got a letter from a university student who is doing his thesis on barns. He wants to spend a week-end here researching the structure of our octangular barn and he's willing to pay for his room and board. He's coming this weekend."

"To stay with you?"

"Yes. Lee's here and I've got a spare bedroom. Besides I need the money. Of course, he might change his mind when he sees the room and how old everything is and he might want to stay in Riverton at night."

"I wouldn't worry too much about it as long as it's clean," he assured her.

"Maybe coffee from that old pot will help put him in the right frame of mind for his research." She pointed to a high shelf above the stove where a coffee grinder and a blue enamel pot were stored.

"Be sure you use them when you make breakfast." Rand chuckled, his blue-grey eyes dancing a moment with mirth. "Seriously, you might like to contact the Riverton Historical Society or the library. See what they have on old buildings in the area."

"That's a good idea. If he's interested in old things, maybe others are too ...and I have to make a living."

Before she could ask Rand what he thought of the idea, the telephone rang. Expecting it to be Beth Taylor asking for Lee, Lindsay was surprised by a woman's voice asking if Rand Dyson was there.

"Just a moment." Lindsay motioned that the call was for him.

His eyebrows went up a notch as he took the phone from Lindsay.

"Yes, Natalie. I know it is your father's birthday and I'm sorry I have been delayed," he apologized. "And, yes, I have the wine, and, yes, I will be there by six."

Seeing the 'how did Natalie know he was here look' question on Lindsay's face, "Country gossip," Rand said. "Natalie called Millie Woodward, Doc Woodward's wife, something about tonight's party and Millie mentioned that you had a beautiful foal and that I was here."

Chagrined, Lindsay murmured, "I'm sorry. I didn't mean to keep you."

"There's no need to be sorry." Rand reached for his coat. "I knew what time it was."

Then, leaning close, his lips brushed hers. "See you soon, City Lady."

And he was gone. But not the feel of his lips.

Eight

Long into the wee hours of the morning, sitting at the kitchen table with a notepad in front of her, her eyes smarting from tiredness, Lindsay finished her draft for a boarding stable for horses at Trailwood.

Rand had suggested she see her grandfather's bank manager, Lyle Edmonds. Before she saw him, she needed a clear outline in her own mind.

Her plan was simple. She had the barn, corral, pasture fields, trails to the woods and river. The barn's octangular shape could be an attraction, a landmark, a focal point for the stable and she would lease the rest of the land, like her grandfather did, to a neighboring farmer in return for hay and straw for her own horses. She and Lee could do the work: Art could be their adviser.

Lindsay needed a "hook." Something that would attract people with horses, people who wanted to get away from the city for a weekend, spend it on a farm riding their horse. She would need to advertise—a weekend in the country with your horse—something that would tease the mind of a horse owner looking for a boarding stable.

On paper it seemed feasible.

Lindsay also had her porcelain painting—a hobby that could be expanded into a small business, but it would take time to establish a solid customer base. She could even tie it to Trailwood, paint horses instead of flowers or combine the two.

There was another option. Pack it in. Go back to the city. The supermarket manager had promised her a job anytime she wanted to return.

That didn't solve Lee's problem. "Get him away from his so-called friends," the juvenile judge had said. And she had. Lee had new friends, new interests and Art Winston was a good role model for the thirteen-year-old.

Tired, exhausted, she finally pushed her draft away and turned out the lights.

~ * ~

The next afternoon, Lindsay dressed carefully for what she felt was one of the most important meetings in her life: three quarter length winter coat, black slacks, her hair held back from her face with two clips and a briefcase full of papers. She didn't have an appointment. She hadn't even thought about it.

Like an omen, the sun peeped out from behind dark clouds. All the same, her courage wavered when she reached the marble pillars flanking the entrance to the bank. Telling herself she was Lindsay Macaulay, the new owner of Trailwood, she straightened her shoulders and walked calmly toward the woman sitting at the receptionist desk. "I would like to see Mr. Edmonds, please."

"Have you an appointment?" the receptionist asked.

"No." Lindsay shook her head. "Sort of a spur of the moment decision." Lindsay smiled. "I was drinking a cup of tea, thinking—and here I am."

The receptionist smiled and she said she would try and work Lindsay in between the manager's appointments.

A half hour later, the receptionist escorted Lindsay into Lyle Edmonds' office. A pleasant looking man with a receding hairline stood and held out his hand to her. "I'm Lyle Edmonds, Miss Macaulay and I'm very glad to meet you. Your grandfather and I were good friends."

He motioned for her to take a chair across from his desk. "Old Jeb was a very proud man when he was able to pay off his mortgage a few months ago."

That mortgage again. "I don't understand why he needed a mortgage in the first place. Trailwood always seemed to show a profit, albeit a small one," Lindsay said, hoping Edmonds would supply some information as to why Old Jeb had needed a mortgage.

Instead, he asked, "What can I do you for you, Miss Macaulay?"

Disappointed, Lindsay took a breath and proceeded. "Although I would like to follow the Macaulay tradition of breeding and racing, it isn't a practical choice for me. Instead I would like to open a boarding stable, and, possibly, later, a bed and breakfast. Right now, what I need most is advice and money."

She explained that city residents who owned horses, needed a place to board their horses and a place to ride. Trailwood, with its octangular barn, its woods and trails along the river, was ideally suited for such a venture. She and her son would look after the horses on weekdays, with Art Winston's guidance, of course. She saw Edmonds smile.

"Before I can advertise Trailwood as a boarding stable, the stable needs to be upgraded and repaired," Lindsay continued. "I know I can sell the property, but..."

"Have you had an offer?" Edmonds looked up from the papers he was studying from her briefcase.

"Asher Honeyborne mentioned that a numbered company was interested."

"Do you want to sell?"

"No. Trailwood is our home now." Lindsay's gaze never wavered from Edmonds'.

"It is a good place for my son to grow up." As she spoke, she realized that she truly loved Trailwood. It was her heritage, her link to the past and hopefully the gateway to their future. Unfortunately, her assets were limited: two brood mares and an-almost perfect day-old filly.

Lindsay sat quietly watching Edmonds study the outline she had worked out. "Your best bet, Miss Macaulay, is to put a small mortgage on Trailwood. A mortgage would entail yearly or half-yearly payments, plus interest." He explained that if she defaulted, the bank would take over the property. They in turn would sell it, pay off the mortgage and Lindsay would receive whatever was left.

"An alternative is a short term loan. Payments could be spread over a one or two year period which would give you time to get Trailwood on a paying basis. For that, I'm afraid, you will need a co-signer."

Just then, Edmonds' secretary buzzed him on his intercom. "Sir, your next appointment is here."

Edmonds got to his feet. "I like your plan to turn Trailwood into a boarding stable, Miss Macaulay. I think you could make it a paying proposition." He walked around his desk. "But it's certainly going to take time and work...and money." He offered his hand. "Give me time to study these figures. In the meantime, think over your options, a loan or a mortgage...and leave your telephone number with my secretary."

The meeting was over and Lindsay was no further ahead than before she came. But she didn't want to go home. She wanted her family. She wanted her father *who hugged her and whispered "I love you" in her ear* and her grandfather *who shielded her from her mother's wrath.* Why did those thoughts creep out of the shadows of her lost memory?

Lindsay hadn't realized how much she loved Trailwood until she had talked to Edmonds. She wanted to stay there and raise her son. If she could only talk to her dad...and she could in a way by visiting his grave site.

When she came to the crossroad of her road and the Cemetery road, she turned north, parking the truck on the side of the road opposite the Pioneer Cemetery stone archway. Winding an old scarf that was in the truck around her head, she walked carefully over the ice-crusted snow, searching row after row for her family.

The quietness of the cemetery, glazed in the soft golden light of a winter sun, was like balm to Lindsay's troubled soul.

A rabbit darted from behind a monument. A crow cawed his ragged note of objection. A tear caught in her eye as she came to a headstone with an angel on its brow. Maryann Dyson, aged two. She read the date. She must have been Rand's sister. How awful it must have been to lose a child.

At the end of the fourth row, she found a blue marble stone with Macaulay carved across the top. In smaller letters was Jeffery Jebediah—her father—the date of his birth and the date of his death. Below the letters was a mural of a horse, sulky cart and driver at the finish line and the inscription *"the Best of the Best.* Lindsay started to cry, giant gut-wrenching tears for the father she didn't remember and the grandfather her son would never know.

It was a long time before she noticed the names carved inside a heart on a similar monument next to her father's. Jebediah and Martha Macaulay, the grandmother she loved and the grandfather she had hated for the last twenty years. Jeb hadn't meant for the truck he was driving to run over her leg. It had been an accident. He must have been devastated. Her dad had just been killed and Maria, his daughter-in-law, was leaving and not taking her daughter. Lindsay was screaming for her mother. Until then, Lindsay had only thought about herself, but what about her grandfather's loss, his pain?

Here in the tranquility of the cemetery, her tears washed away the hurt, the pain and the animosity. No matter what happened in the future, she would stay at Trailwood.

Suddenly, she realized that Lee would be home ahead of her. And he was. His boots were in the boot tray outside the kitchen door and his school books were thrown on the kitchen table. For a fleeting second—he usually didn't throw them about like that—she wondered if something was wrong.

She didn't have to wait long.

A few minutes later, Lee stomped in from the barn, plunked his butt down on a kitchen chair and demanded that they move back to the city.

Open-mouthed, Lindsay stared at him. "For heaven's sakes, why?" Then she saw his face. She grasped his chin, turned it to the light. Lee had an inch-long cut on his left cheek and a bruise around his right eye which was already turning black. "What happened?"

Lee jerked his head away. "I got in a fight."

"I can see that."

"Oh, Mom, we shouldn't have come here!" Lee cried. He jumped up, pushed past Lindsay and vaulted up the stairs, slamming his bedroom door.

Lindsay rushed up the stairs and flung his door open. "Lee, I want an explanation and I want it now."

Lee lay face down, flopped across his bed. His fists scrunched the coverlet. "I can't go back to *that* school. Ever!" he cried. "Please, Mom, don't make me!"

His distress broke Lindsay's heart. She saw on the bed beside him, her hand gently rubbing the tightness between his shoulders. "Suppose you tell me what happened," she asked softly.

For a long moment, Lee didn't say anything. Then he began slowly, "This morning, Mrs. Taylor was looking for money she had put away in her dresser drawer the day of the skating party. The money was gone. So she called the police. An officer came to the school. He questioned everyone that was at the skating party." Lee gulped a sob. "Ian Hardesty told him that he had seen me leaving the upstairs bathroom next to Mrs. Taylor's bedroom."

"Surely other kids used that bathroom," Lindsay said.

"None of them had ever been in trouble with the law," Lee cried out. "The police questioned me again. I guess they found out from my school records. Anyway, they said that I had the opportunity and it would go easier for me if I confessed." Lee raised his head and looked at Lindsay. "I tried to get you on the telephone—the police said I could make one call—but you had left Mr. Edmonds' office. Then the officer called the house. You weren't there either." Lee rolled onto his back and sat up. ""Oh, Mom, I was so scared. Where were you?"

"I was at the cemetery," she whispered. "So what happened?"

Lee turned over. Sat up. Knuckled his eyes. Gulped a sniff. "Mr. Taylor came home. His wife told him that someone had *stolen* her money. He laughed and said that he was the thief. He needed to make change for a customer, so he used the money his wife had put away to make the change. He promised to give it back."

"What's the problem?"

"Ian Hardesty. He's telling everyone that I was in trouble in the city. That I'm a thief. He keeps calling me a juvie and some of his friends are calling me a juvie too. Mom, it is so awful."

"I thought the judge said those records were sealed and as long as you stayed out of trouble, they wouldn't be opened."

"Well, someone found out because it was Ian Hardesty that told the police that I had a record. And I sure didn't tell anyone."

"Neither did I," she said, urging Lee to come down to supper. But as Lindsay went down the stairs, she remembered she had told someone.

She had learned a lot about suspicion at the supermarket, when to think the worst and when not.

She also learned that a well-founded suspicion sometimes could save the store hundreds of dollars. Deep pockets, hidden merchandise, brazen attitudes were all part of the above suspicion package. This was different. This was a confidence she had shared with Rand. But how well did she know him? He was Art's trusted friend, a man of means, a man who didn't believe in love. Breed only *the best to the best* was his motto. She had to think.

Supper was a solemn affair. Neither she nor Lee ate much. "We have to discuss this," Lindsay said.

"There's nothing to discuss. I want to go back to the city."

"This will blow over. This is your home now and you love it here." Lindsay reached across the table, touched his arm. "Lee, there are going to be Ian Hardestys wherever you go, someone who wants to rake up the past, hurt you, make you feel small. Are you going to run every time that happens? And it *will* happen. Or are you going to stand tall, tell them to go take a flying leap...and get on with your life? It's your choice."

Lee didn't answer her. He just pushed his plate aside and went upstairs to watch the small television set they had brought from Toronto.

Lindsay's movements seemed weighted as she cleared the table and washed the dishes. Lee's pain was her pain. Instead of running upstairs to her son, as she wanted to do, she got her paints, brushes and buttercup plate from her grandfather's downstairs bedroom which had become a storeroom. She critically viewed the plate. The leaves needed a little extra color to make them more realistic. She arranged everything on the table, pulled the hanging lamp a little lower and prepared to drown herself in her work.

A sharp knock on the veranda door startled her for a minute.

Rand!

She opened the door.

"I'm Alice Taylor. We met the other night at the play..." the woman said hesitantly.

"Oh, yes, Alice. I remember you." Lindsay stepped back. "Please come in."

As Alice removed her boots and Lindsay took her coat, she said, "I came to apologize, to explain what happened this afternoon...about the money, the police." She took the chair at the end of the table that Lindsay offered. "I feel this whole mess is my fault."

Lindsay had never been a tea-drinking person, but watching Alice rubbing the back of one hand with the other, now seemed a good time to start. "Would you like a cup of tea, Alice?"

Alice smiled, although it was a bit on the wobbly side. "My dear old granny always said that a cup of tea can diminish almost any trouble."

After the tea was made and poured, Alice began her confession. "Ever since we started the garage, I've always tucked a little money away in an upstairs' drawer. Because, when you're in business, money is often in short supply."

Lindsay nodded. She knew the feeling.

"There's a man who hangs around the garage, does odd jobs for Russell...I don't like him and I don't trust him, but Russ says he's perfectly harmless. Just a guy down on his luck." Alice added another teaspoon of sugar to her already sweet tea. "I had to go into town for groceries, pay some bills. A friend and I went to lunch, and then we went shopping. I spent more than I should have, so when I got home, I went to the dresser drawer to get some cash. The money was gone. The man I suspected had a sound alibi.

"When the police found out about the skating party yesterday, they started questioning the kids. When there was a line outside the downstairs bathroom, Beth suggested that some of the kids go upstairs and use the bathroom next to our bedroom. Three went up. Lee was one. The police questioned the kids further and somehow they found out that he had been involved in a robbery in the city."

"Lee never robbed anyone!" Lindsay exclaimed. "He's as honest as the day is long."

"I know that now, but by the time Russell came home, the damage was done. If only I had waited, none of this would have happened."

"Well it did happen." Lindsay tried to manufacture a smile as she poured Alice another cup of tea. Lashing out at Alice wasn't going to solve anything. "Maybe we all are too quick to pass judgement." Like she had been doing a few minutes ago.

Alice nodded toward the buttercup plate. "A hobby?"

"Yes. And I enjoy it. Makes me forget my troubles."

"How did you get started?"

Lindsay smiled, remembering. "I was in rehabilitation at a Toronto hospital. The pills dulled the pain; they didn't take it away. The hours were empty, endless. My therapist tried to involve me in different crafts. I wasn't interested. One day, she put me in a wheelchair and took me to the craft room, pushed me in front of a table with paints and handed me a plate with a crack in the middle. I asked what am I supposed to do with that and she said, paint it. Be creative...and then she left me."

"And I sat there. Angry. Alone. Staring at that damn plate. I grabbed a brush. Stuck it into the green paint. Swished it onto the plate. Part of the crack disappeared. I calmed down and, using a thinner bristle brush, I slowly covered the crack and to make my story short, that crack became the stem of a flower and the flower became a rose. Although I must admit that first rose looked more like a cabbage." Lindsay grinned at the openmouthed Alice. "And that's how I got into china painting."

"Have you ever painted horses, foals, farm scenes?" she asked.

"No, but I've been thinking about it ever since our foal was born."

"You should put some of your work on display at the horsemen's show at the Tamarack Lodge," Alice said. "It's coming up soon."

"I've read about it in some of the horse magazines, but I'm afraid going there is out of my budget."

"You would learn a lot about horses and you would meet a lot of people. There's always a dance and a snowmobile ride through the countryside to finish up, weather permitting of course."

"Sounds like fun," Lindsay admitted as Alice got up to go.

The two women hugged.

As Lindsay locked the door, put away her paints and turned out the lights, she wondered what the coming day would hold.

And what would she do if Lee refused to go to school?

Nine

Before Lindsay realized it, it was Friday and researcher, Marshall Armstrong, was coming in on the five-fifteen train. She hadn't been to the railway station since she and Lee had arrived in that awful blizzard six weeks earlier.

The train braked to a stop and a man in his thirties with black-rimmed glasses and dark curly brown hair alighted from it. He was carrying a small suitcase in one hand and a briefcase in the other.

Lindsay couldn't believe this was the student she was expecting. This man was much older than the usual student. She had never asked Marshall Armstrong's age, presuming that he would be in his early twenties since his voice had sounded young. She had forgotten that people went back to school at different ages.

With Lee's problems at school, the Macaulays didn't need more gossip floating around about them. She couldn't even give the man back his money. She had already spent most of it. Yet she knew it would be inappropriate for him to live at their house. It would certainly lead to more gossip, given he seemed near her own age. Lindsay walked toward the man, holding out her hand. "I'm Lindsay Macaulay."

"Marshall Armstrong...Marsh for short, "he said. He quickly tucked his briefcase under his arm and took her hand. "You're awful pretty for a landlady," he grinned.

Although her cheeks grew warm, Lindsay ignored his compliment. "My truck is over here. As I told you in my letter, our transportation is rather primitive. It doesn't have power brakes or power steering and the heater isn't that great and we don't have a radio."

"The past is coming to life," he quipped as he stowed his suitcase under a tarp in the back of the old pickup. "Old truck. Old barn. Old ideas...

Lindsay wasn't sure if he was being facetious or not, but she had to admit his smile would melt an iceberg. And he certainly wasn't afraid to ask questions. The rattletrap came first. How old was it? Who built it? Was it a Ford or Chevrolet? How many cylinders did it have, six or eight? Was it a gas guzzler? How many miles did it go on a gallon of gasoline? Lindsay didn't have answers to all of his questions.

Then his questions swung to Riverton and the surrounding countryside. A half hour later, as Lindsay turned into their lane, Marsh suddenly stopped talking. Framed on three sides by a perimeter of tall pines was the house and behind it was their octangular barn, its field stone foundation twinkling with tiny time-imbedded diamonds. Added to the panorama was a small flock of wild turkeys pecking through the snow for their supper in a field next to the barn. Even before Lindsay stopped, Marsh jumped out of the truck. As he stood, legs apart, hands on his hip, he uttered one word. "Wow!"

A half hour later, as Lindsay was placing dinner on the table—she had put a tuna fish casserole and apple cobbler in the oven and set the timer before leaving for the station—Lee showed Marsh his room and the location of the facilities. Half way through their meal, when he accepted a third helping of casserole, Lindsay realized that their guest had a good appetite, something she needed to keep in mind when preparing meals.

Marshall only stopped talking long enough to chew. He wanted to know about their house, how long they had lived here, could he go with Lee to feed the horses? Later, Lindsay showed Marsh a file of old clippings she had found relating to Trailwood and the barn. He asked questions and Lindsay answered the best she could. The answers to many, though, could be found in the historical files at the Riverton County Library. She would take him there the next afternoon. Finally, noticing that Lee had gone up to bed and Lindsay was turning off the outside lights, Marsh took the hint and went up to bed.

Saturday morning, Lindsay and Lee were both up at their usual time. She made breakfast and Lee set the table. But there was no sign of Marsh. Maybe he was a late sleeper. She told Lee to knock on his door. He did, but there was no Marshall Armstrong. "Mom, he's gone," Lee yelled down the stairs.

"He can't be gone!" Lindsay exclaimed, running up the stairs to view his empty room.

Where is he then? Pulling on their boots, Lindsay and Lee grabbed their coats and ran to the barn. Marsh wasn't in the stable. They went up the ladder to the loft. And there he was, sitting on a beam high above the hay mow under the cupola, a measuring tape in one hand, a pad in the other, a pencil tucked behind his ear, taking the measurement of the beam's circumference.

Aghast, Lindsay stared up at him. *My God! What if he fell?* Would her insurance cover him?

Hands on her hips, anger bristling from every pore, she ordered. "Get down from there!"

Marsh acknowledged her command with a grin, a bow of his head and a nifty salute before swinging down a rope to the hay loft floor.

"Would you kindly tell me what you're doing up there?" Lindsay demanded, irritation stressing her every word.

Looking much like Lee did when Lindsay caught him with his hand in the cookie jar, Marsh said, "Just trying to find any square corners in your barn where a devil might hide."

Then, realizing that Lindsay was taking his morning climb very seriously, he explained, "An octagon and a circle are kissing cousins. Quakers drew inspiration from the circle. In my thesis, I compare the circle to the octagon. Decades ago, many farmers believed that devils hid in their barns. When a calf or a sheep died unexpectedly, they believed it was the work of the devil."

"Whether the devil is in my barn or not, I don't want you climbing up on those beams," Lindsay said. Then, turning to Lee, who was grinning, "And don't you get any ideas about climbing up there." Glaring at them both, she turned on her heel and threw the words "Breakfast is ready," over her shoulder like a handful of darts.

The mood was still tense when they sat down to breakfast. Marsh apologized. "I'm sorry, Lindsay. I didn't mean to upset you. I was careful...I'm used to climbing and measurements are important to any thesis."

With a sheepish grin on his round face, he said, "I'm afraid I like to tease. I'm sorry.

By the time they had finished breakfast, Lindsay's anger had mellowed to miffed.

"Why do you want to write about barns anyway?" Lee asked.

"Because they are part of our culture, our past and we have to understand our past in order to prepare for our future." Then he smiled, exposing a row of uneven bottom teeth, "And don't wait until you're thirty-two to do it."

"Why barns?" Lee persisted.

"Because they're rare, because there are so few of them still in existence." Marsh went on to explain that many people, especially those who live in big cities, had never seen a barn, much less an octangular one. "And you have one right here in your yard."

"Octangular buildings have been around for a long time," Lindsay said as she cleared the table. "There's an article in that file I showed you about an octangular summer house that President Jefferson built for himself in 1806."

"Touché." Marsh nodded his head. To prove his theory, he said that he needed to take more measurements, especially from the center post to the barn's outer perimeter. After lunch, if Lindsay was still willing, he would like her to drive him to the library in Riverton.

Lee said it was too bad Art Winston wasn't available—he was still away looking after the horses for a man in the next county—as he had more knowledge in his little finger than most books had between their covers.

"Art says barns, just like houses, need good ventilation. 'I'll bet you didn't know that horses can get the flu just like people, only it isn't called flu, it's called....equine influenza...the symptoms are the same, running nose, cough, fever, loss of appetite."

Marsh's eyes crinkled at the corners with laughter. "No, I didn't know that...and I would like to meet your Art Winston."

"Do you think Art will be home before Marsh leaves Sunday afternoon, Mom?"

Lindsay said she didn't know, adding that if she was going to drive Marsh to the library after lunch, she had household chores to see to: beds to make, potatoes to peel and a pot roast to put in the oven. "And you can do the dishes," she told Lee.

His, "ah, Ma," brought a grin to Marsh's face.

At the library, while Marsh concentrated on Riverton's early history and articles related to the octangular barn, Lindsay went to the newspaper reels section to see if there was any information about the Macaulay family. From a faded hand-written manuscript, she learned that Trailwood got its name from an old trail that ran along the side of the river, through the town and out to Georgian Bay. She found several stories written about her father. One told about the accident and his injuries. Another paid tribute to her father's skill as a driver, naming some of the prestigious races he had won and adding that a few weeks before his death he had been chosen to represent Canada at an international meet in Europe.

Lindsay wondered if Maria knew about that trip, or if he was keeping it as a surprise. Her dad wouldn't have gone without Maria. He loved his wife, despite her parenting eccentricities. And he loved being a Dad. How did she know that when she couldn't even remember the man's face?

Lindsay wasn't even aware that she had brought up a picture of her father and his funeral cortege on the screen, or that she had started to cry as little tidbits of the past broke through the barriers of her lost memory—*her dad, tucking her into bed at night, kissing her on the brow, hearing his whispered words, "sleep tight, don't let the bedbugs bite."*

"Is that your dad?" Marsh asked, looking over her shoulder at the picture.

When she nodded, he gave her shoulder a gentle pat.

"Have you found anything on octangular barns?" she asked, struggling for composure.

"Only that they're rare," he said, "And yours is one of the last ones in existence."

While she rewound the news reel and returned it to its rightful shelf in the history section, Marsh told her that the librarian was going to send him copies of anything she found when she searched through some old files in the basement.

Later, driving in the lane at Trailwood, Lindsay was surprised to see Rand's pickup truck parked close to the barn. What was he doing here? She hadn't seen him for several days as he had been a guest teacher at an equine college in Alberta. *Probably he is checking on her new filly*, she thought, parking the rattletrap next to his new Chevrolet three-quarter ton.

Lindsay had been so busy she hadn't had time to see the filly and when Marsh suggested they "see how she's doing," she didn't hesitate.

Rand was in Princess's stall checking the filly's hooves. "They're doing just fine, Lee." When he saw Lindsay and Marsh, he gave the filly an extra pat, smiled that extra special smile that wrapped around Lindsay like a caress. He then stood holding out his hand to Marsh as she introduced the two men, who were as different as day was to night.

Both men were casually dressed: Rand in his usual jeans and sheepskin and Marsh in a blue nylon jacket with frayed cuffs. While Rand was fair, strands of cinnamon hair peaked out from under his pushed-up Stetson, Marsh was darker with shadows of a late afternoon stubble appearing along his jaw line. One was country-born, the other city savvy. One was trying to get an education; the other already had a degree. Both men had qualities she admired. Only one made her heart race.

Her intuitive instincts told her Rand already knew Marsh was much older than the student she was expecting. Gossip, she supposed was the same in the country as in the city. According to an old fable that Bonnie often quoted, gossip could go around the world while truth was putting on its shoes. Someone had evidently seen her meet Marsh at the station, ~~and~~ knew he was their weekend guest and told Rand.

The chores for the night were completed. It was time to go to the house for supper and with Rand still hanging around, like March weather in May, she felt obligated to ask him to join them. In spite of her misgivings, supper was an animated affair. Marsh said Lindsay looked pretty in her turtleneck sweater, praised her cooking and talked to Lee as an equal, complimenting him on his knowledge of horses. Rand, on the other hand, let his eyes do the talking, speaking with a soft eloquence that surpassed speech.

Lee surprised even Lindsay when he told them that he wanted to go to agricultural college, learn all he could about horses and breeding and be a horse-breeder like his grandfather and great-grandfather.

When it came to octangular barns, it seemed both men wanted to show off their knowledge. "Circular structures went back to the bronze age in Europe," Marsh said. "Families and animals occupied the same shelter with a small passage between cooking area and stable."

Rand said, "Circular and polygonal barns came to North America in the second half of the nineteenth century. They influenced our society."

Marsh argued that barns provided a documented history of our past and that Lindsay's barn was one of the last of its kind in Ontario.

And the debate went on.

Tired of just listening, Lindsay said, "Cupolas save hydro, you know. They allow extra light to filter down to the stable."

Both men stared at her for a moment before continuing their conversation. She thought they acted like men of centuries ago when a woman dared to voice a thought.

Seething inside, Lindsay cleared the table and emptied the last of the coffee into their cups. She hoped when Rand finished his coffee he would go home. But he stayed and the two men continued talking. Like two adversaries, Marsh talked, Rand challenged. And vice versa.

Lee yawned. He excused himself, saying he was going to bed. Lindsay wanted to go to bed too. What on earth was the matter with Rand? Why didn't he go home? She didn't want to be rude, but "It's getting late, so why don't you postpone the rest of your discussion until tomorrow?" She nodded to the kitchen clock. It was past midnight.

Marsh pushed his chair away from the table and stood. "I didn't realize it was that late." He held his hand out to Rand. "I enjoyed our discussion. You brought out some interesting theories about barns and their place in the evolution of farming." Then, turning to Lindsay, he said, "Good night, my pretty hostess. I'll see you in the morning."

"Sooner than that, if he has his way," Rand grumbled as he reached for his coat, which was hanging on a peg on the back of the kitchen door. "I thought he would never go to bed."

Lindsay wanted to say, "Then why didn't you go home?" But for once she kept her words to herself and only said, "It's been a long day."

Rand still dawdled. He reached for her hand, brought it to his mouth, kissed each finger. Then gently he pulled her closer. Lindsay had the greatest temptation to rest her head on his shoulder and leave all her burdens there. Instead she looked up into his face, such a solid face. "Just what do you think you're doing, Rand?"

"Making a statement." His voice was low, deep, sensuous.

Seeing the desire in his eyes, feeling his need, Lindsay's head warred with her heart as he lowered his head. His lips touched hers. What began as a gentle kiss deepened as his tongue dueled with hers and Lindsay's world spun out of control. But the slamming of the bathroom door brought reality.

"Good night, Rand." Gently, Lindsay pushed him away.

Another quick stolen kiss and, "Good night, City Lady, and don't forget to keep the *barn* door closed."

Ten

Lindsay watched Marsh Armstrong board the train for Toronto with a "thank goodness the weekend was almost over" feeling. She had learned some of the pitfalls of having weekend paying guests. She would certainly need a set of rules, like "no climbing up to the cupola."

She wouldn't have to make supper as there was plenty of left-overs from dinner, so she could relax with her painting, but before she had removed her boots, Lee was telling her that Rand had dropped by and they were invited to Windcrest for supper the next night.

"I accepted for us, Mom, I hope that's all right." Lee looked at her hopefully. "If it isn't, you're to call him." Lee looked at her hopefully. He loved the busyness of Windcrest as Art had taken him there several times. "And, just think, Mom, you won't have to cook. Won't that be a treat?"

Lindsay agreed, but later as Lee watched television and she concentrated on a new design, she began to have doubts, not only about her feelings for Rand,—he was way out of her social league—but also about the scene she was trying to create. It was a new design which had a barn silhouetted against the late afternoon sun with a flock of wild turkeys pecking in the snow in the foreground. Scenes, however, were not one of Lindsay's strengths and she'd become frustrated. After several wipe outs, Lindsay called her best friend Bonnie Tobin in Toronto, a skilled porcelain painter, for advice.

"Your design is too busy," Bonnie had told her. "Try getting rid of some of those turkeys. Try just one or two with a few tufts of grass poking through the snow. A tall pine and that barn will give the scene realism."

Like always, Bonnie's advice was good. The two had met twenty-one years earlier in the Toronto Hospital where Bonnie, with her newly earned degree from Queen's University, accepted a position in the physio-rehabilitation department. That same day she'd met a frightened, freckled-faced, fifteen-year-old teenager who, after four operations, was in danger of losing her leg. Believing strongly in the new concept that exercise was as important as bed rest, Bonnie had cajoled, bribed and browbeat Lindsay into exercising her leg...and her mind. During those angry, heart-tugging months, a deep and lasting friendship had been forged between the short, pudgy therapist with the topknot hair style and the red-headed teen from Trailwood—her reward, seeing *her girl* leave the hospital carrying a book and walking on her own leg.

The Macaulays' move to Trailwood hadn't dampened their friendship as the two women talked on Sunday nights when long distance telephone rates were cheaper. Always part of Bonnie's conversation was, "What's that favorite nephew of mine been up to?"

"Raiding the fridge as usual," Lindsay laughed as she said goodbye.

Following Bonnie's advice, she wiped out several of the turkeys and it was past midnight before the scene came together.

~ * ~

Lindsay awoke, glanced at the clock, threw back the covers and vaulted out of bed, yelling, "Lee wake up. It's nine o'clock. You're late for school."

The smell of burned toast and Lee's loud "Don't get your shirttail in a knot, Mom," came from the kitchen. "It's Heritage Day. No school, remember?"

Lindsay took a deep breath and sat down on the bed. She had forgotten that the government had set aside the third Monday in February as a holiday to encourage the preservation of Canada's history. At the supermarket, it had been just another working day.

"Did you tell Aunt Bonnie we were going to Windcrest tonight for supper?" he asked as she came for breakfast.

"Yes. And I'm looking forward to it. I know you have been to the stables several times with Art, but all I've seen of Windcrest are those fieldstone posts at the lane entrance. I want to see the house, the barns, the horses—and," she grinned, "his invitation to supper is the icing on the cake, so to speak."

Lee lifted his eyebrows in an "oh, Mother!" expression.

~ * ~

The "icing on the cake," was far different than she expected.

Windcrest was beautiful. The 19th century sandstone house harmonized with modern barns and white fences. Before she had parked, Lee jumped out of the truck, running across the yard to watch two yearlings cavorting around a large paddock. Two boys about Lee's age were leaning against the fence, their chins resting on their arms watching the horses. Lee adopted the same pose.

For a few minutes Lindsay just sat in the truck and watched Lee. He needed a new pair of jeans; the frayed edges above his ankles testified to the fact that he was growing out of his clothes. She was so engrossed in her own thoughts that she didn't notice Rand walking across the yard.

"What are you thinking about so seriously?" Rand opened the truck door for her to alight.

"I was just thinking that Trailwood is good for my son."

Rand's words, "and good for you too," brought a glow to Lindsay's cheeks.

"Who are those boys?" she asked. "I didn't see them at the school play."

"Mac Townsend's two sons. He's my farm manager. He and his wife live apart and this is the weekend the boys are here with their dad," Rand explained, cupping Lindsay's elbow in his hand as he guided her toward the largest of his three barns, which he said, were built apart because if fire, heaven forbid, should destroy one, the others would survive.

It had been a long time since she needed a steadying hand under her elbow when she walked. Yet it still gave her a warm, comfortable feeling.

The long narrow barn had about a dozen horses, all moving noisily around in their separate stalls. "This is where we keep the yearlings," Rand said as several horses poked their heads out over the Dutch doors of their stall, some nickering, some just bobbing their heads. "If it's a nice day tomorrow, we'll turn them outside for a few hours." He talked about their qualifications, which ones he would keep, which ones he would sell at the spring auction. He considered them Windcrest's cash crop.

Desperately needing a distraction from the feelings that Rand's closeness was creating, she nodded to the old grey tomcat dozing beside a loose bale of hay. "Are you thinking of putting him in the auction too?"

"Old Tom's part of the fixtures," Rand laughed, as the cat strutted off, his tail whipping back and forth, emphasizing his displeasure at being disturbed.

From the yearling barn, they walked across a narrow yard to the barn where Rand kept his mares. Unlike Trailwood's barn, there were no heat bulbs dangling from the ceiling, no tarpaulins draped along the walls, no drafts seeping in around the doors. In this well-lighted, heat-regulated barn, hot water pipes attached to the rafters provided a uniform warmth to the mares and their foals. Lindsay sighed. *Oh, what money can do!*

So that visitors would know who-was-who, each of the mares had an engraved wooden nameplate above the Dutch door of her stall: Starcest Jewel, Wind Mystique, Beauty Crest Lady etc. "Where did you get such fancy names?" Lindsay asked.

"Combination of sire, dam and breeding stable," Rand said as they strolled along the stalls. "Actually our mares have two names, their registered one and our name for them: Starcest Jewel is Jewlie, Wind Mystique is Misty and this one Mac calls Lame Brain." The nameplate above the door said Beauty Crest Lady."

"Lame Brain!" Lindsay exclaimed. "Why, for heaven's sake?"

"Because her mothering instincts are so poor."

"Then, why do you keep her?"

"She throws a beautiful foal and her shareowner doesn't want to sell her," Rand answered, closing the sliding door of the mares' barn.

Moving on, they passed a small cement block building with "Laboratory" and a "No Trespassing" sign above the padlocked door. "All our technical equipment is in there."

Although the barn was fairly new, Lindsay noticed that rust dripped from a crack in its eave trough. "Only Mac and I have the keys to that building," he continued, holding the stallion barn door open for her. "Ever since Starmist's progenies have been doing so well at the racetracks, his semen is becoming a big part of our profit margin."

"Did you ever race Starmist?" Lindsay asked.

"Oh, yes. He was a winner big time, but when he got kicked in the knee by another horse, we put him to stud. Then to our surprise we found he was more valuable at stud than as a trotter."

While the stallion barn was the smallest of the three, it was the most lavish. Gold nameplates hung above the doors, larger windows lighted the stalls and a wider passage allowed for extra room for grooming. Two stalls were used for hay and straw; blankets, bridles and other equipment were kept in a smaller stall at the end of the passageway with a catch-all stall for wheelbarrows, forks, shovels, pails, brushes and curry combs.

Rand slid the door on the first stall open, reaching for the stallion's halter. "This is the big fellow who has made all this possible," Rand said as he cross-tied the liver-colored chestnut in the wide passage. "Starmist, meet the lady in my life," he reached for Lindsay's hand, drawing her closer to the stallion.

A breath caught in her throat. Rand had called her the lady in his life. Evidently Starmist approved, as the stallion snorted softly, bobbing his head.

"He's a beauty, Rand," Lindsay tilted her head viewing Starmist from all angles, his friendly eyes, his dark mane, his long flowing tail.

"That picture I saw in *Trot* magazine doesn't do him justice." She stroked his nose.

"I agree," Rand said. "Now you can see...."

With *the lady in my life* still ringing in her ears, the significance of his words "now you can see" was slow to register. The stallion's white blaze, liver chestnut coloring and four white socks, were almost identical to Princess's foal. Although the foal's coloring was lighter, it would darken with age.

"But how...?" She continued to stare at the stallion.

"The usual way," Rand grinned, as color flooded Lindsay's cheeks. "Seriously, the moment I saw your filly, I knew Starmist was the sire. Besides their major coloring, both have tiny black spots at the top of their left white stocking."

"There's *no* documentation, Rand," Lindsay protested. "My grandfather kept meticulous records. He even kept track of every ounce of bran he fed to each horse." She stepped back pulling her hand away. "And why didn't you say something the other day?"

The barn creaked. Starmist's head bobbed. A horse nickered.

His hand reached for hers again. "Two reasons, really. You were so happy. I knew there hadn't been that many happy moments in your life, and I didn't want to spoil it. Secondly, I needed to know if this was an isolated incident or if someone was black-marketing Starmist's semen. Incidents like that can destroy a stable."

"You keep your laboratory locked and you said that only you and Mac have a key. So how did your stallion's semen get into the vagina of my mare without you or Mac knowing?" She was uncomfortable talking about semen and vagina and tried to lighten the situation. "And don't tell me…immaculate conception."

A slight smile flitted across his face as he shook his head. "Seat of the pant investigative research on the computer. I started with the possible time of conception. Who had access to my lab? Who had keys? Where was I? Where was Mac? Had he given his key to anyone? Who knew Princess was in heat? Only one name kept coming up."

"Art!" Lindsay silently breathed his name.

Rand nodded. "Since insemination takes two people to administer, I called Doc Woodward. I made some offhanded remark about watermarks obscuring the date on my record book page, and I just wanted to verify that the date on the computer page was correct. Woodward said that last March he had helped Art inseminate Princess. All the documentation was in order and your foal proved that everything went well. Before he could say anything else, I broke our conversation by saying that someone had just come in the office. Now, I knew what I only suspected: Starmist was the sire of Princess's foal."

"I don't believe it!" Lindsay exclaimed, shaking her head. "Art is my friend, Lee's friend, too. I don't know how we would have survived these last few weeks if it hadn't been for Art. He taught us how to look after the horses, listened to our troubles, even contacted Herb Haggitt, the antique dealer on our behalf." Lindsay kept shaking her head. "It isn't true!"

"I didn't want to believe it either," Rand continued. "Art is my friend too. When my wife Rita left me—took almost everything I had—Art worked without wages helping me stay afloat. He knows as much about Windcrest as I do. I owe him...big time, and he does have share in a couple of the mares. Beauty Crest Lady is one.

"I called Art. That was the hard part," Rand continued. "He came. We talked. He admitted taking the semen and even though I understood his reason, I couldn't condone it."

Lindsay nodded. Whether it was a candy bar from a grocery store or semen from a laboratory, theft was theft. And what was she going to tell Lee—that the man he looked upon as a role model, friend, confidant, was a thief? There had to be some justification, but how do you justify taking something that doesn't belong to you?

She needed to talk to Art. Lindsay wanted him to tell her what had happened that day, but he was away. "Art loved my grandfather..."

"*Love,* Lindsay. That's what put this bizarre miracle in play. After your father was killed and Maria and you left Riverton, Old Jeb was alone. Art was alone too. Each became the family the other didn't have. They talked about the past, the present, and a lot about Old Jeb's dream of someday breeding a golden cross. Jeb had come close a couple of times."

"What *is* a golden cross?" Lindsay interrupted. "Everyone talks about it, but nobody says what it is."

The taut lines on Rand's face softened slightly as he tried to simplify the intricacies of good breeding. "A lucky spin of the genetic wheel...breed the best to the best and hope for the best," he said. "Old Jeb always believed that Princess was an outstanding mare and he was right. Over the years, she had thrown many exceptional foals. Still for her to birth a golden cross she needed to be bred to a horse that was as exceptional as she was. Starmist was that stallion. But Old Jeb could never afford the fees.

"Three things happened last March that put this bizarre miracle in motion. I accepted an invitation to speak at a convention in Texas, which I combined with a two-week vacation in California. I left Mac in charge with Art as his backup.

"The second thing indirectly affected Windcrest—Mac's wife decided to leave him and take their two boys. It was the same morning an order came from a Western breeder for three vials of Starmist's semen—we had four vials in stock.

"Since Mac wanted to get home, he asked Art if he could look after packing and shipping the order and gave him the key to the lab. Art was also looking after your grandfather's horses since Old Jeb was in the hospital. He had been diagnosed with cancer of the colon. He had always doctored his horses, so when he became constipated or had diarrhea, Old Jeb doctored himself. By the time he had a colonoscopy, it was already too late. The cancer had spread into his lymph nodes and other parts of his body.

"Art looked after the shipment to the West, checked on Queenie and Princess, who was in heat and went to see Old Jeb at the hospital. The news was devastating. Jeb's cancer had metastasized. His time was limited. And because Art loved that old man, he wanted to give him his dream—a golden cross."

Rand unhooked the snaps on the tie ropes and led Starmist back into his stall.

"To shorten the story," Rand continued as they moved on to the next stall. "He knew there was one vial of Starmist's semen left in stock. On the spur of the moment, he made a decision. He filled out the necessary sperm papers and called Doc Woodward. Woodward, who often helped with the inseminations, had no reason to question the papers or the vial of semen."

A tiny tear slipped unnoticed down Lindsay's cheek.

"That's what happened, and why it happened and that, my dear Lindsay, is how you happen to have such a beautiful filly. I also called the Standardbred Association. They have registered your filly but will you have to choose a different name because Surprise is already taken."

"There is one thing I don't understand. If my grandfather was the horseman everyone believed him to be, why didn't he know that Princess was in foal? He must have gone to the barn because he was fairly active right to the end."

"According to Art—when we talked—your grandfather didn't go to the barn very often. When he did, the mares were usually covered in the summer with fly netting and so he didn't notice that Princess's stomach was larger or that it drooped lower."

Only the horses' stomping feet and their soft nickers broke the silence of the barn as Lindsay made her decision. She couldn't condone what Art had done, but she understood it. She also needed to show Lee that theft, in whatever form, or for whatever reason, was wrong and that there was a consequence.

"Rand, I don't want to see Art charged. I'll give you the filly if you don't press charges."

It was Rand's turn to look startled. "You would do that!"

"Art looked after my grandfather and the horses when there was no one else to do it. And he has looked after Lee and me." Although she didn't have a clue where she would get the money, she added, "I'll get him the best lawyer..."

Rand grasped her shoulders, shook her gently. "Lindsay, I have no intention of prosecuting a grieving man for trying to give his friend his dream. How could you think that of me?"

She wanted to put her head on his shoulder. Cry. Instead she sniffed, "The records..."

"Are all in order," he said as he reached for her hand again as they moved along to the end stall where Aprilmist waited impatiently for attention. She watched Rand take a butterscotch candy from his pocket and give it to the young stallion. Her eyebrows lifted. Rand grinned. "He's got a sweet tooth."

Lindsay's world had just been turned on its axis. Everything was out of kilter. Her head was pounding. For a moment she longed for the zing of a cash register and a customer complaining, "That's not the price listed in the flyer."

"Aprilmist will make a good mate for Princess," he continued. "Don't forget you have to breed her within the next week or so." He stood away from Aprilmist's door but back far enough that Lindsay could see the young stallion. "It is too soon for Aprilmist's offsprings to prove themselves at the racetrack so in lieu of monetary fees, I would be willing to consider a half interest in Princess's next foal."

Giving the stallion another pat on the nose, he slid the door closed.

Eleven

As they started up the path toward the house, Rand called to Lee, "Supper's in half-an- hour." Lee acknowledged with a wave of his hand.

The tranquility of the winter scene reflected in the narrow windows of his old house provided Lindsay with a focus away from her troubled thoughts.

"The stone mason who built your house must have taken a great deal of pride in his work," she said, feeling Rand's hand in the middle of her back gently guiding her.

"My great-great-grandfather, Ira Dyson, built it in the early eighteen hundreds for the woman he loved, whose surname incidentally was Macaulay."

"You're kidding!"

Rand shook his head. "Her family forbade her to marry Ira. They said he was a no-account drifter with no money and no prospects. Ira decided, no matter how long it took, he would show her folks they were wrong. He got a job as a stone mason's helper. He learned the trade. Probably worked on your barn. He bought this land and, during his spare time built this house. By then, Hannah was married and had three children. Years later when her husband died, Ira took up his pursuit. The two were married and lived happily for the next thirty years."

"What a wonderful story," Lindsay said as she hung her coat beside Rand's in the small mud room just inside the back door. "Does that mean we're related?"

"Distantly, perhaps, but not close enough to cause any problems."

Before she could ask, "what problems," she saw him sniff his shirt cuff. "I smell a little horsey. I need a shower and a change of clothes...and while I'm doing that, why don't you have a rest in the family room, put your feet up and enjoy some of my good 'down home' country music."

Rand took her hand and led her to a large room dominated by a vintage fieldstone fireplace, with the flames dancing across the cedar logs. There wasn't anything vintage about his state-of-the-art walnut console with its television, radio, cassette player and multi rows of tapes. "What kind of music do you like—classical, rock, country?" At her nod of *country* he slipped in "one of my favorites," an Anne Murray tape.

Cradled in the arms of the deep padded chair, the rich alto voice of the "Canadian songbird" drifting around her, Lindsay tried to relax. but there was so much to think about: stud fees, stolen semen, Lee. Yet it was Rand's *"the lady in my life"* that slipped into her thoughts. For a few moments, here in this room, in this chair before the fire, she felt as if she had come home.

Rand wasn't the best looking or the tallest man she had ever met but there was something in the way he moved that set him apart. His body had a rhythm all its own. And when he talked to her, his words wrapped around her like a caress. Yes, he got angry. And he got upset. But he dealt with his problems in an understanding way. He understood the devastating misery of Art's grief and he made allowances for it. Was it any wonder she was falling in love with him?

"I can't see how you can keep your mind on business when we have all this….," she told Rand a little while later, when he took a chair opposite her.

"I'm glad you like my home. This is my favorite room too," he said softly. "But I almost lost it."

Lindsay looked at him questioningly.

The ambiance of the room seemed to lead to shared confidences as Rand continued, "I had only been married a few months—I came home unexpectedly—two men were ripping out the fireplace. They said my wife had hired them to replace it with a modern electric one. I confronted her. She cried. She said she was just trying to please me; the whole house needed modernizing.

"We made up, of course. Then, one afternoon a few years later, I came home and she was gone…and the only thing left that I valued was the fireplace and these chairs."

As if he had said too much, Rand quickly stood, offered Lindsay his hand and pulled her up out of the chair.

"While we wait for the oven to heat our supper, I'll show you my office and the computer." He indicated an open doorway at the opposite end of the room. "Helen, my housekeeper, prepared everything before she went to her daughter's this morning, even set the table."

"Has she been with you long?"

"Oh, several years. Natalie found her for me shortly after my wife left. Helen's husband worked for the racetrack, looked after the barns, kept them clean, watered the racetrack on race day—that sort of thing. Unfortunately, he got cancer and died and Helen was left with only a small pension. She needed a job and I needed a housekeeper. On the whole, it has worked out well for us," Rand said. "Monday is Helen's day to visit her daughter, who is a nurse at the Riverton hospital and it's usually her day off too."

The computer room was small and compact as old harmonized with new. A mahogany desk with a high pigeonhole back, sat comfortably beside a small table with a computer on top and a printer on a shelf below. Rand pulled out a swivel chair so she could sit in front of the screen.

Lindsay smiled as pictures of Windcrest scrolled up: mares munching grass, Starmist galloping around the paddock, yearlings frolicking in the field. With Rand leaning over her shoulder, Lindsay found it hard to concentrate. The fragrance of his aftershave spoke of spring and mountain streams and his voice close to her ear whispered of closeness and intimacy.

Then she saw the service fee for Starmist. She gasped. The fee for stud was listed below one of the stallion's pictures. My God. Stolen or not, the breeding fee would have to be paid. How would she pay when she had no money, no job and a craft that paid figuratively in cents and satisfaction, not in dollars?

"Quit worrying." Rand's hand patted her shoulder. "I've taken care of everything."

Lindsay had heard almost those same words fourteen years ago, and they put a dart into her heart. Derek Wilson, Lee's father, had assured her that he would, "take care of everything," and he had, but not in the way she or anyone expected.

Derek Wilson had been Lindsay's first love. They had met in the craft room of the rehabilitation hospital. She had just come from a rough therapy session. Pain racked her leg and Bonnie Tobin, her therapist, had told her that she had to work harder on her exercises if she hoped to get out of the hospital in a few weeks.

To say that Lindsay wasn't in a good frame of mind was a slight understatement, when a man in a left shoulder and right leg cast rolled his wheelchair too close, bumping her arm and asked, "What are you doing?"

A crazy question when any dumb jackass could see she was trying to paint a flower on a china plate and not doing a very good job of it even before his bump had sent her brush swigging upwards. Through gritted teeth, she exclaimed, "I'm trying to paint!"

"I can see that." He had smirked. "Is that animal, mineral or vegetable?"

God, she hated men with beards and unkempt hair and brown eyes that danced with mischief! She glared. He grinned. And finally, after a long moment, she laughed. "I don't know."

Derek's therapy, like Lindsay's, was long and painful and the time went slowly. They commiserated with each other and soon became an inseparable pair. Although two months younger than Lindsay's twenty-two, he was an inch taller and outweighed her by sixty pounds. He was having treatment on his back and shoulder; he had crashed his motorcycle into a hydrant and came off second best. She was having treatment on a leg whose splintered bones were slowly healing

They ate together. They laughed together. They played one-handed games. They talked about everything...anything. Each had a family: Lindsay had Maria who was always busy. Derek had a father and a sister who had written him off as a bum. Two lonely people fell in love. After a very intimate moment, Derek asked Lindsay to marry him and she had said yes.

When their therapist urged caution, they didn't listen. They were happy. Derek got the cast off his leg. Lindsay graduated to crutches, and an overjoyed Maria was happy to plan her daughter's small wedding, and pass her responsibility on to someone else.

She bought Lindsay a three-quarter length white dress with embossed roses and a full skirt which hid the brace she wore on her left leg. She took Lindsay to the hospital chapel where Bonnie and a few friends sat in the pews. They waited. And waited. An hour later a policeman came. Derek had been in a motorcycle accident. He had been going too fast and missed a curve going the wrong way out of the city. He was dead.

~ * ~

Seven months later, Lee was born in the maternity wing of the same hospital where she had met Derek. Her gimpy leg had brought her Lee, but Derek's broken promise of *"taking care of everything"* still rankled, leaving deep scars on her heart.

Over the years Lindsay had dated salesmen, shopkeepers and manager's assistants, men who were always moving to a better job, a better place, men without staying power.

"Don't you want to get married?" Rand's words teased the top of her ear.

"Of course, I do." Lindsay fidgeted with the mouse, trying to bring up the taskbar that would give her access to the Standardbred Association. "When I do...if I do, it will be for the right reason."

Determinedly, she kept her eyes on the computer screen, her fingers on the mouse. Oh God, how she wanted to turn around. That would mean disaster— for her and for Rand. He was educated. She was not. He was a breeder, lecturer, and well-to-do; she was the owner of a rundown stable teetering on bankruptcy.

"And just what is that right reason, Miss Macaulay?"

Lindsay stood, moved away from the computer before turning to face him. "Love like my grandparents had."

"You can't even remember your grandparents!" Rand exclaimed.

"Oh...but I can."

Every once in a while, like now, a memory would break through the fetters of her past-chained mind and she could see Martha, her plump little grandmother, who had died when Lindsay was not-yet six, sitting in a rocking chair by the window. Bending to kiss her was Jeb, her grandfather, his cap pushed back above his forehead, a day-old stubble on his face and a warm love in his eyes.

Jeb never left the house without kissing his wife, whether it was to go the barn to do chores, or to the mail box to get the mail. Nor did he care who saw him—their gossipy neighbor, the implement salesman, or his granddaughter, who often stayed while her father and mother were at the racetrack. "I'll see you in a little while, old thing," he would say softly.

Martha had told the little girl, who sat cradled on her lap, that "old thing" was her husband's way of calling her darling without anyone knowing. Theirs was an all-embracing love. That was what Lindsay remembered. That's what she wanted.

"Money or security doesn't enter into it, Rand. Love and the way two people feel about each other is all that matters."

"And just how should a man feel about you?"

"I want my man to love me, honor me, not because he's duty bound by some piece of paper. I want him to be proud of me and I want to be proud of him. I want him to love my son as his own because Lee is a part of me, just as I am a part of him.

"The man I marry must accept my gimpy leg and when I can't dance at somebody's wedding, I don't want him to feel ashamed or apologize for me. Instead, I want him to hold me and tell me he loves me and that we will dance later in the love-light of our bedroom."

"That should be *some* dance, Miss Macaulay!" Stormy, grey eyes warred with tranquil blue as Rand grabbed her, yanked her close. "You're worse than my ex-wife. Do you know that?" His fingers bit into her shoulders. Shook her. "Rita wanted my money. You want my soul!"

"That's not true!" Lindsay exclaimed as tension roped around them like invisible bands of steel.

"Well, you're not going to rope me," he interrupted angrily, shaking her. "And while you're mourning your failure, dream of this." His head bent forward. His mouth rammed against hers. His tongue invaded and the heavens exploded.

From somewhere, a voice called, "Mom, where are you?"

And another voice. "Rand. I'm here."

"Damn!" He swore as he raised his head. "I forgot Natalie was coming over."

Seconds later, Lindsay was standing alone. Her clothes askew. Her hair mussed. Her senses reeling.

Lee called out again, sounding worried.

"Rand, where are you?" Natalie demanded impatiently. "I've brought those papers for you to sign."

"Straighten your blouse." He grated out the words as he ran his fingers through his hair—as if anything could comb away the passion that had just raged between them. "You look like you've been attacked."

I have been, she wanted to shout. Instead her, "I'm here, Lee," was partially muffled by Rand's calling, "We're coming." He moved quickly to block Natalie's view of the computer room. He didn't block Lindsay's view of him, bending forward, kissing Natalie on her cheek. "I was just showing Lindsay our Standardbred program..."

"Not your etchings?" Her testy teasing belied the smoldering anger in her tone. "You're definitely slipping, my dear."

"Helen left our supper in the oven," he said, taking Natalie's arm, he turned her toward the kitchen. "Would you like to stay...beef stroganoff?"

"I'd love to stay. Daddy is away. He's having dinner with Lyle Edmonds and his wife."

Lindsay recognized the bank manager's name, just as Lee interrupted, "Rand, Mac said to tell you that he would look after the chores tonight. He doesn't have to have the boys back until nine."

Rand nodded, propelling Natalie ahead of him. "If you ladies will be seated..."

Lindsay noticed the fourth place setting. Her heart nosedived; Rand had known Natalie was coming. Then she heard him explain, "Art was coming, but Jake Miner—he's that horse breeder in Norfolk County—called him just before noon. Jake needed someone to look after his horses, he said he had to fly to Edmonton…his brother died suddenly." Rand pulled out a chair for Natalie.

So he hadn't known. Lindsay's self-assurance went up and another notch was added when Lee remembered his manners and pulled out his mother's chair and waited until she was seated before gently shoving it in.

"Would you like to give me a hand, Lee?" Rand asked.

They were barely out of hearing distance when Natalie leaned forward, her voice hissing, "I hope you're not getting any ideas about Rand. He's only being neighborly. He and I have an understanding…"

Her words confirmed Lindsay's suspicions that this was no casual drop-in, get-some-papers-signed visit. Everything from the enticing neckline of Natalie's elderberry blue dress with its pencil-thin skirt to her open-toe heels embracing the lie of the casualness of her visit.

Lindsay glanced down at Natalie's hand…no sign of a ring. "Oh?" Before Natalie could answer, Rand's backside was pushing the kitchen door ajar so he could carry in the hot casserole. Lee followed with the rolls and salad.

"Smells delicious," Natalie sniffed. "Helen is such a good cook."

As Rand spooned stroganoff onto their plates, he and Natalie kept up a continual chatter about people and events that were foreign to Lindsay and Lee.

"The Riverton Hospital Benefit is coming up in a few weeks." Natalie smiled at him. "Will you make the same donation as you did last year? A considerable one, if I remember."

His answer, "probably," was barely uttered before Natalie was asking, "And will you be able to donate, Lindsay? It is such a good cause."

How could she donate when she had no money and Natalie knew it. Suddenly Lindsay recalled that Bonnie always had a humorous reply for people who asked for money before payday.

"You'll have to excuse me. Right now, I couldn't afford a scrapping jacket for a louse." That recall succeeded in bringing a lightness to Lindsay's tone and she was able to say with aplomb, "I'm sure it is a good cause, Natalie. I'll speak to my accountant about it."

Unaffected by the undercurrents swirling around him, Lee ate hungrily. He loved Beef Stroganoff. Lindsay simply moved her food from one side of the plate to the other. All her life she had accepted being second best, being not-quite-good-enough. That's how Maria saw her; that's how Lindsay had always seen herself.

But that was no longer acceptable. She was the daughter of one of the best sulky drivers in harness racing. She was the granddaughter of one of the best breeders in the Riverton County. And she owned Trailwood. Be dammed if Natalie with her fine clothes, perfect manners and *do you remember*s were going to make her feel second rate.

"Rand, I would like you to compliment Helen for me on this wonderful supper...and this green bean salad is the best I've ever eaten." The surprised expression on Lee's face almost made Lindsay laugh. He knew she hated green beans.

"We often serve it at our club luncheons," Natalie said. "Would you like me to introduce you to some of my friends in the club?"

"That's thoughtful of you, Natalie." Rand endorsed her idea. "You need to make friends in the community, Lindsay, especially if you intend to stay."

"Oh, do you intend to stay?" Natalie inquired.

Lee broke into the conversation. "Of course, we're going to stay." The episode at the Taylors' skating party was evidently forgotten. "We love it here, don't we, Mom!"

"Yes, we love it here," Lindsay answered, holding her head a little higher, her back a little straighter. "We're going to stay." At that moment she knew it was true. Come hell or high water, no matter what happened between her and Rand, Trailwood was their heritage—and no one was going to take it away from them.

"You certainly sound determined." Natalie shifted slightly in her chair. "Trying to do it alone...well..."

"Lindsay isn't alone," Rand intervened. "She has Lee and Art to help her."
"I know, but Lee is just a boy and Art is a cantankerous old man."
"He is not!" Lee exclaimed. "Art is my friend and Mom's friend too."
Natalie backtracked a little. "I'm sure he knows a lot about horses, but he's certainly not a good role model for any boy." She looked to Rand for confirmation, but none came.

"How can you say that?" Lee stood, knocking his chair over backward. "Art cares about people. He looked after my grandfather for months when he was sick and he's been kind to us. He doesn't look down his nose at us either because we're poor, or we don't know anything about horses!" Lee's voice kept rising. "And maybe he forgets to wash sometimes or change his clothes. But he's my friend and I love him!"

Lindsay was astonished at Lee's outburst. She was proud too. She stood. "It was a lovely dinner, Rand. Thank you. It's getting late and Lee and I have chores to do." Her watch said five minutes to six. "We'll be on our way. Good night, Rand, Natalie."

As Lindsay turned to leave, she caught a glimpse of Rand as he threw his serviette on the table. But he didn't follow them.

Twelve

Lindsay had just begun her morning exercises when she heard Lee bounding down the stairs. Moments later.

"Mom! Mom! There's something wrong with the water."

Lindsay paused, her left leg still in lift position. "What do you mean? What's wrong with the water?" she called back.

"...only a few drops coming out of the tap. It's all rusty."

Grabbing her housecoat, Lindsay was soon standing beside Lee in the bathroom.

"See...all that's coming out of that tap are a few drops of rusty water," Lee said as he pulled up his slipping pajama bottoms. "Now there's nothing."

"Probably a blown fuse," Lindsay said. She went downstairs to check the fuse box which was located in the upper wall of the basement stairs. None were blown. She then returned to the bathroom.

"Call Art, Mom. He'll know what to do."

"I don't think he's back yet."

When Lee started to say "call Rand," he remembered and asked instead, "How am I going to wash?"

"That shouldn't be a problem. Water and you have never been bosom friends." Lindsay grinned in spite of herself. "There should be some water in the tea kettle. Just dampen this and wipe your hands and face." Lindsay handed him a face cloth. "I'm going to get dressed."

While Lee ate his cereal and toast, Lindsay called the pump specialist. His name was at the bottom of the list by the telephone. Reg Weaver, owner of

Weaver Pump Service, said he had been looking after Old Jeb's pump for years. "Told Old Jeb he needed a new one," Weaver said, adding that he had a couple of other calls to make and would be there in a couple of hours.

"What about the horses, Mom?" Lee asked. "They have to have water."

"Did you leave any water in the pails in the barn?" Art had taught them to leave a pail of water outside each horse's stall. In this cold weather, though, they weren't doing that since the water often froze over during the night.

"I guess I can melt some snow for them," she told him.

While Lee got ready for school, Lindsay grabbed her coat, pushed her feet into her boots, got a couple of empty pails from the pantry and went outside. Shoveling snow into the pails, her fingers soon began to tingle as she hadn't worn her mitts.

Placing the pails on the burners, she expected that by the time she finished her coffee and toast and had a bowl of oatmeal porridge, she would have two pails of water for the two pails of snow. Instead she got only four inches of water speckled with tiny globs of impurities.

Straining the water through a sieve, she took it to the barn, giving a small portion to each mare. Working quickly, she dished out a scoop of oats for each horse, threw them a fork of hay, hugged the filly and hurried back to the house. And it was just nine fifteen.

While she waited for more snow to melt, she shoveled a path to the pump house, an exaggerated name for the small lean-to shed at the back of the garage that protected the pump, heat lamp and wires from the elements. Lindsay still hadn't figured out how she was going to pay the repairman when he came. Of course, she had choices: a loan, a mortgage, or the hutch which Art had said was a family heirloom.

She was still mulling over her choices when Reg Weaver drove into the yard. Weaver, a big man in winter coveralls and a John Deere ear flaps cap, waved and headed toward the pump house where Lindsay caught up with him.

"Pump was always freezing up," Weaver told Lindsay as he pushed the hinged front of the pump house aside. "Finally talked your grandfather into putting this heat lamp over it a couple of years ago."

"Any idea what's wrong?" Lindsay bent low, peering into the shed.

"Not sure. Probably the valve." Weaver simplified his explanation for Lindsay. The pump had two valves, one at the top and one at the bottom of the pipe. If it was the valve attached to the pipe at the bottom of the sixty-foot well, it would take five to seven hours and he would need to get another man to help him pull up the pipe. If it was the valve at the top of the pipe, it would take a couple of hours. The cost—a couple of hundred dollars one way, a thousand plus the other.

Lindsay called Herb Haggitt, the antique dealer. While she waited for Haggitt to return her call, she strained some snow water into the coffee pot. She'd missed her morning fix. A few minutes later, looking out the kitchen window, sipping coffee from her mug, she saw the police cruiser driving into their lane. It was Sergeant Joe Riley, the same officer she had talked to when Lee was accused of stealing Alice Taylor's money. Lee was sitting beside him.

What now? Her heart plummeted.

Lindsay met them at the door. "What's wrong?" she cried. "What's happened?"

Lee looked at his boots, not at his mother as Sergeant Riley guided him into the kitchen. "Lee pulled a knife on Ian Hardesty."

"He what?" Lindsay stared incredulously at Riley whom today was wearing his police uniform with three yellow chevrons on the sleeve. "I don't believe it." Lindsay looked from the Sergeant to Lee and back again to the Sergeant. "Lee doesn't even own a knife!"

"Lee admitted it, Miss Macaulay." Riley pulled a small jackknife from his pocket and placed it on the table in front of Lindsay.

"Lee! Where did you get that knife?"

"In the hutch drawer." Lee's words were muffled against his coat front. Finally he looked up. "It was my grandfather's."

"It's an old jackknife, Miss Macaulay and it has Jeff Macaulay's name engraved on the handle." Sergeant Riley flipped the knife open, exposing a narrow two-inch blade at one end and a bottle opener at the other. "It's old, but it is still a knife."

"We tried to get you earlier, Mom, but there was no answer." Lee's voice wavered.

Lindsay said she was outside. "What's going to happen now?" she asked.

"Lee is suspended, of course. There will be a hearing in a couple of days and what the school board's final decision will be, I don't know," he said, adding that he was leaving Lee in Lindsay's custody and he was not to leave the farm under any circumstances. "Miss Ormstown said she would be in touch with you about his homework and as soon as I learn the date of the hearing, I'll call you." Meanwhile, he said, he was going to do more investigating into the bullying problems at the school.

After he had gone. Lindsay got two Cokes from the fridge. She took a chair opposite Lee. "Would you like to tell me what really happened?" she asked quietly. When Lee had gotten in trouble in the city, Lindsay had read numerous articles and books about teens searching for their identity and the problems they faced; how to manage competition, how to avoid conflicts and cement friendships, how to find their place in the world.

She read that even good kids spent more time *looking* for something rather than *doing* something and because they were lonely it was often easier to say *yes* than say *no.*

Slumped in a kitchen chair, Lee ran his forefinger around the top of his Coke bottle.

"Lee, please. I can't help you if you don't tell me." Lindsay poured some of her Coke into a glass. She hated drinking from the bottle.

Suddenly, like a dam that just broke, the words flowed. "The kids hang around in little groups. They won't talk to me. If they see me coming they just turn away. The only one who is nice to me is Beth. She sits beside me on the bus and in our home room and helps me with my assignments." He paused, gulping a swallow of Coke before he continued. "Although most of the subjects are the same, science is totally different. When I ask anyone to see their notes, they tell me they didn't take notes or they can't find them.

"Ian Hardesty is the worst, especially on the bus. He talks loud, makes sure everyone one can hear him. And he's always riding me, trying to make me look stupid." Lee gulped back a sob. "And it isn't just about school. He says our truck is ready for the junk heap. He calls our horses crow-bait. And everyone hee-haws. Oh, Mom, it's awful."

"Why didn't you tell me?"

"I couldn't, Mom. He said *things...bad things*...about our family, about you." Lee wiped his eyes. "Oh, Mom, I just couldn't tell you..."

Lindsay's stomach tightened into knots. She knew what they were saying—an unwed mother with a son couldn't be trusted around men—their men. She was loose, *an easy lay*. She had heard it all at the store from hand-covered mouths, but never so blatantly.

Lee continued, "Hardesty gets real crude. On the bus he told Beth that if she kept associating with me, she'd turn out just like you—dirt poor with a brat and no husband. When he said that, all his friends stomped their feet and laughed. Beth cried, Mom. That's when I knew I had to do something."

Lindsay's hand smothered a gasp. "Oh, Lee...

"I just couldn't take it anymore, Mom!" He paused. Took a drink of Coke.

"I waited until Ian was alone in the boy's washroom. I slammed the cubicle door in his face. I knocked him down. I sat on him. I held the knife blade above his throat. I yelled at him. I told him if he ever said any of those things again, I would slit his throat. And that's when one of the other boys came in and he ran for Miss Ormstown and she called Sergeant Riley."

Lindsay stared at her son, his long legs stretched out before him.

In the city, where more than a quarter of the kids in Lee's class had single moms, he melded in. Here in the country, he stood out like a sore thumb. Roots went deep. Names stood for influence and traditions

She had once heard her grandfather say, "a person with a bad name is already half-hanged." Where did that come from? But this wasn't the time to explore her memory recall. "What else did Hardesty say?"

Lee hesitated, taking another swallow of Coke and for a second Lindsay thought he wasn't going to answer. Then in a low voice, he finally continued, "Ian says I didn't even have a name, that I'm nameless because I don't have a father." Lee's head came up. "But I have a name, Mom!" His eyes met Lindsay's, questioning, defying her to say it wasn't so. "I knew I had to stop him."

Lindsay gulped back a sob.

"I'm sorry, Mom."

She felt his lips touch her cheek before he turned and ran upstairs.

My God. What was happening to them? A sharp knock on the door broke her thoughts. Reg Weaver. He gave her his bill. Would she like to pay it now or send him a cheque? She would send him a cheque, she assured him. But at that moment Lindsay wasn't quite sure where the money was coming from to cover it, nor did it matter right now. All that mattered was Lee.

Lindsay picked up her glass still filled with Coke. Poured it down the sink. Cried. Paced the floor. She got a package of ground beef from the refrigerator. She put it back. She paced some more.

Over the years, Lindsay's only anchor had been Bonnie Tobin. Unfortunately, Bonnie was in Toronto and Lindsay was here. Lindsay dialed. Prayed that Bonnie would be home and on the third ring a familiar "hello" came over the line.

"Oh, Bonnie. I was so afraid you wouldn't be home," she sobbed. "And I need to talk to you...."

"It's the first day of my two-week holiday," Bonnie explained before asking what was wrong.

For the next half hour, Lindsay poured her troubles into Bonnie's listening ear. Just to have someone to talk to, to listen, somehow put them into perspective.

"Oh, Bonnie, what would I do without you?" Lindsay wiped the tears from her eyes.

"Don't you know that a trouble shared, is a trouble halved?" Bonnie chided when Lindsay apologized again for calling.

As they talked, commiserated, Lindsay was able to get a handle on Lee's problem but a niggling sense of guilt still remained. She had brought Lee to Trailwood to get him away from the bad influences of his so-called friends in the city. Instead she had brought him to Trailwood where his only companions were a sixty-year old man, an eleven-year-old girl, and a horse named Queenie.

~ * ~

As Bonnie predicted, life would go on. It did. Lindsay and Lee went to the barn. They did the chores. Lee didn't talk. Lindsay didn't question. They forked hay, added extra straw to Princess's stall, hugged the filly, patted Princess's nose. When they were leaving, Lee went back and gave Queenie a hug "I didn't want her to feel neglected," Lee said. "Horses have feelings, just like people."

They walked to the house.

Lee went back upstairs.

Lindsay got her paints, but she didn't paint. She just sat at the table. Lee had never lied to her. Oh, little fibs. But he had never *really* lied. So where had he gotten the knife? She went to the hall where their hutch stood, which according to Art wasn't a hutch; it was a *jardiniere* and it had belonged to her father's grandfather. Whatever it was, it had to go, this hutch with a secret drawer. Only there was no *secret* drawer.

Lindsay stood back. Looked at it. It wasn't even a good-looking piece of furniture. Plain, awkward, small table with open bottom attached to four bowed legs. It's only claim to beauty was the carved motifs that decorated the front panel. Lindsay ran her fingers along its thumbnail edging downward over one of the rosettes. The rosette moved. Startled, Lindsay paused. She slowly turned the rosette and a thin drawer slid out. Lee hadn't lied!

She ran upstairs, tapped on his door, opened it. Lee was asleep, curled into a protective ball like he had done years ago when he was a toddler.

She closed the door and went downstairs.

She got her paints, pulled the hanging lamp lower and began to sketch the head of a horse with a black head, white face and big friendly brown eyes. Not bad. While the image was still fresh in her mind, she sketched it onto one of the mugs that she had purchased at the Goodwill store when Lee bought his skates. The mug had a flaw on the side but the horse's mane would cover it. There was no paint, though, that would cover the flaws in her own life.

A single mom with a child. A horse farm teetering on bankruptcy.

~ * ~

The next morning began with an apology to Lee and a heart-warming hug, and a call from the antique dealer saying that he was still interested and agreed to give her six hundred and fifty dollars for her hutch. He would pick it up in a couple of days. Lindsay wondered if he knew about the secret drawer. Was that what made it so valuable?

Then Sergeant Riley called. With the principal still on sick leave, Miss Ormstown and the chairman of the school board, Broderick Hunter, had set Lee's hearing for the next morning at ten o'clock in the school's boardroom.

The day dragged. Lee was out in the barn with the horses and Lindsay touched up the mug with the head on the side.

Early in the evening a car drove into the lane. How dare Rand bring Natalie here?

The woman wasn't tall and slim; instead she was short and stocky and carrying a suitcase.

"Bonnie! Oh, my God!" Lindsay cried as she ran out the door. "Bonnie..."

The suitcase dropped. "Well, you might let me in the house before you turn on the water works," Bonnie quipped as she folded Lindsay into her arms.

Suddenly the day wasn't so dark.

"Aunt Bonnie! How did you get here?" Another pair of arms went around the two women.

"Well," Bonnie drawled in her homespun way. "I called a certain man who teaches at a certain college and that certain man gave me a lift to Riverton and here I am."

"Oh, Bonnie, I'm so glad to see you." Lindsay couldn't hide her tears.

Instead of supper being a dismal affair, it turned out to be a jovial one, especially after Art, who had just come home, dropped in to see how Lindsay and Lee were doing. And the short stocky little woman with the topknot and the big gangly man who never took off his cap got along as Bonnie later said, "like a house on fire." Art's whimsical, "I taught Lee..." and Bonnie's "I caught him in my arms when he took his first step" upmanship went on and on until Lindsay's and Lee's troubles were temporarily forgotten.

Thirteen

Lindsay and Lee arrived at the school five minutes before their scheduled hearing and were directed to the board room by the school's secretary. It was a friendless room with Venetian blinds which closed out the sunshine from its only window. A long table with six high-back chairs dominated the room. Lindsay and Lee chose two nearest the door.

Lindsay drew her coat a little closer. What was in store for Lee?

A tall man, slightly stooped with balding head and dark-rimmed glasses, carrying a brief case, strode into the room and took the chair at the head of the table. Broderick Hunter, Natalie's father. Lindsay recognized him from a picture in the school's yearbook which the school secretary had given her when she'd registered Lee for classes two months earlier. Miss Ormstown and Sergeant Riley followed. Both nodded to Lindsay and Lee, then sat.

Hunter called the hearing to order.

Miss Ormstown gave her report. She stated that early in January Lee had transferred from a Toronto elementary school. Despite the differences in the schools' curriculums, he had adjusted well and was trying very hard to fit in. Since she believed that Lee was trying to protect someone, she recommended that he receive counseling and the mandatory five-day suspension for carrying a sharp object.

Sergeant Riley gave his report next, stating that Lee had been in trouble with police back in Toronto and had been warned by the judge the next time he would end up at the juvenile detention center. Shortly afterward, the sergeant said, the Macaulays had moved to Trailwood. He stated that a week ago he had questioned Lee about some missing money at the Taylors. "Since there was *no* theft, sir, I just filed the report."

After flipping through several pages of the reports, Hunter ordered Lee to step forward. "Lee, you are charged with attacking Ian Hardesty with a knife. How do you plead?" Hunter peered over the top of his glasses.

"He's a thirteen-year-old boy, for heaven sakes." Lindsay wanted to jump to her feet. Shout. "This is not a court room. Lee's not a criminal!" Instead, she followed Bonnie's earlier advice. *"Grit your teeth and keep your mouth shut!"*

Lee looked straight at Hunter, only his hands, tightly clutched behind his back, reflected his fear. Instead of answering "yes" or "no," he said, "I know I shouldn't have pulled a knife on Ian, sir. I was wrong. He was wrong, too, sir. He shouldn't have told lies about me. He shouldn't have made Beth cry. He is guilty too, sir."

"Beth?" Hunter turned to Miss Ormstown.

"Beth Taylor, sir. Her father owns the local garage. Beth used to be Ian Hardesty's friend."

"And this is what they fought over?" The lines on Hunter's face deepened.

"I believe so," Miss Ormstown said. "Yes."

"Ridiculous!" Hunter gritted out the word as he again flipped through the report. "Where did you get the knife? Did you bring it with you from Toronto?"

"No, sir," Lee answered. "It was my grandfather's."

"Your grandfather's!" Hunter scoffed. "Jeff Macaulay never carried a knife. He had more sense. So where did you get the knife?"

Lindsay could feel Lee's anger. She had taught him that truth and love were the cores of their mother-son relationship. It was precious to them. Now, Hunter was calling Lee a liar. She held her breath, afraid that Lee's quick temper would explode.

"Sir, it was a small one-blade pocket knife," Sergeant Riley quietly defused the situation. "Jeff's Macaulay's initials were on it. He probably carried it when he went to school."

"Jeff Macaulay was a good man." Hunter's face reddened as he glared at Lee. "You've dishonored his name. Do you realize that?"

"I think he would have approved, sir."

"Approved!" Hunter scowled. "Approved. Young man, I think you need parental guidance. Where's your father?"

"My father is dead sir. There's just my mother and me."

Silence. Nerve shattering silence broken only by the tapping of Hunter's forefinger as he again leafed through the reports.

"Considering the circumstance I think the Children's Aid Society should get involved here." Hunter looked at Miss Ormstown, then at Sergeant Riley. "This *family* needs monitoring."

Lindsay gasped. Surely they wouldn't think of taking Lee away from her. He was her life, her reason for living. In her distress, she didn't notice the man who slipped quietly into the room.

Hunter looked up at the intrusion. "For the record," the deep lines around his face curved into a slight smile. "Our third committee member, Rand Dyson has arrived...late."

Lindsay tensed. After Lee's outburst at his house the other night, Lindsay wasn't sure if his presence was a good thing or a bad thing.

"I apologize, sir. Our district school board meeting ran late."

"I'm sure you've read the reports that were sent to you yesterday, Rand. Have you anything to add?" Hunter asked

"Yes, I have." Rand moved forward to stand beside Lee. "I know this boy. He's not a troublemaker." He put his hand on Lee's shoulder.

"Last fall, there were rumors of bullying in this school, although there were no official complaints. Sergeant Riley was asked to keep a watchful eye on the situation—you were ill at the time, Broderick—and it was the consensus, although not unanimous, that 'boys will be boys.' And no further action was taken. I didn't agree then. I don't agree now. Perhaps if we had done something then, we wouldn't be here today.

"This boy chose to do something. True, he threatened Ian Hardesty with a knife. That was wrong and I agree he should be punished. Miss Ormstown has recommended that Lee receive a five-day suspension, and the two days already served. I would recommend that both boys go for after-school counseling and each boy must write a thousand word essay on bullying and read it before the class. Lee had a knife and therefore must receive extra punishment."

"Such as....?" Hunter asked.

"Twenty-four hours of community service at the public library."

"A bit lenient, don't you think, Rand?" Hunter looked over the top of his glasses.

"No, I don't. Hardesty provoked this situation. Lee was responding the only way he knew how."

The lines tightened around Hunter's mouth.

"Anything else?"

Lindsay noticed that Rand had stepped away from Lee.

"Yes. Bullying has been a constant problem at the school, and we have all looked away. We need to discuss it in the classroom, get it out in the open. And as teachers we have to listen. Scars from bullying can last a lifetime.

"Bullying begins in subtle ways: one student calling another a name, a bump against a desk so that papers *accidentally* end up on the floor, a faint innuendo added to someone else's answer, exclusion—still sitting when everyone else has been chosen, finger pointing, negative laughter. Often the bully is not really a bad kid, just one with misdirected morals who likes the feeling of being a leader, being the center of attention at the expense of someone else.

"Broderick, we have to start here in the lower grades, in schools like this one, to teach our kids better ways to handle the 'bullies" of society. We need to give the Miss Ormstowns and the Sergeant Rileys the resources to combat it. And I would ask this committee to take steps toward this end."

The muscles on Hunter's face tightened. He consulted with Miss Ormstown and Sergeant Riley. He made notes. Fearfully, Lindsay waited. Lee's bottom lip trembled. Seconds seemed like minutes.

Finally, Hunter read the sentence: five-day expulsion added to the two already served. After-school counseling, a thousand word essay and twenty-four hours of community service. "And if you ever come before this committee again, Macaulay, I will personally see that you are expelled from this school."

The hearing was over. Tears clogged Lindsay's throat. She opened her arms. Held Lee close. And she wanted to thank Rand, but the door had already closed behind him.

~ * ~

Bonnie had soup and sandwiches waiting for them when they got home from the hearing and as soon as Art heard their truck drive in the yard, he had come to the house. Of course, he stayed. Now, he and Lee had gone to the barn, probably to rehash everything that was said at the hearing.

"I learned something today. About Lee. About myself," Lindsay said as she carried the dirty dishes to the sink.

This was the first chance Lindsay and Bonnie had time to talk.

"What was that?" Bonnie asked, filling the sink with hot water.

Lindsay always found that working together—like washing and drying dishes—made talking easier. One washed. One dried. One talked. One listened. Problems got aired, discussed, lessened. She often wished she and Maria had done dishes together...maybe they would have had a better relationship.

Lindsay got a clean dish towel out of the drawer. "I thought Lee didn't care much about not having a father in his life. Today, I learned different. When Hunter asked him where his father was, Lee's whole body tensed, little beads of sweat broke out above his lip. He squared his shoulder as if he were expecting a punch...and he got it." Hunter's deep gravelly voice *where's your father* still echoed in Lindsay's ears. "He cares, Bonnie, and he isn't going to let anyone know it, especially me."

"I remembered something else," Lindsay continued, putting a glass on the shelf. "Last Fathers' Day, Lee's class was asked to write a story about their dads. Lee missed school that day—he was sick. I tried to think— remember— other Fathers' Days. He was sick on those days too. And when anyone talks about someone's illegitimate kid, he makes some excuse and leaves the room."

"Thank God illegitimacy doesn't have the stigma it once did." Bonnie drained the sink.

"I know, but it's still there. Always will be, I guess. And kids pay for the sins of their parents." Lindsay hung the dish towel to dry on a bar attached to the back of a cupboard door, surprised that the dishes were finished.

"Do you think what happened today will stop the bullying?" Bonnie asked as she applied some lotion to her hands.

"Slow it down for a while, I guess. Time will tell."

"Coming here was the right thing," Bonnie assured her. "For him...and for you."

"Bonnie, after the hearing, I tried to speak to Rand...thank him for speaking up for Lee, but he left so quickly, I didn't have a chance."

"You really care about him...?

"I suppose I do." Lindsay accepted the hand lotion from Bonnie. "Right now, though, all I can think about is that appointment with Lyle Edmonds," she said.

Bonnie had told her the bank manager's secretary had called when she was at Lee's hearing. Lindsay had an appointment with him at three o'clock.

~ * ~

Sitting on a straight back chair in front of the bank manager's desk wasn't that much different from sitting in a straight back chair at Lee's hearing. Her mouth felt dry. The palms of her hands were sweaty. Her heart beat was erratic. So much hinged on this meeting.

After their initial greeting, Lyle Edmonds opened her file. "Miss Macaulay...Lindsay, if I may..."at the nod of her head, he continued. "Your idea to turn your farm into a boarding stable is a good one. For a novice, you've laid out your plan very well. You have a good location, the Macaulay name is certainly well-known in the county and your octangular barn and trails along the river can be drawing cards. I also think that offering accommodation to owners so they can spend a weekend in the country with their horse is a sound one."

"Boarding stables with weekend accommodation for owners has been successful in other provinces," Lindsay said, "But I couldn't find any in this area."

Edmonds agreed. The bank had also checked. "Lindsay, the bank has gone over your proposal very carefully..."

Lindsay's hopes nosedived.

"The bank is prepared to grant you a ten-year mortgage so that you can develop your boarding stable." He smiled across the desk at her. "Interest will be paid semi-annually with a principal payment at the end of the second year. This will give you time to get the business established."

"Thank you." A tear trickled from the corner of her eye.

"My pleasure." Smiling, Edmonds handed her a copy of the mortgage agreement.

"This is a standard mortgage document. Take your time. Read it carefully." He stood. "While you're reading it, I'm going to get a coffee. Would you like one?"

Lindsay shook her head. Her stomach was tumbling around like clothes in a dryer. Oh, she wished she had a better knowledge of legal documents. "He's an honest man, girl. Trust him." She heard her grandfather's voice. She looked up. No one else was in the room.

Then Edmonds was back. "Any questions?"

She had dozens of them, but at the moment only one came to mind. "If I should miss making a payment, what would happen to Trailwood?"

"Not all businesses succeed, Lindsay. Poor management is most often the cause of failure. However, the bank wouldn't grant you a mortgage if it didn't feel you were a good risk," Edmonds said, one leg dangling as he sat on the corner of his desk. "If you miss a payment, we will call you. No big deal.

"If you missed two or three, we would be concerned. Maybe ask you to come in, talk, find out what the problem is, and possibly make a suggestion or two on how to solve it. If the default became longer in duration, the bank would make arrangements to operate the business, possibly sell it. Then, after all the debtors are satisfied, the balance would be turned over to you or your estate." Edmonds studied her face. "You can always sell, Lindsay. You have that option. And there are buyers out there. A year or so ago, a numbered consortium approached your grandfather about buying Trailwood. Jeb told them he was keeping it for his family."

Lindsay paused before handing him back the document. "Everything looks okay."

Edmonds buzzed for his secretary. He needed her to witness the signing of the agreement. While they waited, he asked Lindsay about her new filly.

Relaxing a little, Lindsay smiled. The birth of the filly was one of the brighter moments in her life.

"She's a beauty. Perfect in every way."

"Are you going to breed that mare to the same stallion again?"

"Oh, no. I couldn't afford...I just don't think it's wise to use the same stallion again." Lindsay added that it seemed awfully soon to breed Princess again. Maybe she would give the mare a rest for a year. That would give her time to find just the right stallion.

"Sounds like a sensible approach," he said as his secretary hurried into the room.

"I'm sorry I took so long, sir. I got waylaid by Mrs. Granby again."

Edmonds returned to his managerial position behind the desk. "Mrs. Granby is one of our oldest customers," he told Lindsay. "She's in her nineties—a little on the lonely side, and sometimes she just needs assurance that her portfolio is secure."

A load lifted off Lindsay's shoulders. If the bank took time to assure an old lady about her portfolio, it would surely look after Lindsay and her mortgage.

"Have you given any thought as to a tentative opening date?"

She shook her head. Until a few minutes ago, she wasn't certain if the bank would even grant her a mortgage. Now, there were so many things she had to do: order lumber for new stalls, fence posts around the paddock to check, potholes to be filled in the trails and the list went on and on.

"Lindsay, you should seriously consider going to the horsemen's convention at Tamarack Inn this weekend. You would not only meet other people from the horse industry, but you might get answers to some of your questions like business license and the best places to advertise. I know it is short notice."

She stood. "I simply don't have the time, if I am going to have my boarding stable operational by mid-spring." She couldn't wait to get started. Besides, every penny of the mortgage money was earmarked for her stable. None could be spared for a convention.

"The bank is one of the convention sponsors." Edmond walked her to his door. "As a gesture of their appreciation, the horsemen give us complimentary accommodation for the entire convention. Since I have other commitments, my assistant manager is going in my place and he intends to travel back and forth each day as his young wife is expecting. So there is a complimentary room available and personally, I would like to see you go."

"Mr. Edmonds..."

He held up his hand. "Go home. Think about it. This is Thursday and the convention begins on Saturday. Meanwhile, take this with you." He handed her a large envelope which contained a copy of her mortgage. Stapled on the side was a smaller envelope with "complimentary" typed in the corner.

Fourteen

Lindsay parked the truck and hurrying along the snow-coated path to the veranda, she almost slipped twice, but was too excited to slow down, even though she knew she should. She had paid a heavy price the last time she had fallen—a broken leg and months of pain and therapy.

"Bonnie! Bonnie! I got it!' She wrenched open the kitchen door, waving a large envelope. "Look at this. Tell me what you think." She handed Bonnie the envelope containing her mortgage.

Clasping her in a bear hug, Bonnie exclaimed, "I just knew they couldn't turn you down."

"That's more than I did," Lindsay laughed as she pulled free. Then, turning, she impulsively hugged Art who has having an afternoon tea-for-two with Bonnie.

"Where's Lee?"

"Rand picked him up. He took him to the library. Said he wanted to introduce him to some of the people he would be working with for the next few weeks."

Deflated a tad, Lindsay poured herself a cup of tea, noticing that Art was not only drinking tea but had removed his cap, another first for the day.

"What's this?" Bonnie asked, noticing the "complimentary" envelope attached to the mortgage envelope

"Complimentary accommodation at the Tamarack Convention. It was certainly thoughtful of Mr. Edmonds. Of course, I can't go, but it was a nice thought."

"Why can't you go?" Bonnie asked. "You told me a few days ago that Alice Taylor said that if you went, you could display some of your porcelain in their gift shop."

"I did think about going...that was before this trouble with Lee at the school." She had thought she might get away for one of the day's sessions. "I wouldn't think of leaving him alone now."

"Alone? Who am I?" Bonnie challenged.

"My wonderful, wonderful friend." Lindsay grinned. Spunky, rebellious, determined, persistent, impatient, all described Bonnie Tobin.

"It seems to me that fate just smiled on you. I don't have to be back to work for another week. Art can help Lee look after the horses. So...why don't you just go?"

"Complimentary feels like charity to me and I'm not ready for charity yet," Lindsay said defensively. To her, the two were synonymous. When she was in her early teens, after missing months of school because of her leg, the gym teacher, Miss Horst, had looked at her scruffy shoes. "There's nothing wrong with your leg except your shoes. There's so old they're falling apart." It was true, her shoes were falling apart but they were the only ones that were comfortable. Maria had refused to buy her better shoes until Lindsay learned to walk without limping.

When the kids in her class had seen the lace-ups sitting on the teacher's desk and heard Miss Horst say to Lindsay, "Put these on. Compliments of Goodwill," everyone had laughed, and laughed even harder when Lindsay had to limp up to the front to get them. A long time ago, but it still rankled.

"Charity!" Bonnie exclaimed. "For heaven's sake, Lindsay. It's business. They give and you take and vice-versa."

"It will give you a chance to meet other people, maybe meet someone who has a boarding stable," Art added his two-cents worth to the conversation. "And have some fun for a change."

"Before I forget, Maria called," Bonnie interrupted. "I wrote her number on that pad beside the telephone."

"I wonder how she knew I was here. I only told a couple of people I was moving. I didn't want any of Lee's *friends* contacting him." Only the supermarket owner and their ex-landlord had their address. "To be honest, in all the frenzy of moving, I forgot about Maria."

"Maybe she still keeps in touch with someone here," Bonnie said.

"It's possible, I suppose. Sometimes, years ago, when I was supposed to be asleep, I would hear her talking on the telephone to someone. Once I heard her laughing about some ugly old stone pillars. The other day I noticed that the bank has tall marble-stone pillars at their entrance."

"The bank manager!" Bonnie raised her eyebrows skeptically.

"More likely Asher Honeyborne," Art answered. "He was always sweet on Maria."

Music suddenly blaring in the background over the line put an end to their conversation as Lindsay said, "Hello, Mom."

"Don't call me that!" Maria snapped. "You know I hate it."

"Sorry." Lindsay held the receiver away from her ear. She reminded herself to remove the amplifier Jeb had installed because of his hearing problem. "It just slipped out."

When Lindsay heard Art chortle, she realized he and Bonnie could hear every word Maria was saying.

"What on earth were you thinking, moving to the country? Trailwood is no place for you. You don't know anything about farming or horses."

Lindsay sighed. Not even a, "hello, dear," or "how-are-you" before Maria started to complain. She hadn't changed. Years earlier, when Lindsay had to do her leg exercises every morning, Maria said the exercises were the cause of her pain, the reason she limped. And the wool sweater with the teddy bears on the front Lindsay had bought for Lee, Maria wanted her to take it back. It was costly and would make Lee itch. So Lindsay had learned it was easier to give in than argue.

Of course, Lindsay wasn't the only one Maria criticized. Pointing out people's faults was second nature to her. But her mother had her good points, which were often overlooked. When Lindsay had her accident, Maria had stayed with her night and day; even moved permanently from Trailwood to Toronto. Once when Lindsay was hospitalized at the Hospital for Sick Children, one of the nurses told her that her mother had worked nonstop for twenty-four hours at a senior center using a charcoal burner to make coffee and heat soup for residents in a seniors' home.

Somewhere in the years between the Hospital for Sick Children and Trailwood, Lindsay had grown up, had a child, been widowed without a husband and worked in a supermarket part-time. Then *fate,* or as Shakespeare put it so eloquently, "a divinity that shapes our ends," took a hand.

Leaving Lee with a neighbor, Lindsay was on her way to the drug store to get some Vick's Vapor rub for Lee's cold when she fell on a patch of ice on the sidewalk just outside their building. The fall not only broke the femur in her left leg again, but the break had spiraled above and below her knee.

This time, instead of being airlifted to the Children's Hospital, Lindsay was taken by ambulance to University Hospital where the doctors had decided to use a new technique, intramedually nailing, developed in Turkey during the war years to set and rebuild soldiers' broken bones.

Before the operation, her doctor had explained that a rod would be inserted in the medullary cavity (the marrow) of the femur bone and this rod would be held in place by locking nails or screws inserted diagonally in the leg bone itself. After the operation, her leg would be immobilized in a cast for eight to ten months from the tip of Lindsay toes to her upper hip. "When it heals, we expect you to be able to walk without a limp."

Walk without a limp!

Lindsay never heard the doctor telling her that recovery would be long and slow or that it would be costly. She only heard that she would be able to walk without a limp.

Maria had heard something else. 'Walking without a limp' also meant freedom for her. She could chuck her responsibilities. Lindsay would be able to work and look after her young son on her own and for the first time in her life, Maria would be free of responsibility, be herself, do what she wanted, go where she wanted, when she wanted, without a thought for anyone else.

Ever since she had been a kid, someone was always depending on her: her family, especially after her mother took off, her husband Jeff and later their baby and Old Jeb and the farm. Maria had never been free to *just be herself.*

"I'll find the money for the operation," Maria promised, and Lindsay believed her.

Whenever Lindsay questioned her, she said she had heard about a charitable organization that funded rehabilitation for accident victims. She had applied on Lindsay's behalf and their expenses would be covered until she could get back to work again.

Lindsay's intramedullary nailing had done more than strengthen her leg...it strengthened her belief in herself. By balancing herself on one leg, crutches under her arm, she could even pick up things she dropped—stretch cast straight out behind her, balance on good leg, lean forward—one hand on back of chair for safety, and *voila!* Pick up a knitting needle, even a pain pill. And she learned to oven-cook their meals. Saucepans were heavy, awkward to lift, and she had several burns to show for it. So she used the oven and smaller dishes.

There were bad moments during those months too. There had been a fundraiser at the rehabilitation center, the prize, two tickets to a Blue Jay game. When the committee learned that the winner was in a wheelchair, they said they would provide transportation for her and her son to and from the stadium. Maria said Lee was too young to go to a ball game; she would go instead. Although Lindsay couldn't see the faces of the players from the wheelchair section above the seats, Maria had a birds-eye view. She still complained. She hated sitting alone. Why couldn't Lindsay have stayed home and let her take a friend?

Her worst day—the day the doctor removed her cast. Lindsay naively expected that she would automatically walk without a limp. The cast had come off, nine months after it went on. Her leg felt cold, naked. "Take your time," the doctor had advised as Lindsay stood. He was on her left side holding her arm, Bonnie was on her right side holding the other arm. If it hadn't been for the doctor and Bonnie, Lindsay would have fallen flat on her face. Her leg wouldn't hold her. It had no strength.

"Not to worry," the doctor assured her. "Your leg's weak. After all, it hasn't been used for nine months." He gave instructions to Bonnie:

"Whirlpool bath every day for three weeks at least. Massage. Exercise. Then, we'll see..." And he was gone.

"I tried so hard, and I can't even take a step." Tears had streamed down Lindsay's face.

"You will. It's just going to take time." Bonnie had given her a hug. "Rome wasn't built in a day, you know."

Lindsay had learned to walk again, first on crutches and putting a little weight on her leg; then with just one crutch and more weight and finally on her own. Lee had used the time—in Bonnie's words "to grow like a bad weed." Lindsay had gone back to work part-time; Lee had gone to school full time with day care supplementing the needed hours.

Although they had lived together in the same apartment, they saw little of Maria. She still worked nights as a hostess at a night club, and she had a busy social life. Jeff's insurance money was almost gone and she had sold her car. Then, Maria wanted to move to a different apartment closer to her work, but it was miles from the school and there were parks in the area where she could take Lee on her days off.

Lindsay refused to go. They argued. Maria shouted. Lindsay stood firm. In the end, she and Lee moved to a small third-floor apartment near a school in the same area where Lindsay worked and Maria moved west. She had been offered a hostess job by a major hotel chain, whose owner she had met one night at her club.

That was almost seven or eight years ago and, although they talked occasionally on the telephone, they had not seen each other since. Lindsay and Lee were at Trailwood, had a home, new friends...and a mortgage.

"I should have inherited Trailwood." Maria was still continuing her tirade. "I was Jeff's wife. His heir. Not you." And her harangue went on and on and Lindsay finally hung up the phone.

She was crying, not tears of sorrow, but tears of frustration. "She does it to me every time," she sniffed. "Makes me feel guilty that I somehow allowed Old Jeb to run over me."

Bonnie gave Lindsay's shoulder a pat as she emptied out Lindsay's cold tea and poured her a fresh cup. Art declined a "freshin' up."

It was a long moment before he broke the poignant silence.

"If anyone needs to feel guilty, Lindsay, it's me. I was responsible for your dad's accident."

Perplexed, she gave him a quick look as she reached for a facial tissue on the counter. "You weren't even there."

While the nod of his head showed that he agreed, Art continued, "Just the same, I was responsible. I was scheduled to drive that night. I had been out drinking the night before. I drank a lot those days. I had a hangover. Shortly before race time, I called in sick. Jeff, who was getting ready to go home, took my drive." A tear trickled down Art's cheek. "It was an important race for the owner. He needed the purse. And Jeff took my place and he was killed." Art's voice wavered.

"That doesn't explain..."

"Your dad had planned for him and Maria to go out on the town that night. When I called in sick and Jeff volunteered to drive in my place, Maria was furious. She accused Jeff of putting the horses and racing ahead of her. She'd had enough. She was going to show Jeff Macaulay she wasn't going to stay home and wait for him. She called someone—she had minor flirtations over the years. She was leaving. For good. Jeff hadn't told her that they might be going to Europe. He was saving it as a surprise; he was going to tell her that evening."

"Mother was leaving us...for good!" Lindsay whispered.

"I don't think so," Art said. "She was upset. Disappointed. She said she had enough of horses and work...she was going to have some fun for a change. Old Jeb told me that he tried to talk some sense into her. Maria grabbed the keys for your grandfather's truck—Jeff had their pick up at the track—and ran out of the house. That's when the call came from the racetrack that there had been an accident.

"Your grandfather said that he ran outside. Yelled for Maria to stop, tell her ....," Art continued. "She was already in the truck. You must have heard the commotion. You were outside too, running toward the truck. You grabbed the door handle. Maria didn't see you. She put the truck in gear. You lost your grip—fell—and the rest is history."

"And you've blamed yourself for what happened that night!" Lindsay stared at Art incredulously.

Art wiped his sleeve across his nose. "Don't you see? I was responsible for everything that happened: Jeff driving, Maria leaving, you getting hurt..."

Lindsay glanced from Art to Bonnie and back again to Art. "Maria said..."

Suddenly tiny bombshells of memory began exploding in Lindsay's head, shells which had been lying dormant for twenty-six years, just waiting, and out of the explosions she saw a truck, a little girl running, crying "Mommy, Mommy....door slamming, truck moving, turning, little girl crying, grabbing the door, grasping, slipping, falling, screaming. "Mommy! Mommy! Mommy!"

Lindsay covered her face with her hands and Bonnie's arms went around her. "It's all right, dear. It's all right," she comforted.

"Why didn't someone tell me?" Lindsay wailed. "All these years I've been blaming Grandpa..."

"Until you returned to Trailwood, Lindsay, no one knew you blamed Old Jeb for the accident. After Jeff was buried, your grandfather went to the hospital. He tried to see you, but there was a "no visitors" sign on your door. And the nurse in charge insisted. "No visitors.""

"Jeb never understood why you didn't try to contact him, because he wrote to you, sent you gifts..."

"I never received any gifts, any letters..." Lindsay sniffed.

"Because they were always returned. Stamped address unknown," he said. "And the years went by. Then, when Maria called about eight or so years ago and told him there was an operation that could strengthen your leg and she didn't have the money to support you and the boy during the rehabilitation and the extras that would be needed..."

"He mortgaged the farm!" Lindsay exclaimed. "To pay my rehabilitation bills."

Art nodded. "But he was having problems of his own. He had just been diagnosed with cancer and he had to go for an operation. That's when he called me to come and look after his horses. We talked, became friends. And when I told him that Jeff was filling in for me the night he was killed, your grandfather just said, 'I'm glad you told me, Art. I always suspected...'

"Later, I took the semen. I wanted him to have his dream, a golden cross, "Art said, wiping a tear from his eye. "Now he's gone and he'll never know."

"He knows," Bonnie said, putting her arm across Art's shoulder. "And Lindsay knows about Starmist, too."

"Yes, I know," she nodded. "Rand told me, and he also said you sold your mare, Lame Brain, to pay part of Starmist's stud fees."

"And you don't hate me?" Art asked.

"How could I?" Lindsay hugged him. "You looked after my grandfather, you've looked after Lee...and me. You found someone to buy those old antiques." She was interrupted by headlights, Rand's Lincoln stopping outside the path to the veranda. He had brought Lee home from the library.

"Rand said he couldn't come in because he had to help Mac with chores," Lee said as he bounded into the kitchen. "How did it go with the bank manager, Mom?"

"I got it," Lindsay said, explaining bits of what getting a mortgage entailed.

Meanwhile, Art was putting on his coat. He said he would check on the mares and the foal before he went home. His truck was parked near the barn. And he would see them tomorrow.

When the door closed behind Art, Bonnie turned to Lee. "Your mother forgot to tell you...she's going to the convention this weekend." Bonnie grinned when Lindsay tried to shush her. "And I'm going to stay here with you and Art's going to help you look after the mares and foal."

"Neat!" Lee's hand went up in air and he was off to the barn to catch up with Art.

Fifteen

Long after the radio DJ had signed off, Lindsay fell into bed...every bone, every muscle in her body screeched its tiredness. Yet she lay wide-awake, thinking about all that had happened: Lee's hearing, Rand speaking in his defense. Afterward, taking him to the library, introducing him to the custodian, the librarian, people with whom he would be working. True, it was part of Lee's punishment—his expulsion from school—but it was punishment administered with a soft glove approach, a learning experience from which Lee could profit.

Art's confession that he had been responsible for her dad's death was a catharsis for him, but to Lindsay, it brought the pain of lost memory: the teacher who belittled her shoes, the laughter of her fellow students, the pain of being singled out.

Art had tried to make up for his problems by helping her grandfather. He stole Starmist's semen so her grandfather could realize his dream of a golden cross, but it had come too late for Old Jeb, but not too late for her.

Lindsay still wasn't quite sure what a golden cross was. Rand's theory was the mating of the best qualities in stallion and mare and the result a near-to-perfect foal, and her golden cross brought prestige to Trailwood and the Macaulay name. But could it make up for her ten lost years of memory?

Maria's claim that Trailwood should have been hers had surprised Lindsay. It shouldn't have, as her mother was just being her mercenary self. Old Jeb had left Trailwood to his granddaughter.

Those years between, for Lindsay, had brought something more precious…a son, to love and her reason for being.

Bonnie, her dearest friend, had helped her pack her case with porcelain, even stayed up late to fire her kiln and finish the pieces Lindsay had brought from the city. "This plate with the wild turkeys, and this one with a mare's head, are both suitable gifts for men," she said as she had put a price sticker on the bottom. "Women always like buttercups and roses," Bonnie had added as she packed two vases in the suitcase. Lindsay was busy printing a short history summary of porcelain painting to go with each piece. "Porcelain painting began in China long before Columbus discovered America…"

Wafting between wakefulness and sleep, she tried to count her blessings. Lee had a job, a little one which gave meaning to those enforced hours of community service. Even in the shadows of sleep she could hear his "Mom! Mom, I've got a job!" And his grin reached from ear to ear. "A paying job! Just a few bucks a week, but it'll help, won't it, Mom?"

"And just what is my son who forgot to take off his boots and left snow on my kitchen floor going to do that earns him a few bucks?" Lindsay had asked, her heart beat jumping pridefully.

"Dusting the high shelves for the library custodian. He's got arthritis in his arms and it's hard for him to reach, so after I finish my community payback service, I'm going to dust all those high shelves for him—and he's going to give me a ride home when he closes up, and he's going to pay me." Then as if he were trying to curb his enthusiasm for a crime that was paying dividends, "It's only two days a week, Mom."

However, it was the thoughts of a tall man with cinnamon hair, grey-blue eyes and caring hands who once had massaged her leg, a man of contradictions, that had finally lulled Lindsay into the world of sleep.

~ * ~

Lindsay was on the road at seven o'clock the next morning, the weather forecast, "cold and clear," making winter driving conditions almost perfect. The two-lane highway to Tamarack was like a silver ribbon winding between the snow-crusted fields and forests. Lindsay hummed to herself, old remembered tunes, Pattie Page's "Doggy in the Window"—she should see about getting Lee a dog. Every boy needed a dog. As the miles rolled up on the speedometer, the words of Loretta' Lynn's "I'm a Honky Tonk Girl" seemed appropriate.

Two hours later as Lindsay came over a small hill, she saw the Tamarack Lodge. With its multi-turret roof, white stucco facade and shuttered windows open to the sun, it looked more like an inn from a Bavarian fairy tale than a lodge in Ontario.

Lindsay had never been to such an elegant place and her old feelings of insecurity crept in. Her grip tightened on the steering wheel. Hadn't Bonnie said there were only three kinds of people in the world, the wills, the won'ts and the can'ts? The last just gave up without trying. She had come too far to give up now. Hadn't she met people of all stripes at the supermarket? Not all the shoppers were regulars. Not all were rich. Not all were poor. And she wasn't a nobody—she was a *somebody with two horses, a filly and a rundown stable.*

Sighting a number of vehicles similar to her own rusty pickup in the parking lot, she turned off the ignition, grabbed her suitcases and marched up the three steps to the lodge entrance.

The foyer was overflowing with people. Some were checking in. Others were at small tables registering for the different lectures. Right then a friendly face would have been welcome, but she didn't see anyone she knew.

Lindsay set her suitcases on the floor. "Miss Macaulay?" A young man materialized out of the crowd. "Sorry, I got sidetracked for a moment. I've been watching for you since eight o'clock," he explained hurriedly "Both Alice Taylor and Rand Dyson said I was to look for a pretty red-head carrying two suitcases. And you're only the only red-head in the crowd." He reached for her cases. "By the way, I'm Aubrey Monahan, the owner's son and keeper of the craft room." His grin was infectious. "If you will come this way, please."

The craft room, which was parallel with the front of the building, was overflowing with everything from liniments to horse blankets. "I saved several shelves for you," he said as he opened a glass display cabinet that was just to the side of the cash register. "I wasn't quite sure how much space you would need. If there's too much, you can spread your porcelain out a little more," he told her as he explained the fee structure. He surprised her by saying he would take orders. "Mrs. Taylor said your porcelain was valuable so if I have to be elsewhere, the cabinet will be locked."

"I expected to see Mrs. Taylor," Lindsay said as she handed him the different pieces.

"She and her husband usually come just for the awards dinner and the snowmobile ride," Aubrey said as he took her other suitcase and headed for the stairs. Lindsay went to the check-in counter where the clerk asked her name, address and the license number of her truck.

"Your room is on the second floor at the end of the corridor. I hope you find it comfortable."

The room was more than comfortable. It was elegant, Lindsay thought, as her feet sank into the thick pile of the blue carpet. Tiny forget-me-nots, in the same blue color, were woven into the border design of the white bedspread and matching drapes. Laughing like a schoolgirl, her arms outstretched, Lindsay whirled round and round. Then after a quick use of the facilities, she combed her hair, patted a little powder over her freckled cheeks and touched up her lipstick. She was ready to take on the convention.

The seminar was scheduled to start at ten o'clock. She had two minutes to make it. She hurried down the stairs and as she approached the registration table she noticed that the woman was getting ready to leave. Two unclaimed folders lay on the corner of her desk.

"Are you Lindsay Macaulay?"

Lindsay nodded.

Birdie Pike, Director, was on her name tag. "Any relation to Old Jeb Macaulay?"

"He was my grandfather."

"Old Jeb was a fine man...and a good horseman." Birdie walked with Lindsay to the conference room. "Everyone liked him."

Lindsay agreed as she looked about the auditorium, its walls plastered with advertising folders, everything from harness to patent medicines. The usher at the door told them there were only two empty chairs in the whole place, one in the director's section and the other on the outside aisle in the second row from the front.

She had just taken her seat and opened her agenda folder when Bart Bartholomew, the chairman of the Standardbred Horsemen's Association, called the meeting to order. After extending a welcome to everyone, he said they were fortunate to have as their opening speaker a man they all knew. Lindsay glanced at her agenda and her heart did a somersault: Rand Dyson. Her folder skidded to the floor. The chairman had barely said Rand's name when a hand reached down beside hers to pick up the folder and a voice just above her ear whispered, "I'm glad to see you decided to come."

Before she had recovered from her shock, Rand, who had come in through a side door, was already standing on the platform, shaking hands with Bartholomew. With a smile that encompassed the entire room, Rand said he was happy he was able to adjust his schedule so that he could be at the seminar. Despite her shock, Lindsay couldn't help admiring the breadth of his shoulders in the corduroy sports jacket and the nice way his pants hugged his muscled thighs.

For a second their gaze met across the crowded room and her pulse rate increased tenfold. Silently she scolded herself. She had come to this convention to learn about horses and breeding and farming, not to get in a dither about Rand Dyson.

He talked about breeding and management. He spoke without notes, confident of his ability to say what he wanted to say. Not even a cough disturbed the quiet of the room. But Lindsay had a hard time concentrating on the speech. Her mind kept wandering to the man. A few strands of his light brown hair had fallen across his brow. She wanted to push it back.

"Brood mares fit into one of three categories: mares who are family pets, mares who are bred for profit, and mares who need to be culled. If your mare has a weak maternal family or a tendency to decrease productivity, she should be culled without hesitation."

"Before you cull, don't you think your mare should have a second chance?" Lindsay recognized the voice of Birdie Pike.

"It goes back to what kind of foal you want, Birdie. Do you want a foal that will be a pet or a moneymaking race horse or a foal that when sold as a yearling will bring a good price?" Rand said. "And when you choose a stallion for your mare, check his qualities and make sure his qualities will offset any poor qualities in your mare."

Rand certainly had all the right qualities. But he wasn't perfect, that was for sure. Unpredictable. She never knew which Rand she was going to meet. On the train when they had first met, he had been polite, friendly, helpful. When Lee told Art they weren't just visiting Trailwood, but staying permanently, he became waspish. At Trailwood, when she couldn't walk from the snowmobile to the house, he had carried her, massaged her leg, even mopped the floor. Oh, yes, Rand had all the right qualities if you liked to roll the dice.

"Sometimes the stallion you choose for your mare won't produce the right results. The cross will fool you—a leaden one instead of a golden one," he continued. Did she imagine it or did a fleeting shadow cross Rand's face? Was he thinking of his former wife and their failed marriage—certainly not the subject at hand which, of course, was horses?

"Rand." A man sitting in the row behind Lindsay got to his feet. "How important is it to visually inspect the stallion before breeding him to your mare?"

"I think it is important to see what you're getting. Just because the statistics say it is right, doesn't necessarily make it so." For a second, his gaze again lingered on Lindsay.

Chemistry? Ball games? What was he talking about? Lindsay had come to Tamarack to learn about breeding horses and boarding stables; instead she was experiencing sensations and feelings that had nothing to do with Trailwood or her horses.

"And keep records. They are vitally important. Jeb Macaulay, whom many of you know, kept detailed records until a year or so ago when he became ill. He firmly believed that a good grade mare, like his Princess, bred to the right stallion, could produce a better-than-average foal. And he was right. Unfortunately, because there are no records, his granddaughter, who took over Trailwood after he died, has had difficulty proving that Old Jeb actually achieved his dream of breeding a golden cross."

An "ah" rippled through the crowd.

Lindsay stared at Rand. This was the first time anyone had mentioned that Princess might have given birth to a golden cross foal. Doc Woodward said the mare had delivered a beautiful filly. Rand said the foal was perfect in every way. Art, who couldn't keep from smiling, gave both Princess and the foal a big hug. *No one* had mentioned golden cross! In fact Lindsay didn't know what it was until she had read an article on foals in one of the horsemen's magazine that still came to the house, despite the fact the subscriptions had run out.

"What's the name of the new filly?" a woman in the audience asked.

"You'll have to ask his granddaughter. She's sitting here in the second row."

Grinning broadly, Rand urged, "Stand up, Lindsay."

People strained to see her. The Macaulay name was well-known in the area. Some had bought horses from Old Jeb as he was affectionately known. Others had seen Jeff, Lindsay's father, race, win, even get killed. Many had recently been to Jeb's funeral. Since Lindsay hadn't been one of the mourners, few people knew that Old Jeb had a granddaughter. Now Rand was saying that, after the man's death, his mare had given birth to a golden cross and people were curious.

"What are you going to call the filly, Miss Macaulay?"

Until she had awakened this morning, she had no idea what she was going to call the little filly. Now, stamped on her forehead with an invisible branding iron was a name.

"Why, *Jeb's Dream*, of course," she said proudly as she stood.

Sixteen

The rest of the morning session was by a man from a local co-operative who talked about feeding and feed supplements, vitamins and minerals. After a buffet lunch, the seminar split into smaller groups. Lindsay chose "Surviving as a Small Breeder." The leader was Birdie Pike, the slightly built, pixie-faced director.

"I'm a small breeder like you," she began, looking directly at each of the twelve people in the room. "A few years ago I had one horse and a dream. Now I have seventeen horses, two kids and a husband, although I didn't get them in quite that order."

Lindsay liked her approach…it was friendly and informative and it gave her a feeling that she really did have a chance at rebuilding Trailwood into a paying proposition.

"You don't have to have a large farm to be successful. But you *do* have to be selective," she said as she went on to relate how to compete in a very competitive market.

By the time the session was over, Lindsay's head was bursting with facts and figures. She had made so many notes it would take her a week to unscramble them.

Her next stop was the boutique. Aubrey said he had sold two pieces…the mushroom coasters and a vase with tiger lilies winding around its narrow neck. Both of these pieces were painted before she came to Trailwood. There was also some interest in the wild turkeys. Lindsay was thrilled.

Since there was an hour before dinner, she decided to go outside for a walk. Some fresh air might clear her head. She got her coat and boots and was on her way out the door when Jim Everest, one of the directors from Riverton, stopped her. "Miss Macaulay, I wanted to ask you about those back forty acres."

"Back forty acres?"

Realizing that Lindsay didn't know what he was talking about, he explained that for the last five years he had been leasing the forty acres at the back of the Trailwood property from her grandfather. "I would like to lease them again this year."

"As soon as I get home, I'll look up your contract." Lindsay gave him her best 'I-would-like-to-do-business-with-you' smile.

"Well, Miss..." Everest stammered. "Your grandfather and I...we never had a contract. Just a handshake."

"Oh ..."

Rand, who had been looking for Jim about one of the advertising displays, caught the tail end of their conversation. He gave her shoulder a gentle squeeze. "It's all right, Lindsay. A handshake is fine. Jim won't cheat you."

Feeling a little foolish, Lindsay held out her hand. "Then, I guess the back forty is yours, Jim, at whatever price you think is fair."

"Thank you, Lindsay," he said. She was glad that the formal 'Miss Macaulay' was gone.

Stepping outside, Lindsay breathed deeply of the brisk air. As she walked toward a trail that led through a stand of spruce, she noticed that snow clouds were hanging low above the trees. The snowmobilers would be glad if snow came, as snowmobiling was listed as one of the after-hour activities. She hoped a significant accumulation would hold off until she got home tomorrow night.

Lindsay hadn't gone far along the trail when she heard footsteps crunching on the snow behind her and a familiar voice asked, "Like some company?"

"Certainly," she said as Rand fell in step beside her. Lindsay had wanted to thank him for his tribute to her grandfather and for not mentioning the circumstances surrounding the foal's birth. "You said that golden crosses are rare—only one every five to ten years. Since there isn't anything official, how do you know my filly is a 'golden cross.'"

Before Rand answered, he took her hand in his, tucking both in his bomber jacket pocket. "A golden cross is a term that goes way back—not anything official—just a foal that has something special, that little extra, that sets it apart. Conformation, good shoulders, strong legs, deep chest, an alertness in the eyes, strength, attitude, possibly coloring and, of course, blood lines."

"Hundreds of foals have good blood lines," Lindsay reasoned. "There must be something else."

"Chemistry, the same type of chemistry that attracts a man to a certain woman." Then before Lindsay could ask more about that unseen chemistry, he pointed to a bright red crested bird with a sweeping red tail. "Look up there, Lindsay. See that cardinal."

Lindsay looked up. Sounds like he's saying *hurry, hurry*."

"Probably is," Rand agreed. "His mate must be close by. They're year round residents, you know." Sure enough, before they had gone ten feet, a brownish red female swooped from one spruce limb to another just above the male.

As Lindsay and Rand continued their walk through the woods, he pointed out rabbit tracks and deer runs. Scattered about the outer edge of a small pond were feathers and scraps of fur and a partially hidden fox den. Grimacing, Lindsay stepped around the carnage. Rand squeezed her arm lightly and the warmth in his eyes said that he understood her reticence.

"Are you glad you came?"

"Yes, I've learned a lot, met a lot of people. But it will be good to get home, unscramble all the information that I have accumulated."

"You're not staying for the snowmobile party Saturday afternoon?" Rand exclaimed. "That's our most popular activity."

Lindsay's lip curved into an amused smile. "I don't have a snowmobile."

"I do." He squeezed her hand, the one that was still tucked in his pocket.

"Rand, I've only booked my room for tonight." She pulled her hand free. She didn't tell him the complimentary accommodation was actually for two nights' stay at the inn.

"We can easily change that. I'm sure the lodge hasn't booked your room for Saturday night. This is their slow season, and that's why they give us a good rate for the convention."

"Bonnie is already doing me a favor by staying over...

"And loving every minute of it. She certainly has a good head on her shoulders. I didn't have an inkling who she was when she called the college to see if she could get a ride to Riverton with me. I must admit a trip home was never more pleasant."

"She's certainly the best friend I've ever had, and she loves Lee like the grandson she's never had."

"She never married?"

"She was engaged years ago, but she wanted to go to college more than she wanted wedded bliss, and the man wasn't prepared to wait..."

"She seems satisfied with her life."

"I think so. She has a fairly good income, and a two bedroom apartment near the hospital where she works in the therapy department. She has many interests: scrap booking, tatting, readers' club, and she does a lot charity work." Lindsay grinned, "like looking after Lee and me."

"And she wouldn't mind looking after your son for another day, now would she?"

When Lindsay didn't answer, he pressed on. "So, why don't you give in and say I'd love to go snowmobiling with you, Rand." The timbre in his voice was huskily intimate.

"I don't think so. My leg! The cold!" The last time she was on a snowmobile—the only time she had been on a snowmobile—her leg had cramped and the pain had been excruciating.

"You weren't dressed for snowmobiling. The suits are lined, boots thermal, and it isn't supposed to be that cold."

Smiling a little at his persistence, she added, "I don't have a snowmobile suit."

"The inn has suits they rent to anyone who doesn't have one. It's part of their service." He grinned.

If the snow kept falling, tomorrow would be an excellent day for snowmobiling, Rand told her. With a packed layer already on the ground, this new snowfall would let the machines glide over the trails. It would probably be the last chance the snowmobilers got to use their machines this season.

When they had completed their circle walk back to the front door of the inn, an excited Aubrey was waiting for Lindsay. He had sold three more pieces of her porcelain. And had another inquiry about the wild turkeys on the barn bridge. "Wonderful!" She clapped her hands above her heart.

Someone was waiting for Rand, too—one of the Standardbred Association directors who informed Rand the chairman had called an impromptu meeting of the executive board. They were waiting at the bar.

"Probably about booking the inn for next year's convention," Rand said. Then with a teasing, "See you later, City Lady" and a quick kiss on the cheek, he was gone.

Suddenly feeling tired—she had been up since five o'clock—Lindsay decided to have a relaxing bath and sample some of the lovely creams and lotions provided by the inn. It would be even more enjoyable as there would be no Lee yelling, "Hey, Mom." But the mother in her made her pick up the telephone and call home. Bonnie's "Everything's fine," was the assurance she needed to "relax and enjoy."

She didn't make it to the tub. By the time she got off the telephone with Lee and Bonnie, it was time to get dressed for dinner. She had brought her only black ankle-length sheath with the sweetheart neckline that never went out of style. With it, she usually wore a gold rope chain with its matching earrings, an old set of Maria's that she had been going to give to the Salvation Army. What shoes to wear? Now that was a problem. Should she wear the medium heel pumps with the strap around the ankle or the older pair with the low heels that were more comfortable? What the hell! Throwing caution to the wind, she slipped on the ones with the narrow straps and the open heels and taking her time, walked slowly, carefully, down the stairs.

But she found there was more than one way to fall.

Rand was waiting, dressed in a dark brown western suit, white shirt and matching string tie—and, oh, so handsome. "We've got time for a drink," he said as she cradled her palm in his hand before tucking her arm over his sleeve.

Although the bar room seemed full, Rand found a small table for them in a semi-dark corner. When he asked what she would like to drink, the only one that came to mind was a Margarita. She remembered it from a supermarket Christmas party—sugar and spice and brandy. What else? She didn't have a clue.

While she waited for him to come back, she relaxed and listened to Patsy Cline's "Crazy Dreams" on the bar radio. Patsy sang about dark horse runners, long shots, big chance takers and having crazy dreams. Wasn't that what she was doing, taking a big chance by dreaming crazy dreams? Her dream man became real when Rand came back, pulled his chair close and whispered something she couldn't hear above the noise. His eyes said it better as they looked deeply into hers, making her feel alive with emotion.

This was new. Different. Feelings she had only read about were winding straight to her heart. She sipped her drink, tasting the salt that rimmed her glass as the lyrics of "Crazy Dreams" soon drifted into Charlie Pride's, "Someone Loves You Honey." *Falling in love*, she thought, was like being in the clouds and suddenly jumping into the sunlight with only a parachute. It was scary.

"Have you thought any more about staying over?" Rand asked.

Oh, yes, she was thinking about it.

Those thoughts quickly changed direction when Natalie, elegant in a chartreuse semi-formal dress with a tiny jacket and a full skirt that swayed provocatively with every step, hurried into the bar and headed straight for Rand.

With a "damn" audible only to Lindsay, Rand stood. "Hello, Natalie." He kissed her on the cheek. "I didn't think you were coming."

"Father's cold is worse so I'm taking his place at the head table and presenting the Best Horseman of the Year Award."

Before Natalie could say anything more, the gong sounded for dinner and Rand, without saying a word, casually took each woman's arm and escorted them to the dining room. Lindsay wanted to run, get away anywhere. Instead she walked with Rand, her head held high, a smile pasted on her lips.

The banquet hall was quickly filling with people. Dozens of round white-clothed tables, each with a horseman's motif in the center, were closely spaced around the hall with the usual head table on a raised dais at the front to the room.

Halfway to the front, Rand stopped beside Birdie Pike. Each director presided over a table of guests and Lindsay's reservation was at her table. "Birdie will take good care of you." Rand pulled out a chair and when Lindsay was seated, his hand gripped her shoulder for just a second. "I'll see you later." He then took his place at the head table, Natalie smiling triumphantly at his side.

Seeing Lindsay's chagrin, Birdie leaned close. "Natalie wasn't coming to the convention until someone told her you were, and suddenly her father's cold—Broderick is always one of the presenters—became worse and, of course, she was *forced* to take his place."

"Broderick Hunter was fine a couple of days ago," Lindsay remarked, remembering how combative and condescending he'd been at Lee's hearing.

"Yes, but Natalie didn't know you were coming." Birdie laughed lightly. One thing she clearly liked better than caring for horses was gossip. "Natalie's been after Rand for years—she was at college when he married Rita. When *she* took off, Natalie got a second chance. Rand sometimes needs a hostess, a date to escort to a party and Natalie has always been there. Everyone thinks of them as a couple. Now middle age is creeping up on Natalie and she wants a husband. Rand *is* that husband. Beware."

"I'm no threat to her. "Lindsay pushed her cutlery back and forth.

"She thinks you are, and that's the point."

Lindsay noticed that Rand seemed to need to lean closer to Natalie—he was evidently having difficulty hearing her. Lindsay wanted to yell at him, smash a bowl of mashed potatoes over his head, dump hot coffee on Natalie's gown, anything to keep them apart. Although feelings like these were as old as time, they were new to Lindsay. She was jealous.

"They don't have an understanding?"

"Not to my knowledge," Birdie whispered as Bart Bartholomew tapped his glass and asked everyone to stand for the blessing and to stay standing for the toast to the Queen. Lindsay lifted her glass just a little higher. Rand and Natalie didn't have an understanding. No commitment. Then, bending closer to Lindsay, she whispered that Ned had just received word that one of his oil paintings, Ode to Joy—a barn swallow dropping food into the mouth of a newly hatched chick, had been accepted by the National Art Gallery in Ottawa. Lindsay saluted him too.

If people with such diverse personalities and backgrounds as Birdie and Ned could come together in love, why couldn't she and Rand? Hope was like a distant dream.

The after-dinner speaker was Carl Logan, Dean of the Agriculture College where Rand lectured. Logan talked about the multimillion dollar Standardbred industry and its effect on the economy, and the college's desire to own a satellite farm where harness racing drivers could be trained and get an education in horse breeding and farming.

As he spoke, Lindsay's glance strayed to Rand, who was looking her way. Their gaze met. Lindsay could feel her cheeks heat up as a whisper of a smile curved his lips. Unfortunately Natalie saw the exchange and moved a little closer to Rand, her hand closing over his forearm, her breath teasing his ear. Lindsay noticed he didn't move an inch closer, nor did he move an inch away.

Then came the awards. The driver of the year. Art had told Lindsay over their morning coffee that her father had won it several times. Horseman of the Year: a friend of Birdie's copped this award. Horse of the Year: Starmist, and the list went on and on.

"Tonight the Standardbred Horsemen's Association is honoring a man posthumously, a man who after his death achieved every horseman's dream, a golden cross, and I would ask that his granddaughter, Lindsay Macaulay come forward and accept this award in her grandfather's honor."

"Oh, my God!" Lindsay's hand went over her mouth to stifle her outcry. Her smile was a mile wide, although a bit shaky as she blinked back the tears. She sniffed. She never had a handkerchief when she needed one. She stood up and at that moment she realized she was wearing her narrow ankle-strap open-heel shoes and she had to walk to the front, go up two steps to accept the award, and she couldn't—mustn't—limp. Not with everyone in the auditorium, especially Natalie, watching.

As she started toward the speaker's table, Lindsay could hear Bonnie saying, walk slowly, don't think about your leg, hold your head up, eyes straight ahead and keep moving. The next thing she knew, Natalie was presenting her with a miniature statue of Princess and her foal, with the words "Jeb Macaulay, Breeder of the Year," engraved in gold plate on its base and Natalie was begrudgingly saying, "congratulations." Carl Logan and Bart Bartholomew were shaking her hand and Rand, as he turned her to face the crowd, kissed her on the cheek. Everyone was standing, clapping and Lindsay was crying.

Then, holding the statue close, Lindsay accepted Rand's arm as he guided her back to her seat.

She had never limped once.

Seventeen

Still on an emotional high after accepting her grandfather's posthumous Breeder of the Year Award, Lindsay decided that instead of going to her room as she had intended, she would go with Birdie and her husband to the common lounge where the horsemen and their wives were gathering for an after-dinner get-together.

That wonderful feeling began to dissipate when she saw Rand standing in the arch at the other side of the room with Natalie hanging onto his arm. Although Birdie had insisted there was no commitment between them, Lindsay's smidgeon of hope quivered into oblivion.

Birdie guided her to a settee near the floor-to-ceiling fireplace where cedar logs blazed in the screened hearth. The fireplace, although similar, was much larger than the one at Rand's home, another reminder of what she wished could have been. Birdie still insisted there was no commitment between them. To Lindsay their actions spoke louder than words.

Behind the settee was a set of narrow windows and a sliding door which opened onto a deck illuminated by soft overhead lights. The numerous easy chairs and chesterfields with lots of cushions added a friendly ambience to the room, which was soon buzzing with conversation.

Although Lindsay enjoyed the camaraderie that flowed around her, small talk that came easily to others was awkward for her and she was glad when she saw Alice Taylor heading her way.

"I'm glad you came, as I'm sure you are. That china you brought is just beautiful." She squeezed the back of Lindsay's hand.

"Thanks, Alice. And thanks for mentioning my work to the proprietors of the lodge. The Monahans' son, Aubrey, was watching for me and helped me set up in the boutique. I've already sold several pieces."

"Those plates with the wild flowers make you think of spring and that can't come too soon for me," Alice said.

"Me too...and, I'm even getting used to driving a standard shift truck in the snow." She was sure Russ Taylor had told his wife about his horrendous experience he had the day he delivered Old Jeb's truck to her.

"I'm glad they gave your grandfather that Breeder of the Year award. He had come close so many times." She smiled her congratulations and then waved at her husband across the room. "He's found a chair for me..." She gave Lindsay's hand another squeeze and she was off.

Lindsay would have liked Alice to stay, chat and she was relieved when Jim Everest picked up his guitar and started to strum. Although he wasn't a professional, he had an easy style that fit the mood of the crowd. Another man, urged by the crowd to get his violin, soon joined Jim in a Burle Ives tune, "A Little Bitty Tear Let Me Down." No *tear* was going to let her down tonight. Soon she was humming and clapping her hands to the country music like everyone else.

Halfway through another country-western song, Johnny Cash's, "I'll Walk the Line," Rand slipped quietly into the room. Flashing Lindsay a grin, he dropped to the floor at her feet. Since chairs in the lounge were in short supply, many were sitting on the carpeted floor. Birdie silently mouthed "her usual headache" to Lindsay's lifted eyebrow question of "where's Natalie?"

Several times during the next half hour, Rand looked back over his shoulder at Lindsay and smiled. Once he gave her knee a gentle squeeze and asked softly, "Glad you came?"

Her, "Oh, yes." was barely uttered when she suddenly felt chilled by the cold, freezing animosity. She glanced across the room. Natalie had slipped into an empty chair near the archway to the lounge and was staring at Lindsay. Then as the little impromptu band finished the last bars of, "The Green, Green Grass of Home," Natalie jumped to her feet.

"Enough of these sad old songs, Jim," she commanded. "Let's put some life into the party."

In seconds she had the men rolling up the carpet while she selected a disc for the CD player. When someone tried to pull the rug out from under Rand, laughing, he got to his feet and helped roll it up. Birdie and Lindsay stayed where they were, close to the fire. For Lindsay, the chill persisted.

The first bars of a two-step had barely started to play when Natalie grabbed Rand's hand and pulled him to the center of the floor. Smiling, looking up in his face, she made sure everyone knew Rand was *her* man. Even Lindsay had to admit they made a handsome couple.

Birdie's husband Ned claimed his wife for a dance and Lindsay was left sitting by herself. After a couple of sets, Lindsay began to feel conspicuously alone. It was not a new feeling. She had experienced it many times over the years...the lostness, the unwantedness. At school dances she had sat alone; no one wanted to dance with someone with a gimpy leg or someone who didn't know how to carry on a titillating conversation. More times than she cared to admit, she had escaped to the washroom, a hall cloak room, any place she could hide for a couple of dances.

Casually, so as not to attract attention, Lindsay moved slowly toward the sliding doors that opened onto the patio deck. It was her nearest escape route. And the patio offered a shelter from prying eyes.

Leaning against the sheltered wall of the deck, Lindsay breathed deeply of the night air, pleasantly tinged with the scent of burning cedar. She knew the soft buildup of snow would make the trails perfect for the snowmobilers tomorrow, but it wouldn't do much for highway driving. The roads, hopefully, would be ploughed by the time she checked out at noon

The falling snow, the soft lights mirrored against the backdrop of tall spruce, created a winter fairyland, a fairyland that had somehow lost its magic. How could a night that held such promise be torn away so easily, so painfully? Lindsay had dared to dream. She should have known better. Hadn't the past taught her anything?

Lindsay was so caught up in her thoughts that she didn't hear the patio door slide open or shut. "You'll catch your death of cold out here without a coat." Rand wrapped a sweater he had picked up from the back of a sofa and placed it around her shoulders.

"Now, what is so interesting out here that it takes you away from the warmth of the fire and the dancing?" he asked, pulling her back against his chest, his arms wrapping around her, his chin resting on her hair.

A tiny smile tugged at the corners of Lindsay's mouth. You, she wanted to say. You bring out strange feelings in me. Feelings I don't understand. Feeling I'm not sure I want to feel. Instead, she whispered, "The snow. I like watching the snowflakes swirl round and round. They have six sides, you know."

Rand chuckled. "How do you know that?" His breath tickled the top of her ear.

Lindsay wanted to turn around, bury her face against his shoulder. Instead she explained in a schoolmarm voice. "Nature studies in high school." She felt his tongue touch the tip of her ear. "One of our professors had us look through the wrong end of a pair of binoculars. The flakes were magnified and you could see all the different shapes."

"You have a perfect shape." His tongue continued to tantalize the tip of her ear.

"That professor..." She stopped. She couldn't remember what she was going to say.

"Oh, Lindsay," Rand gently reprimanded as he turned her around to face him. "What am I going to do about you?" His voice was low, soft, sensual.

Looking up, their gaze met. Lindsay could feel the beat of his heart as he pressed her against him. Slowly he took her arms and put them around his neck. Then his arms moved low and lower on her back, tucking her closer.

The potent maleness of his thighs, the firmness of his manhood, pressed against her, sending wild currents through her veins. Before she realized it, they were slow-dancing, their feet sliding through the wet flakes which melted as quickly as they fell on the deck. Lindsay could feel the raspy brush of Rand's night shadow against her cheek as he pulled her even closer.

As they swayed to, "Can I Have This Dance for the Rest of My Life," the colors of the night caught them in its embrace. There on the deck, sheltered from the weather, neither noticed that the snowflakes had turned into raindrops. Then as if a fairy had waved her magic wand, a faint arc of color began to emerge across the tall spruce trees that bordered the trail where she and Rand had walked. The light from the windows angled against the falling raindrops created an arc of soft colors...soft yellow drifted into light green, into indigo.

"Oh, Rand, look. A rainbow in the snow. Just for us."

His lips brushed against her forehead. "Make a wish, darling."

Oh, how she wished as another voice wafted across time, her father's voice, singing a little ditty in his daughter's ear as he held her between his legs on the sulky as they jogged around the racetrack—a rainbow at night, a horseman's delight. She remembered the ditty.

And the past became the present and the present was so wonderful.

Until the patio door slid open.

Eighteen

Lindsay snuggled a little closer as Rand softly hummed Anne Murray's love song in her ear. Neither of them realized the patio door had opened, that their rainbow had faded nor that the music had grown louder. She and Rand were in their own wonderful world of falling in love.

"Dancing in the snow, darlings? Oh, how romantic!" Natalie said mockingly.

Lindsay felt Rand's muscles tense. "Natalie, there are times...!" he rasped as he cradled Lindsay even closer.

"Snow dancing?" She swayed to the music. "Looks like fun." She looked inquiringly back at Jim Everest who had followed her on deck. She and Jim had been dancing when she saw Rand follow Lindsay outside. Two other couples, curious about where Natalie was going, followed.

"Natalie, I think we're interrupting..." Jim touched her arm.

"Oh, nonsense." She dance-stepped closer and closer to Rand and Lindsay.

"For God's sale, Natalie!" Jim exclaimed. "Can't you see...

Suddenly Natalie's foot started to slip on the wet deck and she *accidentally* lost her balance. "Rand!'' she cried.

"What the...?" Rand turned, caught Natalie before she actually hit the floor.

Somehow in the confusion Lindsay was pushed aside and Natalie was in his arms as Jim angrily looked on. The man who moments ago had been crooning a love song in her ear was now holding another woman in his arms as she was whimpering, "Oh, darling, I've twisted my ankle."

Lindsay saw Rand glance back at her and raise his eyebrows before bending forward to look at Natalie's ankle. Jim just stood motionless, glaring at them both.

Lindsay heard Rand ask, "Can you put some weight on it, Natalie?"

"I'm not sure," she whimpered, leaning heavily against him.

"Why don't you try..." Rand urged as he helped her to her feet. "....try taking a step."

Lindsay watched hopefully.

"Oh, Rand. I can't," she cried. "It hurts too much."

He glanced at Lindsay again before picking Natalie up in his arms.

Lindsay turned away. She just couldn't watch her man stride away with another woman in his arms. Jim Everest was watching too. She saw the same pain, lostness, hopelessness that she was feeling mirrored on Jim's face. *Why he's in love with her, just as I'm in love with Rand,* she thought, as she skirted the crowd of onlookers who had drifted onto the deck.

Did someone call her name?

With tears blinding her, she limped to the stairs and up to her room, flinging herself face down across her bed.

Once before, she had fled from a dance and a group of onlookers. It was before her last operation—Lee was just a baby—Lindsay was working part time at a supermarket. The management held a Christmas party and dance for all the employees of its five stores. On her feet for most of the day, Lindsay was tired, her leg ached and she was sitting off in a corner when a man whom she liked, who worked in the hardware anchor store, danced by. He called to her. "You shouldn't be sitting out, Lindsay. You should be dancing." The song finished just as his partner explained loudly, "Oh, darling, she's not sitting out, she's just left out!" And everyone had laughed.

Tonight she wasn't left out, she was pushed out and she sobbed into her pillow.

~ * ~

Someone tapped on her door. Rand had come. But it was too late. She didn't want to see him, talk to him, listen to him. She wanted a man who "forsaking all others" would love only her...and her son. But he *evidently* had other commitments.

The tap came again. "Lindsay, let me in."

She recognized Birdie Pike's voice, but Lindsay didn't move. She didn't want Birdie or anyone to see her red-rimmed eyes or her swollen cheeks.

"You might as well open the door," Birdie's voice was firm. "Because I'm not going to go away."

Slowly Lindsay got off the bed. Reluctantly she flipped the lock on the door.

"Are you all right? Of course, you're not." Birdie answered her own question. "You've been crying."

That was an understatement, Lindsay thought as she blew her nose. Her cheeks felt raw and her legs felt like they were made of jelly. She sat back down on the bed.

"Natalie can be a *bitch* sometimes." Birdie used the vernacular of the stable.

Lindsay didn't respond, struggling to control her emotions so she wouldn't say something she'd regret. Waiting, Birdie reached for a chocolate from the complimentary box that the management had left on the bedside table, popped it in her mouth. "Rand was worried about you."

"If he was so worried about me, why didn't he come?" Lindsay sniffed.

"He was, but he got an urgent telephone call from Mac Townsend. Starmist has a slight sinus infection. They needed to decide what to do." Birdie smacked her lips. "Mm, that chocolate was good."

"A slight sinus infection...

"Lindsay, a sinus infection can be a serious problem for any horse. A horse doesn't breathe through its mouth like we do, so a sinus infection can affect the flow of air from the nostrils to the lungs. For a valuable horse like Starmist, even a minor sinus infection can be dangerous."

Chastised, Lindsay murmured. "Sorry, I didn't know."

"That's all right." Birdie took another chocolate. "Lindsay, do you care for Rand? I mean *really* care for him?"

Lindsay repressed a sob. There was no use pretending. The evidence was written all over her tear-blotched face. In the beginning, he had been her neighbor, her friend. Then, after she called him and told him that Princess had a foal and he had hurried over, their friendship had grown into something more, and it had happened almost without Lindsay realizing it. "I suppose so," she whispered.

"Then, fight for him, dammit!" Birdie snapped.

Lindsay shook her head. "I can't."

"Why not, for God's sake?"

"Because...we're so different."

"Sure, you're different. That doesn't mean you can't fall in love." Birdie patted Lindsay's hand comfortingly. "No two people can be *more different* than Ned and me. Yet we love each other, and that love is stronger now than when we were married ten years ago."

"Birdie, there's more to it than that. There's Lee. He needs me." Lindsay swallowed. "And there's Trailwood, which is on bankruptcy row. And I wouldn't be here now if the bank manager hadn't given me a complimentary reservation." She gave her nose a good blow. "So I don't need a love affair that's going nowhere."

"Maybe a love affair is exactly what you do need. A man with a gleam in his eye, who thinks you are the best thing since God created an apple tree." Birdie took another chocolate.

"How long since your last serious affair?"

Lindsay almost said, "none of your business," but Birdie was trying to be kind. "About seven years ago. He was the manager at the supermarket. I was just getting back to work after my surgery. We became–well, you know…and when he got promoted to a larger store, he didn't ask me to go with him."

"And Lee's father?"

"More than thirteen years ago. We were going to be married. Derek was on his way to the church when he was killed in an accident on his motorcycle—going in the opposite direction"

"Maybe it's time you gave love another chance," Birdie suggested thoughtfully. "Rand is a good man, a little on the arrogant side, but he has a good heart. And he's lonely. And you, Lindsay Macaulay, bring out his protective instincts." Birdie smacked her lips, her eyes dancing with laughter as she waved the chocolate box in front of Lindsay's face. "Have a chocolate. They're good for what ails you."

"He has Natalie," Lindsay replied.

"Oh, yes, Natalie." Birdie replaced the lid on the chocolate box before she continued. "Rand needs someone to love *him*, not who he is or what he is. Him. Someone to sympathize with him when he's hurt, tell him how wonderful is when he isn't…just love him no matter what."

"He doesn't believe in love."

"How do you know that?"

"He told me. Shortly after Lee and I moved here. He said that the next time he got married—if he got married—he would choose his mate scientifically—the best to the best."

"Oh, I know that theory. There's nothing wrong with it—for horses. But we're not talking about horses. We're talking about people." Birdie continued, "Rita hurt him very badly and it has taken him a long time to get over it. The pain is gone now, but I think the fear of loving again still lingers."

"What was Rita like?" Lindsay's words were muffled as she blew her nose.

"Beautiful, a good socializer, hungry for the good life. I've always believed the main reason Rita went to college was to find a rich husband. She and Rand met at a fraternity house party. She liked him and he was certainly attracted to her. They became inseparable." Birdie licked a bit of chocolate off her finger. "Rand hadn't had a great deal of love in his life. His father, Fred, my uncle, cheated on his mother. That's why Edna left him and went to live in Vancouver for a time. When she discovered she had cancer, she came back to Fred, for Rand's sake more than her own. Fortunately, with treatment, the doctors were able to keep the cancer in remission for almost twenty years.

"A few months before Rand received his degree in equine management, Edna's cancer returned. She wanted to see Rand married, *settled* and the day he married Rita in a lavish ceremony was one of the happiest in her life. She died when the couple were on their honeymoon in Hawaii.

"After the funeral, Rand decided Fred shouldn't live alone at Windcrest and he decided to return home, even though he and Rita had leased an apartment near the college where he had a teaching position. Rita wasn't too keen on the idea but she agreed. Windcrest had been in the Dyson family for more than a hundred and fifty years. It didn't take Rand long to see how rundown Windcrest had become or that it had been Edna's small annuity from her grandparents that had been paying the bills. Fred loved Windcrest too, but he loved to party more.

"Rand was determined to put the heritage farm back on its feet. For the next several years, Rand worked his tail off during the day and partied into the night with Rita. Gradually Windcrest came back to its rightful place in the horse industry. Sometimes, when Rand couldn't go with Rita—a foal was being born or a horse was sick—his best friend from his college days, Terence Norman, who was a lawyer and wealthy to boot and always seemed to be around, accompanied Rita.

"One night Rand came home unexpectedly from a buying trip. He often bought horses for other owners at auctions in United States...the house was empty. Rita was gone, along with his car, the furniture and everything else of value. She filed for divorce the next day. She wanted half of everything; including the farm which she insisted was the cause of their marriage breakdown. You see, Lindsay, she had received good advice from Terence, Rand's lawyer friend.

"Hurt, angry, betrayed, Rand vowed to keep Windcrest. It was his heritage and he wasn't going to part with it. He sold the hired man's cottage and its ten acres in the corner of the property to Art, who still had a little money from his racing days, and they signed an agreement that if Art ever wanted to sell, he would sell it back to Rand. He auctioned off all his horses except the young and untried Starmist and several nondescript mares and put a second mortgage on the farm. By still teaching at the college, working the farm at night, and with Art's help, he was able to save Windcrest and slowly build it back up to its prestigious place in the horse-breeding industry.

"Rand's crowding forty-one now, and he wants a family and he sees Natalie as a compatible partner. He's certainly not in love with her." Bonnie popped another chocolate in her mouth. "Mmm." She grinned. "You had better take the last one. Your figure can stand the calories."

Then casually as though she was proposing a trip to neighborhood grocery store, Birdie changed the subject. "Now go wash your face, powder your nose and let's go back to the party."

"Maybe in a little while. We'll see." She followed Birdie to the door, kissed her on the cheek. "Thank you."

"Oh, Lindsay, I meant to ask you…" Birdie turned for a moment. "Did you hurt your leg when you were dancing on the deck? I noticed you were limping."

Lindsay stilled. Birdie wasn't asking out of curiosity; it was sincere concern. "No," she answered slowly. "I injured it many years ago. Sometimes it gives me a little trouble...and I limp."

"I never noticed it before," Birdie said as she headed back to the party.

Lindsay stood motionless for a long moment. What had Birdie said? She hadn't noticed Lindsay's limp until tonight—not until she was leaving the deck. And a shimmer of truth began to dawn in Lindsay's mind. Her limp was far more noticeable to her than to anyone else. So her leg wasn't the problem. Her confidence was.

She knew it had been shattered right along with her leg. It was Bonnie, bless her, who had rebuilt it pain by pain by telling Lindsay over and over again about a little train that said, "I think I can. I think I can. I can!" And Lindsay had walked finally without a limp.

When she had seen Rand holding Natalie in his arms, her confidence had taken flight and she had limped away. Hadn't Rand glanced back at her before reaching for Natalie? What had he tried to say...that he had to help her. If he had let Natalie fall without trying to save her, what would that have proved—that he loved Lindsay less? It was Rand's nature to help. Whether or not Natalie was manipulating him was secondary. Even a new love needed to learn to trust and right now it was her confidence that needed rebuilding. "I think I can, I know I can, I can!"

The first step in building any new relationship was trust.

They had seen a rainbow. Made a wish. Fallen in love. But at that love's first test, Lindsay had limped away

She needed some quiet time to think, not return to a party. And what better place than soaking in a long, hot bath? She had been going to take one earlier but had stayed on the telephone too long talking to Lee and Bonnie. The party could wait. Her *thinking* couldn't.

Long after her skin had become wrinkled, she patted herself dry, wrapped one of the inn's big fluffy towels around her body, and feeling at peace with herself, opened the bathroom door.

Her peace vanished.

Rand was sitting on her bed. One knee was pulled up, his arms locked around it. His hair was mussed as if his fingers had threaded through it several times. He was watching her.

"How did you get in?" she demanded, pulling her towel a little higher over her breasts.

He dangled a key from a forefinger. "I bribed Aubrey. Told him we were lovers, that you were waiting for me and I didn't want to wake you if you were asleep." His tone was nonchalant, but there was nothing nonchalant about the fire that burned in his eyes.

"Well, you can just tell Aubrey you made a mistake and give the key back to him," Lindsay snapped.

"Oh, but we never finished our dance..." In one fluid movement, Rand was on his feet, standing, reaching for her.

Lindsay stepped back. "Are you crazy?" She pulled the towel higher. He was so tall and in her bare feet she was so short. "We danced ..."

"And we kissed." His voice was as soft as the snowflakes that had fallen on the deck.

He cupped her chin in his hand, tilting her face upwards as his wood-scented aftershave mingled with the freshness of her lily-of-the-valley bath powder. He kissed the tip of her nose before savoring her lips.

Her body grew warm. Tingled. "Rand, what if someone saw you come in here? What would they think?"

He chuckled, a mischievous light in his smoke-grey eyes. "That we're doing what comes naturally."

Emotions, need, overrode good sense. Her towel slipped. His mouth lowered to hers. Her arms stole around his neck. Her nipples became taut. He nibbled. Her body throbbed. Sensations she had not known existed pulsated through her body from the top of her head to the tip of her toes.

Her mind was saying, "Rand, you've got to go," but her body was telling her something different. She had never felt so needy, so wanting. Searching for sanity, she hung on to thoughts of Lee. He became her anchor.

They needed to slow down. "Rand...I can't..."

She couldn't let what happened before with Derek happen again. For her, sex meant commitment; for Rand. it meant *doing what comes naturally.*

"Say you like what I'm doing to you." Another kiss feathered her eyelids.

God help her, she wanted him so! Wanted him to touch her, love her, say that he cared, that this wasn't just a sensuous fling, a one-night stand. For her it meant more, a life together beyond tonight, a commitment...but for Rand it meant fulfilling a need.

He gently pushed her back onto the bed. His hands roamed. His hard manhood pressed against her special place and her smoldering need grew into a consuming fire.

"There's too much between us." He snatched another kiss. "Don't move."

He rolled away. He shrugged out of his jacket, shucked his shirt, his pants, toed his shoes, pulled down the zipper on his pants. She watched.

Déjà-vu.

An isolated hospital room. A man shedding his clothes. A bed, Kisses. Needs. No words of love. And an unbelievable aftermath!

Subconsciously. Deliberately. She rolled away.

Rand made a grab for her. "Lindsay, what the hell are you doing?" His voice was hoarse with emotion, desire. "I need you."

Still no words of love. No words of commitment. Just need.

She grabbed her towel. Wrapped it around her body. Ran for the door. Yanked it open as tears ran down her cheeks.

Rand stared at her. Swore. Angrily yanked on his pants, shoved his feet back into his shoes, shrugged into his shirt, grabbed his jacket, brushed passed her. The black angry look in his yes was darker than the darkest night.

Lindsay closed the door. Locked it.

Turning, she buried her face in her hands and wept

Nineteen

Light poured in around the edges of the bedroom drapes as Lindsay slowly opened her eyes. The hands on the bedside clock said nine forty-five. Oh my God, she had slept in. Was it any wonder? Dawn was breaking over the trees when she had fallen asleep and she had come to only one conclusion: she needed to apologize to Rand, explain. She owed it to him.

It wasn't his fault that Natalie had invaded their paradise, that she had managed to fall and somehow needed Rand to carry her to the lounge, even though Jim was standing nearby.

Afterward, when Rand had come to Lindsay's room, teased her about fleeing before they had finished their dance, he made no secret of his dream of *doing what came naturally.* And for a little while, she let him believe she wanted him as much as he wanted her. And she did. If she hadn't rolled away at that moment, she wouldn't have had the strength.

What an example she would be setting for Lee. If she accepted a casual affair with Rand, she would be saying it was all right for her to play around, but now that he was on the verge of manhood, it wasn't acceptable for him. She had taught Lee that honesty, truth and integrity were the cornerstones of a good life and it was the same for both mother and son. Double standard. One for her and one for Lee. Unacceptable. And she wanted to tell Rand, explain, apologize.

Breakfast was over by the time she got downstairs, although she was able to pick up a coffee and munch on a donut before slipping into the windup session of the convention where Rand was the scheduled speaker. If she could just get a minute to talk to him before the session began—he was talking to Birdie and Ned. When he saw her coming, he turned his back and proceeded to take his place at the podium.

Lindsay stopped mid-step and struggled to keep her tears in check. Someone handed her a program and seeing Birdie waving, pointing to an empty seat beside her and Ned, she continued on.

If the last hours had done anything for Lindsay, besides making her cry, it had strengthened her confidence in herself. Birdie hadn't noticed her limp until she had walked away from the deck. So her problem was no longer with her limp but having confidence in herself. She had come to the convention to learn, hadn't she? Learning was of little value unless you put it to use.

She listened as Bart Bartholomew introduced, "the man who needs no introduction—Rand Dyson." After greeting everyone, Rand said he was going to talk about the importance of a good pasture field. "It can reduce feed costs and still provide high-quality forage as well as add an exercise area for the horses. Horses like to be around horses. They love to roll, run, kick up their heels."

Rand talked in a neighbor-to-neighbor style. He smiled often, but his smiles didn't quite reach his eyes. They had a sadness in them. Was she the cause, she wondered as she made notes about pastures, scribbled facts about nutrients, as ideas came into her head, and with each she became more determined to rebuild Trailwood, make it a profitable boarding stable for horses and their owners.

Rand talked about weed-free pastures, nutrients and different grasses suitable for horse pastures. He made eye contact with many people in the audience, but never a glance at her. His censure was like a branding iron pressed against her heart.

In his lecture Rand said, "Do *not* do that which others can do as well." No other stable as far as Lindsay could learn offered weekend accommodation for owners as well as long term care for their horses. That would be her drawing card...stabling horses with weekend accommodation for their owners. By decorating Old Jeb's bedroom and the spare bedroom and giving up her own room—she could sleep on a cot in the kitchen—she could provide three rooms for guests. And she could provide stable for horses who were on hiatus from the racetrack.

Lindsay was so busy going over the possibilities in her mind that she didn't realize Rand had finished his informal lecture on feed lots and grasses until she saw Natalie hug him and say, "Wonderful presentation, darling!"

Lindsay never knew that someone else's hug could hurt so much and she was very glad when Birdie tucked her arm over hers and together they walked toward the dining room where Bartholomew was to give his wrap-up speech and close the convention.

They were almost there when Aubrey Monahan called, "Lindsay, may I see you for a minute?"

"Of course," she said, asking Birdie to save her a seat.

"Guess what?" Aubrey asked, his face sheathed in smiles. "I tallied up your sales and after deducting our commission, you've made a fair bit of change. And I've got three orders for you—a plate with the turkeys in front of the barn and two mugs with the mare and foal's heads." He handed her a note with the customers' names and a cheque that brought a smile to her face.

"Thank you, Aubrey. You're a good salesman."

When Lindsay went to compensate him for his time, he said he was already paid by the lodge. Then, grinning like a Cheshire cat, the seventeen-year-old handed her a card with her name, address and telephone number on it. "When we're not busy, I like fooling around on my computer. I made these cards for you." He handed her several business cards. "I've put the rest on the shelf beside the daffodil vase my mother bought. I told her it was too pretty to hide in her old china cabinet.

"Oh, Aubrey, how am I ever going to thank you?" Lindsay asked as she gave him a big hug, promising herself she would paint a special mare and foal just for him. "Be sure to thank your mom for me."

Buoyed by the sales and the cheque, Lindsay was smiling when she rejoined Birdie and Ned at the dinner table. Rand and Natalie were nowhere to be seen. Bart was already giving his wrap-up speech. They would have the horsemen's convention here again next year. Noting that several were preparing to leave, he continued, "Since many of you are chomping at the bit to get those snowmobiles revved up, if someone will make the motion and someone second it, we'll adjourn." Someone did and Ned's hand shot up to second it. Others signified their agreement by clapping. In thirty seconds, the room was half empty.

"See you outside." Birdie squeezed Lindsay's arm as she stood up. She was going to her room to suit up.

"Have a good ride." Lindsay smiled up at her.

"Aren't you coming?"

She shook her head. "I'm going home." Then with a rueful grin, she added, "with a few extra dollars in my pocket."

Lindsay finished her luncheon in relative peace, checked out at the lodge desk and went back to her room. She was ready to close the lid of her suitcase when Birdie burst in, plopping a snowmobile suit, helmet, mitts and boots on the bed. "Get into these."

"Oh, Birdie, I can't!" Lindsay cried.

"Why not, for heaven's sake?" Birdie asked. "It's what you really want to do, so do it. Quit running."

Before she could answer, they heard Ned's "Hurry up, Birdie. We're going to be late."

Lindsay snapped the lock on her suitcase. Running? Was that what she was doing?

~ * ~

Lindsay felt like a Martian on an earth walk in her bulky one-piece red and gold nylon snowmobile suit as she made her way along the shoveled path to the side lane where the snowmobilers were waiting in their assigned positions. Many, like Ned Pike, had parked their machines in line before going to dinner. He and Birdie were kibitzing back and forth with some of the other owners. Florida weather, eh? It could turn colder. Storm coming. A pessimist in every crowd. The banter went back and forth.

Jim Everest, who was in charge of the ride, was standing beside his Motor Ski with a clipboard listing all the drivers and their riders in his hand. Anyone who didn't have a machine was assigned to someone who did. Birdie had left a note *"see Jim"* pinned to the chin strap of Lindsay's helmet. Lindsay hoped she would be riding with him or Bart who was next in line.

It was the third man in the black and gold suit, adjusting some minor thing on the seat of his snowmobile that almost made her turn around and go the other way. Lindsay saw the surprise look on Rand's face when he straightened up and saw her walking past him toward Jim Everest. She remembered telling him last night that she wasn't going on the ride…that was before her emotions had taken over her good sense.

Before Jim could get a chance to check Lindsay's name and number, Rand had grasped her elbow and turned her toward his Sno-Hawk, which was parked third in line. "Lindsay's riding with me," he called to the trail boss.

"I am not!" Lindsay tried to jerk her arm away.

"Oh, yes you are.' Rand's grasp tightened on your arm. "You've been trying to talk to me all morning.

"And you've kept walking away," she said, trying to jerk her arm free.

"There's the time and place for everything and a room filled with people isn't the place or the time," Rand answered, turning her toward his machine.

"And I suppose this is," Lindsay snapped. Several people were already looking their way, including Natalie who was just coming out the side entrance of the lodge. "Let go of me!"

"Not on your life, lady. Not until we settle a few things." Rand's words were low and laced with anger. "If you want, I can throw you over my shoulder like a sack of potatoes and carry you."

"That's one way to subdue a lady." Jim Everest laughed as he called out to Natalie, who was hurrying toward them. "I guess you're going to have to ride with me, Natalie."

Struggling to jerk her arm free, Lindsay repeated through clenched teeth. "Let me go!"

"Not a chance, lady." Still holding onto her arm, Rand grabbed his helmet off the snowmobile seat and motioned for Lindsay to put on the one she was carrying in her hand. "Besides, a nice long ride should cool that temper of yours."

"Of all the men I've ever met, you are the most obstinate, conceited…" she hissed as she put on the helmet and adjusted the chin strap.

Not waiting for her to berate him further, he said gruffly, "Shut up, Lindsay." Turning her to face him, his forefinger pressed down on her nose. "Be a good girl and get on that damn machine." Maybe it was his tone, the softness tempered with steel that made Lindsay get on the snowmobile.

Just ahead, beside the lead snowmobile, she could hear the argument that was erupting between Jim and Natalie. "Get *her* off that machine, Jim," Natalie demanded. "We had it planned…."

Lindsay saw the muscles on Jim's face tighten. "Well, I guess you'll just have to unplan it, Natalie." He checked his watch again before getting on his snowmobile. "Either get on my Motor Ski or get out of the way." Natalie got on his snowmobile.

Unaware of what was happening behind him, Rand continued, "I see they've given you thermal-lined boots. That's good." Turning, throwing his leg over the saddle of the machine and adjusting the chin strap, he called back over his shoulder, "If you want me to stop, just tap me on the shoulder."

Lindsay would tap him all right—with a two-by-four—and it wouldn't be any tap. But everything was forgotten, including the apology she intended to make, when she saw Jim's arm go up and motion the snowmobilers forward.

Rand saw it too and called back over his shoulder. "Put your arms around my waist and hang on."

"I know. It's gonna be a helluva ride!"

She felt, rather than heard, his light chuckle as he revved up the snowmobile motor. "Don't forget to let your body shift with mine." He pulled her arms tighter about his waist.

The Sno-Hawk took off smoothly, gliding over the newly fallen snow. The day was perfect for a ride, although a little on the cold side. Every few hundred yards, she saw fluorescent tapes banded around a tree trunk or post, trail markers for their ride, and Lindsay could feel herself relaxing, enjoying the bumps and sways of the snowmobile, despite the fact that Natalie cast an occasionally glaring look back at them.

Little gusts of snow whirled about the snowmobilers as they zigged through fields, zagged over frozen creeks and took steep inclines on full throttle. When Jim motioned for a short stretch break, a large mitten hand helped a small mitten hand off the Sno-Hawk. Standing side by side, her hand in his, they looked out over a small valley of snow-laden evergreens, rail fences canopied by a blue sky.

"Peaceful, eh?" Rand still held her hand.

Lindsay nodded as she gathered her courage. "Rand, about last night..."

"Not here, Lindsay," he said as he helped her back on his machine and they were off again.

Shortly afterward he pointed toward a deer at the edge of the trees and Lindsay saw a fox scamper under a rail fence and they both chuckled when several rabbits bolting for cover ran into each other.

They had been on the trail about another hour when Lindsay noticed that the snowflakes were beginning to swirl in a more animated dance and she saw Jim Everest raise his left arm shoulder height, elbow bent upward, the snowmobiler's sign for stop. Birdie had told her they always stopped every hour or two.

Just ahead, Lindsay could see a flashing sign "Stop and Go" snack bar. The owner had a sense of humor, Lindsay thought, as she read the words below the sign. "Fill up, eat up, empty up." And in smaller letters, "Next pit stop forty miles ahead."

The Mom and Pop snack bar and garage was not equipped to handle thirty snowmobiles at one time and the service was slow. Lindsay didn't mind as it gave her a chance to exercise her leg and use the facilities, the facilities being one cubicle for men and one for women. Unfortunately the queue in front of the ladies' washroom moved very slowly.

When Birdie noticed that the lineup in front of the men's washroom was gone, she commandeered it for herself. Then, she agreed to stand guard for any of the other women who wanted to use it. Lindsay, her bladder bursting at the seams, entered, unzipped her suit and was almost finished when a man yanked the door open and walked in. Lindsay screamed. He backed out. "Can't you read?" he yelled. "This is the men's..."

Red-faced and wishing she could hide, Lindsay emerged, gratefully accepting a coffee and donut from the owner as she walked to the chair Rand had saved for her on the opposite side of the snack bar. She didn't miss the smug look on Natalie's face afterward as everyone chuckled. Birdie apologized too. She said she had only stepped away for a minute to adjust her husband's chin strap.

When Lindsay got to their table, Jim was frowning and Rand had a tight set to his jaw. She had the distinct feeling that the conversation was about her. Yet, when she sat, they were talking about a winter storm that would be moving in from the northeast early in the evening. "We'll have plenty of time to get back to the lodge before then," Jim said, gulping the last of his coffee and heading outside. Rand followed.

When everyone was ready to take off, Rand suddenly got off his machine, lifted the hood and motioned for others to follow the line. He mouthed that a spark plug wasn't firing right.

A few minutes later, without replacing it, he slammed down the hood and instead of following the others, steered to a different trail. Remembering what Art had once said...that snowmobilers never traveled alone, Lindsay hollered in his ear, "Aren't we going with the others?"

Rand shook his head, hollering back over his shoulder. "I want to show you the valley where my great maternal grandfather settled in 1802. Come spring, the area is going to be flooded to make way for a dam."

"What about Jim and the other snowmobilers?" she asked.

"We'll rendezvous with them at Breakwater in an hour or so." Rand motioned for her to get back on his Sno-Hawk.

Lindsay and Lee had heard about Breakwater from Art. It was the area where three creeks came together to form the Riverton River. After years of deliberation—and flooding—the province had finally decided to build a dam just below the forks. Besides holding any flood water, the dam would create a recreational lake for the county. Tamarack Lodge was located about thirty miles east of the proposed dam.

They traveled at a leisurely pace, stopping often to stretch their legs as bluish shadows began to stretch outward from the trees and fences that divided the large fields.

"My great-grandfather built a log cabin on a rise beyond those trees." Rand pointed to a grove of spruce. "Then he sent for his bride, a seventeen-year-old girl he had met only once."

"Your great-grandmother?"

Rand nodded. "In that day, only Anglican ministers were permitted to perform the marriage ceremony. Since neither my great-grandfather nor his bride was Anglican, they couldn't get married. Fortunately there was a law that said if the marriage ceremony was performed at least eighteen miles from the nearest Anglican church, a Justice of the Peace could legally marry a couple.

"Great-grandfather found a Justice of Peace and the young couple went into the woods exactly eighteen and a half miles from the church. The Justice stood on a large stone, the bride and bridegroom on a fallen log, and with a choir of crows cawing in the background, my great-grandfather married my great-grandmother, a marriage which lasted fifty-two years.

Before Lindsay could say she would like a marriage like that too, Rand motioned for her to get back on the snowmobile and they took off again.

Lindsay's leg was beginning to ache and she kept wondering when they were going to meet up with the other snowmobilers. The shadows were deepening and the snowflakes which had been falling gently were agitated, twisting and turning as the wind grew stronger. One area of the snow-covered terrain looked like another and that snow-banked rail fence with a brown vine wound around its angled post looked like the same one they had passed when Rand was telling her about his ancestral grandparents.

She tapped him on the shoulder. "Are we lost?"

Rand shrugged, yelling back over his shoulder that he must have missed the trail when they turned into the valley. "Don't worry. You'll be toasting your toes in front of the fireplace at Tamarack before long."

She hoped so. She was tired, achy and hungry.

"Looks like we're in for a storm," Rand shouted back over his shoulder. "I'm not going to wait for Jim and the others. I'm going to circle through that valley and head back to Tamarack."

They were gliding up a grade, paralleling a snow-banked fence toward a grove of evergreens when the left ski of their snowmobile suddenly caught on something. The ski snapped. The snowmobile shuddered. Flipped, tearing Lindsay's arms from Rand's waist as she hurtled through the air and landed hard on the snowy ground, gasping for air from the shock.

And blessed nothingness.

Twenty

Oh God, she hurt! Every bone, every muscle screamed in agony. Lindsay couldn't breathe. Forcing herself to take short panting breaths, the pressure in her chest gradually eased and she was aware that she was lying face down on the ground.

Rand!

Grimacing, she turned over and slowly sat up. She saw him lying on his back a few feet away, his left leg bent awkwardly to the side. Oh, God, he was so still! Was he alive?

She slid over to him. "Rand. Darling, speak to me," she brushed the snowflakes from his face.

He groaned, opened his eyes.

"Are you all right, love?" he whispered, reaching up to touch her face.

"Yes." She clutched the endearment to her like a precious jewel.

"Put your helmet on. You'll need your body heat...his hand dropped to his side as he slipped into unconsciousness. Lindsay hadn't realized until then that she had lost her helmet. It was lying in the snow nearby.

"Rand! Rand." Lindsay bent forward, pressing her face against his cheek.

An awful fear gripped her. They were alone and he was injured. They had been gliding through an open field on their way home. Suddenly, without warning, their snowmobile had catapulted through the air.

Rand had committed two of the snowmobilers' cardinal sins. He had gone off without a buddy snowmobiler and taken an unmarked trail. No one would even know they were missing until they didn't show up at the rendezvous point, or later at the lodge. It might be too late by then as darkness was already creeping in.

If she could right their snowmobile, get it started, she could go for help. Then she saw their Sno-Hawk, a vine snagged around its left broken ski.

Her courage began to falter she made herself take several deep breaths and calmly assess their situation. Animals lived outdoors in all kinds of weather and they survived, so why couldn't two people wearing insulated suits survive just one night—or until help came?

Their most pressing need was shelter from the wind, which felt like it was coming straight from the Arctic. All Lindsay could see that offered any protection was a grove of evergreens, but they were too far away and a fence banked high with snow, only the tips of the rail posts showing above it. She almost missed the narrow hollow at the bottom of the bank, a hollow big enough to shelter a man.

She struggled to her feet. Grabbing Rand by the shoulders, she dragged him across the snow out of the wind. He moaned but didn't open his eyes. She felt like crying when she realized he was at a right angle to the hollow. How could she turn him without further injuring his leg?

Catching sight of the tip of their snowmobile's ski buried in the snow, she reached for it and slipped it under his leg and secured it with the piece of vine that had caused their accident. "Please, darling, try to help me," she cried.

He opened his eyes. While she lifted his leg, although barely conscious, he managed to shimmy his body into the hollow.

Resting, she looked about. The hood of the snowmobile was an arm's length away. She got it and placed it at Rand's head. Nearby was one of the seats and the repair kit was half-buried in the snow beside it. Finding it easier to crawl than stand, she retrieved them both, using the seat to make a windbreak at Rand's feet.

She opened the repair kit. The only thing of value was a knife and possibly a rope. She slit the kit open, draped it over the boot on Rand's leg and tucked the rope and jackknife into the pocket of her snowmobile suit, a pocket she had found when she was in the Stop and Go facility.

When another gust of wind swept cold pellets of snow against her face, she realized that one side of their little cave was still open to the elements. If only she could have gotten him to the trees.

What if...?

Not waiting for fear to overtake her common sense, she gingerly got to her feet. Body bent, chin tucked into the folds of her snowsuit, she ploughed through the snow toward the evergreens. Much to her chagrin, she found that the lower branches were dry and brittle and the higher; greener ones didn't break off that easily. She had to use her knife but she couldn't hold it with her mitt on. Several cold minutes later, her hand numb with cold, she had enough limbs for a windbreak across the mouth of their hollow cave. Then looping one end of the rope around the branches and the other around her wrist, she pulled her mitt from between her teeth and started back toward the cave.

Instinct was her only sense of direction as bursts of snow eddied around her. Her load caught on something. A little tree—she could smell the cedar. She had read somewhere that cedar bows made a good bed. She reached for her knife, clumsily hacked off several branches and loaded them on top of the larger spruce ones.

She had gone only a yard or two when the muscle in her bad leg cramped. Oh God, it hurt! When she bent to rub it, she lost her balance and fell into a drift. It felt so good to let the storm blow over her, unaware that it had a hypnotic effect and was lulling her to sleep.

A voice cut through the wind. "Lind—say. Lind—say."

She drifted deeper.

"Get up, girl!" Rand's voice. "Get up!" Sharp, cutting like an invisible lifeline, it drew her forward.

Lindsay struggled to her feet.

"A little farther, darling. A little farther."

Lindsay bent lower, battling the biting wind. What felt like a lifetime later, she fell across his chest. He was half out of the cave.

"Thank God!" Rand whispered, cradling her against his shoulder. "I thought I had lost you."

"How did you know I needed you?" she asked.

"Gut instinct, I suppose," he said. "When I, awoke, I guessed I passed out for a while—you weren't here. I called and you didn't answer. Yet, I had this feeling, this intense feeling, that you needed me.

"And you tried to come to me," Lindsay whispered as his arms tightened around her. "It was like an invisible pulley drawing me forward and then I was in your arms. Oh, Rand."

Her heart did a little flip. The wind was still howling; the snow was still sifting through the cracks of their cave but everything was all right between them.

Lindsay got to her knees, pulled her load closer and placed some of the cedar branches behind Rand, urging him back onto them. She then jabbed three larger spruce branches into the roof, praying that the blowing snow would soon fill the cracks. With only a few branches left, she squirmed around and jabbed them into the front opening of their cave, sealing it off.

She had done it! Now they had a chance.

"Stretch out beside me." Rand tugged on her sleeve.

She turned into his arms. "Do you think someone will tell Lee?" she asked. "He'll be so worried."

"I'm sure Birdie will have called him," he assured her, holding her close. "Bonnie is there with him; probably Art's there too. He'll be all right."

Lindsay closed her eyes. She was so tired, so cold. Her hands were numb; she couldn't feel her feet.

"Darling, don't go to sleep." Rand's hand dug into her shoulder. His endearment was like a treasure found in this wilderness of fury. "I want you to lie close and put your left leg on top of mine. Leave your right hand where it is, tucked between our bodies, and put your left hand under my arm. And cuddle close."

She liked that idea

"Lindsay, you have to stay awake! They won't find us now until morning.

"I don't care about morning." Her words were slurred.

"Lindsay. Wiggle your toes."

"I can't feel my toes!"

"Wiggle anyway." The bristles on Rand's chin rubbed against her cheek. "I know you're tired."

Tired! She was beyond being tired.

"Do you know the first thing I'm going to do when we're rescued?"

She could feel his body tense as another pain ripped through her leg. Lindsay shook her head slightly.

"I'm going to cancel my subscription to the *Farmers' Almanac*."

"Farmers' Almanac?" she repeated.

"You've never heard of the Old Farmers' Almanac!" he exclaimed. "Why it's right next to the Bible in every farmer's household."

"Still never heard of it." Her words were muffled against the shoulder of his snowsuit.

"Ever since 1792, the Farmers' Almanac has been telling farmers when to plant their crops, when to harvest them, when the sun is going to shine, when there is going to be a storm," he continued.

"Then how come they didn't predict that a blizzard was coming?"

"Well, that's the reason I'm going to cancel my subscription."

"Because they made a mistake?" What did that say about her? She had made so many mistakes.

"Yes," he continued. "As soon as we get home. I'm going to cancel my subscription."

"If we get home," Lindsay whispered.

"Don't be a pessimist." He shifted his body slightly and a few flakes tumbled down from the roof. "Look at *this* as a positive experience."

"Some experience! You have a broken leg and God knows what other injuries. Your snowmobile is kaput, and you're talking about a positive experience."

She could feel his grin against her forehead. "Well, I have the girl I love in my arms, don't I?" His arms tightened around her.

"*The girl I love, "*she murmured his words. Thirteen years ago another man had said almost those same words to her.

181

As if reading her thoughts, Rand said, "Lindsay, why don't you tell me about Derek, Lee's father?"

"Oh yes, Lee's father," she repeated. "Derek Wilson" She paused for a long moment, thinking, remembering.

"We met in the rehabilitation wing of the hospital. We both had been transferred from active care to the acute rehabilitation unit. He needed at least three hours of carefully supervised exercise on his reconstructed shoulder and hip. And I needed to learn to walk without favoring my muscle-ligament repaired leg as I was throwing my hip out of balance. I was a naive twenty-three and he was a worldly twenty-one. We were both lonely. And he taught me things…"

"Just what *things* did he teach you, Lindsay?" Rand grumbled.

"Oh, things...clothes...people...feelings." A smile crept into her voice. "It was shortly after we met...we were talking, and just out of the blue, he said, 'Why don't you get them up?' I didn't know what he was talking about until I saw him looking at my breasts. '*Those things!* Your boobs. You just let them hang. Are you ashamed of them?'

"I was shocked. Speechless."

"He continued, 'They're beautiful, Lindsay. Get them up.'

"Embarrassed, I stared at him. No one had ever said anything about my breasts except my gym teacher who wrote to Maria telling her I needed a brassiere, that my boobs were bigger than most of the other girls' in my class. Maria got me two cheap ones from Woolworth. Since my limp was the focus of attention, the incident of the bras had been pushed to the back of my mind.

"Now here was Derek saying, 'Why don't you get them up? Get a good uplift? It'll do wonders for you!' Before I could respond, he was off on another subject. He never concentrated on one thing for very long. It was just his way.

"I did get a better bra. Bonnie got it for me…an uplift and it made such a difference. I had a figure then—breasts, a little on the big side, narrow waist, curving hips and a messed-up leg. But I felt better about myself," Lindsay continued. "I guess Derek just made me feel like a woman," she barely breathed the words.

Lindsay didn't let on that she heard Rand's "in more ways than one."

"Derek taught me how to look at people, read their body motions and tell what they were thinking. A smirk meant that they were secretly laughing at me. A lifted eyebrow meant they were dubious. A shrug meant they didn't care one way or the other." There was another poignant pause before she continued. "And he taught me that a kiss between two caring persons was the most precious thing in the world."

"I'll bet he did," Rand muttered.

"Derek taught me to play cards. He always won. I didn't realize he was cheating until he won seven games and took all my pennies, and I saw the smug look on his face. I watched and learned how to palm a card just like he did."

"And did you teach Lee to cheat too?"

There was a faint rumble in Lindsay's throat. "Oh, he doesn't need to cheat. He's a good player."

"Go on," Rand urged.

"One holiday weekend, Maria was away so I couldn't go home and Derek's people didn't want to see him—they were embarrassed by his shaggy beard, long hair and baggy clothes—so we stayed at the rehab center in the hospital. We talked, laughed, hugged and we found that in spite of our injuries our bodies had needs, passionate needs." A long moment passed before she finished. "The result was quite unexpected."

"I'll just bet it was," Rand said, piqued.

"Maria had a fit, of course. She was horrified that she was going to be a grandmother. But the situation opened up another possibility. When Derek was well, he could look after me and she would be free to pursue her own life. She always wanted to go to Vancouver. That was Utopia to her.

"As soon as I could barely walk, she arranged a church wedding for us. I had always dreamed of being married in a long white wedding gown dressed with a lily-of-the-valley coronet holding my veil." Lindsay could feel her eyes tearing. "Instead, I wore a pale mauve dress, bobby pins holding my hair in place and a long skirt to hide my gimpy leg.

"Maria took the day off her, drove me to the hospital chapel—I had been living at home for the last two weeks and she had been driving me back and forth for treatment. Bonnie and several of the people from the rehabilitation unit had come to see us get married. The minister had even opened his Bible, ready, waiting. But it was a policeman who came." Lindsay sobbed softly, remembering. "He said Derek wasn't coming. There had been an accident; Derek had crashed his motorcycle into a bridge abutment. He was dead.

"Maria took me home and went to work. I was alone. Heartbroken, I cried until my eyes were raw. Then a knock came on the door. Bonnie Tobin. She held me, rocked me, cried with me and told me that even though God had taken something from me, He had given me something in return, Derek's baby. So I needed to get off that bed, say, 'thank you, God' and get on with the rest of my life.

"I didn't know until later, at Derek's funeral, when his mother accused me of causing her son's death, that he had been driving away from the church, not to it. It just added to my determination."

"Go on," Rand urged. "Talk about it. Get it out in the open..."

"I worked as long as I could and gratefully accepted the supermarket's maternity benefits. Since I was only part time, the benefits were small. I bought a bassinet and the necessary baby clothes at Goodwill and Bonnie taught me how to knit. She gave me books to read, talked to me about nutrition and baby care and what to expect before and after my baby was born.

"Six and a half months after I was left waiting at the altar, my son Lee was born. He was wrinkled and ugly but his tiny fingers wrapped around my heart. That night I swore on my bedside Bible that no one was ever going to take him away from me. Oh, Derek's parents made noises about wanting their grandson and Children's Aid thought I wouldn't be able to look after him, but I showed them all.

"As soon as I was able, I went back to work. Six months later, I became a full time cashier at the supermarket. That same weekend, Maria left for the west and Lee and I moved to a small, second floor apartments near the supermarket. Baby care was a block away. It was hard making ends meet, and without Bonnie's help, baby bonus and food stamps, we would never have made it.

"Lee's thirteen now and in spite of everything that's happened, I'm proud of him." Her last words got fainter and fainter and she closed her eyes, unsure that she heard his "And I'm proud of you."

"Come on, Lindsay. You've had a little catnap," Rand cajoled. "I listened to your life story. Don't you want to hear mine?"

"Nooo..." She just wanted to sleep. That way she could forget she was hungry, that she needed a facility. It was a long time since the Stop and Go fiasco. She could forget the storm, that Rand was hurt, that he was going to tell her how much he loved Rita...and Natalie. And she didn't want to hear it.

"Come on, Lindsay." A mitten hand cupped her face. "Just stay awake a little longer."

"Nooo," she repeated, but it was another "no" that Lindsay was hearing, a "no" from the past as a kaleidoscope of pictures flashed into her mind:

a little girl crying
an angry woman
suitcase, a truck
a little girl running
a man yelling, waving,
truck, moving, turning,
little girl falling,
screaming "Mama....
Mama..."

Twenty-one

"Lindsay, wake up! Wake up."

Strong arms were holding her.

Glancing up, Lindsay saw a sliver of light which hung like an invisible rope, drawing her upward. "It's all right, darling. It's all right. I got you. You're safe."

Rand cradled her, then kissed her brow and Lindsay relaxed.

"That's quite a trip you've been on," he said as he studied her face. "Are you feeling better?"

She thought for a moment, then replied softly, "I remember, Rand. I remember everything...the truck, the accident, my grandfather. Grandpa wasn't driving the truck that ran over me!" Lindsay's voice gained fervor. "Maria was. And all these years I have been blaming grandpa."

"But you didn't remember, darling," Rand soothed.

"That's why Maria wouldn't bring me back to Trailwood. She was afraid someone would tell me, or maybe that I would remember."

"Maybe a bit of both."

"How she must have hated me!"

"She didn't hate you, Lindsay. She hated herself."

"Every time I limped," Lindsay mused, "It reminded her of what she had done."

Rand gently massaged her shoulder with his mitt hand. "You must remember she did stay with you, looked after you until you were able to look after yourself...and Lee."

"And when Maria's money ran out—we lived lavishly back then—she had to come to Grandpa for money and he mortgaged Trailwood for us. He was old, not well and the farm was all he had left."

"Not everything, darling. He had you."

Lying quietly, mulling over the things she remembered, she felt Rand's body tighten in pain.

"Lindsay, can you move your leg a little? It's resting against mine and my leg's hurting like hell."

Slowly, carefully—their cave was so fragile—she lifted her left leg, moved it back a little. The muscles cramped. How long had it been since they had been catapulted through the air? Seven hours. Nine hours? Would morning ever come?

She was thirsty.

When she brought her mitt up to her mouth—there was a bit of snow on the tip—Rand pushed it away. "Don't do that."

"My mouth is so dry."

"The snow will only make it worse."

"Nothing can make it worse!" Lindsay cried. She was cold and hungry and she ached in places she didn't know existed before the accident.

"Why don't I tell you about my dream?"

"Your dream!"

"What's the matter? Don't you think a man my age can have dreams?"

Her tone slightly whimsical, she asked, "Why don't you tell me about this dream of yours?"

"I want to develop a school for young horsemen," he began slowly, "and older horsemen too."

Intrigued, she urged, "Go on..."

"It would be a school where men, maybe women too, could learn about horses and racing. How to be grooms, trainers, drivers. How to get the best out of their horse. And how to train and race their horses. To prevent drivers from urging their horses beyond their limits by using their skills and not the whip, and how to avoid accidents."

"Like my dad's.

Some accidents like Jeff Macaulay's can't be prevented, like a horse breaking a leg, going down and the driver being thrown," he said. "But, yes, maybe teaching about getting out of the way, perhaps turning your horse when an accident happens." He continued slowly as the ideas began to jell even more. "It would be a private school, open to men and women who are truly interested in the sport of racing."

"Where would you have such a school?"

"Windcrest. I've got the buildings, the paddock and it would be a simple matter to build a half-mile track beyond the barn. The school would be more hands-on than theory."

"And your house? Would you open it up for students or would they live away?"

As Rand talked and Lindsay listened and questioned, the hours passed and more light crept in through the crack in their roof.

"What time do you think it is?" she asked.

"Probably around seven."

Slowly Lindsay turned over, parted a couple of branches along the front of the cave and crawled out. She stood, her muscles shouting at every movement. Everything was covered in snow with only the brown tips of the fence posts and the evergreens breaking the pristine whiteness. How was anyone going to see them? Her red helmet. Atop a post, it could be a beacon of color.

She shivered. Her head felt cold without her helmet. What was a little more cold? She listened. Stretched. Then from across the silence, she heard the faint sound of snowmobile motors.

"Oh, Rand, they're coming." She fell to her knees beside him.

"Yes, love. I heard them." He kissed the tip of her nose, her cheek, pulled her close. She felt his tears on her cheek. They mixed with hers. She hadn't even known she was crying.

Suddenly the sound faded. "NO! No!" she cried, standing up, sending their fragile cave falling in on Rand.

"It's all right, darling. It's all right!" He pushed the branches and snow off his body. "They're just coming through the valley," he said as a rifle shot echoed through the stillness."

Looking back over her shoulder, she saw two snowmobiles flying over the rise. The drivers were crouched low, their bodies bent forward. They reminded Lindsay of two jockeys racing for the finish line.

Lindsay struggled to her feet, frantically waving her arms as she whispered a prayer of thankfulness. Then as they drew nearer, Lindsay could see that the larger machine was towing an ambulance sled. They had come prepared for any emergency.

Turning, she began to pull the branches away from their cave so the rescue team could get closer to Rand. It was such a joyous feeling seeing the rescuers racing toward them and she wanted Rand to experience it too.

Jim Everest was the first to jump off his machine. "Are you okay?" he asked, his eyes scanning Lindsay's face for a moment before reaching for a thermos tucked in his saddlebags.

Lindsay nodded. "Rand's hurt."

"Bad?" Jim poured two cups of coffee as called out a greeting to Rand.

"A broken leg, possibly a concussion," she said.

Jim's mouth tightened as he moved toward Rand with the other coffee. "You sure had us worried, old buddy," Lindsay heard him say. "But there was no way we could get to you last night. The storm came up too fast."

"We made out fine, didn't we, love?" Rand's eyes strayed past Jim to Lindsay.

She nodded as she clutched the cup tighter, letting its warmth seep through her mitts. It was hot and sickening sweet, but, oh, it tasted wonderful.

"Even in the daylight we had a hard time locating you," Bart Bartholomew added as he shut off his machine and manually slid the ambulance sled closer to Rand. "If it hadn't been for that red helmet of Lindsay's, we would have missed you." He gave her a light tap on the head as he walked past. "Do you think you can slide over onto the sled or are you going to need help?" he asked Rand.

"I'll probably need help." Rand grimaced as he tried to move his injured leg.

Jim crouched low at Rand's head, so he could grasp him under the arms.

Since the space was small, all Lindsay could do was watch.

"That's a nifty splint you have there," Bart commented as on the count of three, Jim lifted, Rand slid and Bert gently cradled the injured leg, sliding it to the sled. "Some of Lindsay's handiwork?"

Rand's face was drained of all color and beads of perspiration stood out on his forehead. He took a few deep breaths before looking at Lindsay. "She took very special care of me. No one could have done better."

Bart was just tucking the blankets around Rand when two other machines from different directions, one with Ned Pike trailing an ambulance sled, came racing across the snow.

Seeing Jim on the walkie-talkie, Ned pulled his snowmobile in close to Lindsay. "Are you all right?"

"Cold. Bruised." She managed a semblance of a smile. "Otherwise, all right."

By then, Jim, who had finished talking to someone at the Tamarack Village Clinic had squatted down beside Rand. "Dr. Brown, the staff doctor at the clinic, has arranged for a helicopter to pick you up at the Stop & Go Snack Bar. It's going to transport you to the London hospital where they have all the necessary equipment to look after your injuries. And Ned," Jim looked over to the man who was helping Lindsay onto his ambulance sled, "will take you to the clinic where Dr. Brown will look after you."

As Ned buckled the blankets around her, she heard Rand ask, "Why can't Lindsay go with me?"

"Because, Old Buddy, that leg of yours is going to need some special care, and that bump on your head probably needs to be looked at through the eyes of an MRI and that kind of attention isn't available at the clinic."

Bump on his head! Lindsay hadn't noticed any bump. What other injuries did he have that she didn't know about? Before she could ask Rand, his ambulance sled was off, heading in the direction of the Stop & Go and Ned was readying her for the ride to the clinic. She noticed a couple of others from the rescue unit were loading Rand's Sno- Hawk on a big sled and placing the broken pieces around it.

"Where are they taking it?" Lindsay asked Ned.

"To rescue headquarters. It will be inspected and a report sent to the office of the Department of Transport. As soon as he's able, Rand will have to file an accident report too." Ned gave her shoulder a squeeze before getting on his machine. "Don't worry. Certain procedures have to be followed. It's the law."

And they were off.

Lindsay must have fallen asleep during the ride to the clinic because she only became aware of her surroundings when Ned and a portly grey-haired man were lifting her onto the examining table.

Seeing fear flare in her eyes, Ned quickly assured her. "This is Dr. Brown, Lindsay. He's going to look after you."

"I must have fallen asleep," Lindsay whispered.

"You certainly did, young lady."And it's no wonder. From what Ned tells me, you haven't had much sleep in the last thirty-six hours," Dr. Brown said.

Lindsay nodded her head in agreement.

"Well, for at least the next twenty-four, Nurse Mary McCarthy," he nodded toward the nurse pulling down the zipper of her snowmobile suit, "and her assistant Lillian Adams are going to take care of you." Lindsay could feel someone removing her boots.

Twenty-four hours! "I have to get home to my son," Lindsay protested, trying to sit up. McCarthy chose that moment to pull her snowmobile suit off her shoulders while Nurse Adam tugged on its legs. In seconds, all Lindsay had on were her socks, pants and sweater, and before she could say "Jack Robinson"—her great grandmother's saying—and she was being covered by a white sheet. And Ned was gone.

While the doctor questioned, checked and listened, Lindsay's fidgeted. She wanted to get home to Lee. When her gurney started to move, Dr. Brown said, "The nurses are going to take you to x-ray now, Miss Macaulay. We want to make sure that leg of yours is all right and I think we should have a few pictures taken of your chest and head. Just to be sure you haven't any hidden injuries."

Somewhere between the emergency room and the completion of the x-rays, the formal Miss Macaulay became plain Lindsay. Half asleep from weariness, she was wheeled to a small room, transferred to a hospital bed, an IV inserted in the back of her hand, given a few sips of broth and heard Dr. Brown say, "We're going to let you go to sleep now."

"Lee..." she murmured.

"We'll let your son know that his mom is all right." Dr. Brown patted her arm.

Satisfied, Lindsay closed her eyes and, according to the wall clock, when she opened them, it was more than twenty-one hours later.

"You're finally awake," McCarthy spoke from the doorway. "You've almost slept the clock around."

"Oh, no!" Lindsay exclaimed as she threw the covers back and swung her feet off the bed.

"Not so fast," the nurse cautioned as she put Lindsay's legs back under the covers. "You can't get up. Not until the doctor says so, and he's not here right now."

"Where is he? I have to talk to him," Lindsay said, reluctantly settled back on the pillows.

"Dr. Brown lives at the Tamarack Lodge when he's on call. I'll call him and tell him you're awake."

While they waited, McCarthy explained that Dr. Brown, a retired medical practitioner crowding sixty-five, liked to keep involved in medicine and so he volunteered three days a week at the village clinic. "Doctors are badly needed in these isolated rural areas," she told Lindsay.

She explained, as she straightened the covers on Lindsay's bed, that the emergency center had a direct line to the clinic. "When Jim Everest called, we already knew that two people were missing, possibly injured. When you were found and Jim assessed the situation, he talked directly to Dr. Brown and he decided that the London Hospital was the best place to handle Rand's injuries. He called for a helicopter to pick Rand up at the Stop & Go. He was sure we could deal with any injuries you had."

"Rand? Mr. Dyson...have you heard how he is?" Lindsay asked.

McCarthy shook her head. "But the doctor might have..." She halted as Dr. Brown sauntered in.

"They operated on his leg last night," he said, scanning Lindsay's chart. "And *no*, young lady, you can't go home. That bad leg of yours needs a couple of days of complete rest."

"But I have responsibilities..."

"I'm sure you have." He sympathized but remained adamant. "You've taxed that leg of yours beyond its limits and if you don't want it to break down, you've got to give it a couple of days of complete rest."

However, Dr. Brown did relent a little: Lindsay could make two telephone calls,_providing_she kept them short, and *providing*_they didn't upset her.

Lindsay called home and sighed with relief when Lee's "hello" came over the line.

"Hello, darling."

"Mom! Are you all right? We've been so worried."

"Just a few minor things. Nothing to worry about. I'm just tired, that's all."

"Oh, Mom, I was so afraid!"

"It was an accident. It could happen to anyone." Not wanting to dwell on the accident, Lindsay asked, "Is Bonnie there?" Although she couldn't see him, she was sure he nodded his head.

After asking how she was *really,* Bonnie assured her that Lee was fine, the horses were fine and the filly, according to Art, had grown an inch. "There was a call this morning from that student who was studying barn structure. He wants to come again for a weekend. He said he'd call back later today. What should I tell him?"

"Just get his number and I'll call him in a few days and arrange a date."

"I almost forgot," Bonnie said "You had another call: Asher Honeyborne. He was sorry about your accident and he would call in a couple of days. He said it was very important that he talk to you."

Seeing the nurse in the doorway, Lindsay knew her time was up.

"Just one more short one." Lindsay held her right forefinger up. "And you can dial the number." She had gotten the London Health Science Center number from the telephone directory in the drawer of her bedside table.

McCarthy dialed, got Rand's room telephone and handed the phone to Lindsay. Oh, just to hear his voice! Lindsay waited. But it wasn't Rand who answered. It was Natalie.

"Rand's having his leg x-rayed again. They operated yesterday and put a cast on. Now they want to check and make sure everything's okay." There was a short pause before Natalie continued, "Rand called me early this morning. He wants me to put a special notice in the newspaper for him."

"A special notice...?"

"Surely, you can guess..."

Yes, she could guess. An engagement announcement. Choking back a sob, Lindsay said she was glad Rand was all right and said goodbye. *Rand had called Natalie. He hadn't called her. She had thought*...and the tears flowed like water over Niagara.

That's how Dr. Brown found Lindsay a half hour later. "That's it," he said. "No more calls, and no more crying or you're not going home tomorrow."

Twenty-two

The sun was shining, the snow melting and Lindsay was going home. Dr. Brown had given his provisional okay, if she took it easy; if she didn't overtax that leg, he would discharge her after breakfast. If he'd suspected that she would lie through her teeth to get home to Lee and Trailwood, he hadn't let on. Besides that, Bonnie's vacation was almost over and she had to go back to work at the rehab unit at the hospital.

Lindsay didn't tell Dr. Brown she intended to drive herself home. Her truck and luggage were still at the Tamarack Lodge a half mile away. While she was wondering how she was going to get from the clinic to her truck, the receptionist told her someone was waiting at the front desk.

Lindsay was surprised to see Art Winston pacing back and forth, and when he saw her, he held out his arms, an infectious grin on his angular face.

"Oh, am I ever glad to see you!" she cried. He was part of her family now, the uncle she didn't have, the friend she wanted, the mentor that Lee needed. "There were times...

"I know," Art said, a little embarrassed by his own display of emotion. He asked, "Are you ready?"

"As soon as I say a good-bye to my nurse." Lindsay assumed Art had his truck—maybe she could hire Aubrey Monahan to follow them in her old truck. Minutes later, his hand under her arm, Art guided her toward Rand's Lincoln parked in the patient area beside the front door of the clinic. Sensing her question, he said, "Rand called me last night. Told me to take you home in the Lincoln. You didn't need to be bumped around in any old truck, like yours or mine."

Lindsay really didn't hear anything except *'Rand called me last night.'*

"Ned Pike brought Lee and me over yesterday afternoon to pick up your truck and suitcases," Art continued, not giving her a chance to get a word in edgewise as he held the car door open and helped her in. "Your painting case was sure light. You must have done well."

"The sales were better than I had ever hoped." She looked at him questioningly when he tucked a blanket around her legs.

"I'm pampering you, that's all. Rand's orders."

Rand again. Why couldn't he have called her? The nurse could have brought her the telephone. Unless, unless he felt the accident was her fault, not the accident per se, but the reason he had taken a different route. She remembered that he and Jim were having a heated discussion at the Stop & Go before the snowmobilers took off. She thought it was about her. So, *maybe* in a way she was responsible. Now wasn't the time to think about it. Now was the time to accept the miracle of going home to her family.

"Ned told me that you had named the foal Jeb's Dream, Dream for short." Art stopped at the end of drive, looked both ways before turning onto the highway. "Your grandfather would have loved that."

"It popped out." She shrugged. "I didn't want to say that we hadn't named her yet."

"Jeb's Dream." Art rolled the name over his tongue. "Nice combination. Rand thinks so too."

"I wonder why he didn't tell me that," Lindsay said.

"I asked him if he had been talking to you," Art said, not taking his eyes off the road. "Said he had been talking to Dr. Brown, but what he wanted to say to you was private and he wanted to say it in person."

Was he going to tell her that he was in love with Natalie, that making a wish on a rainbow meant nothing, that it was only casual flirtation at a convention? He and Natalie went back years, had similar backgrounds, similar interests...the best of the best.

Lindsay laid her head back against the headrest as Art extolled the foal's wonderful qualities.

"She even nibbled out of my hand, her little tail going back and forth like a metronome. And she likes to be brushed and curried."

Somewhere over the miles, Art switched their conversation to the accident. He said Birdie Pike had been the first to call the house. She assured them Rand was an experienced snowmobiler and even if the rescue team couldn't get to them until morning Lindsay and Rand would be all right. "It was a long night for us," Art said. He had stayed the night at Trailwood with Bonnie and Lee.

Sooner than she realized it, they were nearing home. There was their white frame house, the octangular barn, their mail box with Trailwood on the side. For one fleeting second as Art turned into their lane, Lindsay thought she saw a stoop-shouldered man with thick white hair waving to her. Her grandfather. He was welcoming her home.

Lindsay didn't have time to think about the apparition as Art stopped, the passenger's door was pulled open and before she could get out of the car, she was wrapped in Lee's bear hug. "Oh, Mom. I'm so glad you're home. I was so afraid!"

"So was I, Lee. So was I." Lindsay held him close for a long moment. Then as she stood, Bonnie hugged her, wrapped an arm around her waist and guided her toward the veranda and the wafting smells of pot roast and apple pie from the kitchen. Art trailed behind, carrying a shopping bag of personal items.

The next hour sped by on winged feet. Art wondered about Rand becoming lost in an area he knew so well. "Must have had other things on his mind." He mumbled the answer to himself.

"How did you find that snow cave, Mom?' Before she could answer, Lee had another question. "Weren't you afraid it would fall in on you? How big was it? How wide?

"About six feet by two feet," she managed between questions.

Everyone laughed when Lee added, "You sure must have had to lay close, Mom."

Bonnie picked the perfect time to assume her aunt-friend-mentor role and ushered Lindsay off to bed. In spite of the hours of sleep at the clinic, Lindsay was still tired. It wasn't until later when Art and Lee had gone to the barn to do the chores and Bonnie was packing for her trip back to Toronto that Lindsay slipped unnoticed down the stairs. She wanted to call the London hospital, hoping to talk to Rand or at least find out how he was.

"London Health Science Center," the receptionist answered.

"I'm calling from Riverton. I would like to speak to Rand Dyson, please."

"I'll put you through to his room."

"Thank you." And Lindsay waited and waited.

Finally a nurse came on the line. "I'm sorry. Mr. Dyson is not accepting any calls," and the line went dead.

Had Rand's condition worsened? Maybe the nurse wasn't allowed to say. On the heels of that thought came another—was Rand refusing everyone's calls or only hers? That question continued to plague her as she crept back up the stairs to bed and relived all the hours and conversations she had with Rand. She could feel his arms about her, taste his lips, glory in the sensual warmness that had flowed through her body. She even remembered the last thing he had said, "Take care of her, Jim. She's special."

And her love was special.

It was that love that had given her the strength to plough through deep snow to get tree limbs to close the opening of their cave, stay awake when she desperately wanted to sleep, share secrets she had never shared with anyone. And hadn't that sliver of light above Rand's shoulder trigger her memory, the memory of those ten lost years?

There were good times too. Lindsay remembered a Christmas party at school when she was eight. She had to recite a monologue about a preacher and a bear, but that night at home everything seemed to go wrong. Daddy was late for supper and Maria was angry. A button came off Lindsay's skirt band and Maria didn't have time to sew it on, so she put a safety pin in it. During the monologue, when the preacher was praying for his life, the safety pin came open, jabbed into Lindsay's side, and instead of saying "Amen," she had cried, "Ouch!" Looking up, she saw Maria covering her nose and mouth with her hands. Daddy was grinning and Grandpa was laughing and clapping.

In another revolving kaleidoscope, Lindsay saw a little girl sitting on a sulky cart wedged between her father's legs, his big hands covering hers as she held the reins. In her mind's ear, she could hear the whiz of the cart's wheels, feel the dust on her face as they had jogged round the track.

Another night was special because everyone was happy. After supper, while Maria and Dad did the dishes,—she washed and he dried—Lindsay and Grandpa played Chinese checkers. Sometimes, when her dad was passing behind her, supposedly putting away a dish, he'd put a finger on hers and move a checker and Grandpa would scold, "No fair. Two against one." And everyone, including Maria, had laughed.

Those years had been taken away by a wheel and an accident that had smashed her leg to smithereens. Somehow, she had remembered little things: to call her mother Maria instead of mother, not to argue with her mother when she was angry, or question any of her decisions. And Lindsay remembered a doctor saying, "Selective memory loss is usually caused by some horrific event."

Now she remembered those missing years: they had come on the threads of a sliver of light that filtered through the roof of their snow cave. And Rand had been holding her in his arms.

Lindsay was proud of that freckled ten-year-old girl, who against all odds had learned to walk without a limp. It had taken courage and guts and tears.

Those same qualities were going to help her rebuild Trailwood to its rightful place in the community. She was proud of her heritage and she was going to continue driving that old rattletrap because it was part of those years. She was going to teach Lee to hold his head high, be proud of being a Macaulay. And if Rand wasn't in their lives, so be it.

First, she needed to practice what she preached, she thought. Put her pride in her pocket and go to the London hospital and see Rand, get things straightened out between them. He said he wanted the best. Well, she *was* the best for him. Not Natalie with her social graces, her education, her rich background, but Lindsay, the girl who danced in his arms, saw a rainbow and gave him her heart. No one could love him more.

The next day after Lee had gone to school and Art had taken Bonnie to Toronto, she was going to catch the eleven o'clock train to London. See Rand. Talk to him.

But as Bobby Burns had said so long ago, "the best laid plans...go awry."

~ * ~

Lindsay awoke hours later to the grinding of the school bus's creaky brakes as it stopped to pick up Lee. She had slept almost eighteen hours. Dressing quickly, she went downstairs where Bonnie's "good morning" was interrupted by a blast of cold air from the doorway and Art's "Truck's gassed. Oil's checked. I'll be ready to go when you are."

By ten o'clock, the house was quiet, even the creaks weren't creaking. Only the radio blared the news that the market price of grain was holding steady and the weather was going to be fine and she had plenty of time to catch the train to London and see Rand.

Her plans changed when a big man with a protruding stomach carrying a briefcase knocked at her door. Asher Honeyborne.

After apologizing for coming unannounced, commiserating with her about her accident, he then explained that he had been ill. "Shortly after I saw you last, I had a major heart attack and my doctor ordered a long vacation. I got back to work on Monday." He opened his briefcase. "I know that at one time you were anxious to sell Trailwood."

"That's true," Lindsay said. "But I have changed my mind. I'm going to rebuild Trailwood."

"The offer was given to me yesterday, and I believe it is too good for you to refuse," Honeyborne continued as if he hadn't heard her. "An anonymous buyer, a numbered company, will pay twenty per cent above market value for Trailwood."

"I agree that's a good offer." Lindsay's eyebrows had hitched up a notch. "But Trailwood is not for sale. It is our home and our heritage and I've no intention of selling."

"Miss Macaulay, you simply *can't* turn down an offer like this," he interrupted. "Think about what you can do with the money—go back to the city, buy a house, put money away for a college education for your son, take a vacation. I'll bet you've never had a Florida vacation."

"No, Mr. Honeyborne, I never have," Lindsay answered. "But I'm still not going to sell."

"Someone who was at the convention mentioned that you had a new foal, a golden cross, I believe," he continued. "Of course, the value of the mare and filly would be added to the initial price."

Lindsay hated being pressured. Customers had often used this tactic at the checkout register of the supermarket when they wanted a product at a lower price. They would argue that it was damaged, a flyer had given a lower price; they only had enough money for the price on the item.

Her chin jutted up a notch. "I am *not* going to sell Trailwood, Mr. Honeyborne, and that's final." She moved toward the door.

"If you should change your mind…" He placed his business card on the table. "It's a very good offer," he added as he closed his briefcase and reluctantly left.

Lindsay was angry. Not just at Honeyborne but at the person or persons behind the numbered company. Why now, when she had secured a mortgage and was preparing to rebuild Trailwood? And she had a golden cross foal. Could there be any connection? Or did someone simply want the Macaulays to leave Trailwood and Riverton County?

Lindsay wished Bonnie were still there. Would Bonnie advise her to sell? That was unlikely as she was impressed with the farm and the horses. Instead, she would have probably advised that Lindsay find out who was behind this overly generous offer.

Suddenly another thought galloped into Lindsay's mind. What if Rand was part of that numbered company? His stallion had sired her golden cross, which would make Starmist even more valuable. She had already offered him Jeb's Dream when she learned that Starmist was the sire of Princess's offspring. He had turned her down.

It couldn't be Rand! Yet if Lindsay remembered her high school literature, didn't Shakespeare say, "Modest doubt is called the beacon of the wise." Right then, she needed to be wise.

She had to talk to Rand, see his face. A customer once had told her that thoughts were often unwittingly transmitted through the eyes. She had caught several shoplifters over the years, but reading their body language and the smidgeon of guilt that was mirrored in their eyes.

She glanced at her watch. She called the station...maybe if she hurried. "Passengers are just boarding," the station agent told her. "Next train west is at eight o'clock."

Lindsay thanked him; she would have to catch the morning one. She knew the extra day would give her body a chance to regain its strength, but she felt jittery, on edge. She needed to keep busy, so shrugging into her coat, tucking her feet in her boots, grabbing a couple of apples from the frig for the mares, she was off to the barn.

Feeding the two mares, talking to them, hugging the foal, was the balm her troubled thoughts needed and she found that she was able to tackle the rest of the day with confidence and aplomb. She would take the train tomorrow.

Twenty-three

Standing close to the window, Lindsay watched the engine of the Northwestern slip into the station as clouds of grey air swished from the train's brakes. It was too soon to go outside. After her sojourn in the cave, she wasn't anxious to experience the cold. *Someone must have felt the same,* she thought, as she watched the station door open. Why didn't they hurry? Didn't they know they were letting in the winter cold?

Then she saw the rubber tip of a crutch and looking upwards she saw a tall man in a sheepskin coat and buttons that three months ago had become tangled with her scarf.

"Rand!"

She forgot about Natalie, Asher's offer to purchase...everything. He was here! She was across the room, hugging him, kissing him, almost knocking him off balance.

"Whoa! Take it easy. I'm fragile, you know," he teased lightly.

"I'm so glad to see you!" Tears trickled down her cheeks.

"Lindsay, we have to talk." He backed her away from the door. "But not here."

"Talk?" She drew back as she traced a line along his cheek, noticing that he was a bit thinner since the accident. "I was coming to London to see you."

"I was discharged this morning," Rand said, holding her away from him. "Mac Townsend picked me up earlier and we went straight to Trailwood to see you. When you weren't at the house, Mac went to the stable to look for you for me. Art was there brushing the filly; he told Mac you were taking the late morning train to the city. So, we came..."

"Rand, should you be out of the hospital?"

"My leg will be in a cast for six to eight weeks. And my head...well, I just have to take it easy for a while."

"But you're here!" She could hardly believe it.

"Lindsay, we have to talk."

She pulled back. Looked up in his face, saw the worry lines, the concern in his eyes. Had he come to tell her in person that he was involved with Natalie and what they had shared was just a light romance, that didn't mean anything?

She had her pride.

Gulping a sob, she searched for the right words. "Rand, when two people are thrown together as we were, they tend to say things, do things they wouldn't do or say under normal circumstance."

She saw Rand's jaw tighten. "You think that's that happened to us?" A coldness crept into his voice as his grey-blue eyes searched her face. "Is that why you were catching the train, to tell me you didn't love me, that what we had was just an interlude?"

Lindsay hesitated. How could she tell him she didn't love him when her heart was breaking in a zillion pieces.

"Well, is that it?"

"I was anxious about you," she whispered.

"Anxious!" His eyes searched the depth of hers. "Anxious?" Suddenly his tone changed. "You should be home resting, not waiting in a station for a train."

"You called Natalie...everyone...but me." She couldn't keep the tremor from her voice.

"No, Lindsay. She came and we talked." He wiped a tear from Lindsay's cheek. "And so that she had a reason for coming to the hospital, I did ask her to put a thank you notice in the paper." He continued, slowly, "Pride can be a very humbling experience and it hurts like hell."

Stifling a sob, Lindsay nodded.

"There was a time, I admit, when I was perfectly content to settle for Natalie," Rand said. "She was a good companion and I respected her. But I never loved her."

"Your scientific approach—the best to the best."

"For horses. Not people." He wobbled slightly on his crutches. "That was before you."

"Before me..."

"Damn it, Lindsay. I can't propose to you standing on crutches in a railroad station!"

Suddenly, her heartbreak exploded into joy. "Why not?" she sniffed. "I fell in love with you in a stable...over the back of a filly."

A warming smile slipped across Rand's face as he moved slowly to the nearest bench. "That long ago, eh?"

Before reaching for Lindsay's hands, he sat, placing his crutches at his feet. Neither noticed the ticket agent watching them from his window.

Leaning forward, Rand kissed the tip of Lindsay's nose. "Woman, I knew you were trouble almost from the first moment I saw you, you and that red hair and gimpy leg." His mouth was a breath away. "I admit I tried to stay away from you. But when you called to tell me about your new filly, I knew that day that you felt something too." His voice deepened as he brought her hand to his mouth, kissed her fingers.

"Love is strange thing; it sneaks up on you, and that's what you did, my darling. You blind-sided me. Then, that night at the lodge, you turned me away and I was angry, hurt, and Natalie was there, saying all the things I wanted to hear."

Lindsay interrupted. "That was one of the reasons I was coming to see you, Rand. Explain. If we had made love that night, and I wanted to, oh, so much! But I would have been setting a double standard. One set of rules for Lee and a different set for me."

"I know." He pulled her into his arms. "After I got over being angry, and frustrated, I understood." He punctuated each phrase with a kiss.

"Rand, I want a marriage like my grandparents had, the death do us part kind. Oh, they had their disagreements and drag-out fights, but before they went to sleep, she would hook her foot over his ankle and wiggle her backside into the hollow between his knees and stomach. And he would gather her close. That's what I want for me.

"It must have been quite a marriage," he mused. "I can see why you would want the same."

"And I want the man I marry to be proud of me, and when my leg gives me trouble and I can't dance at someone's wedding, we'll dance later in the privacy of our bedroom.

He smiled down at her. "Anything else?"

"I have a son…"

"Yes, darling, you have a son, another man's child." He tipped her chin up so he could look in her eyes. "And I admit that gave me a few bad moments until I realized it didn't really matter. He was *your* son and I loved him because he was part of you. And I wanted to teach him things, about horses and friendships, but then I discovered much to my chagrin that he was learning all those things from Art and I was jealous."

"Oh, Rand…"

"When Lee got into trouble at school, beat the crap out of that bully, I was so proud of him. I'm sorry I couldn't tell you that day. If Hunter had seen me talking to you, he might have sensed how I felt about you and had second thoughts. After all, he is Natalie's father."

Rand cupped her face between his hands. "I love you, Lindsay Macaulay."

"And I love you."

He pulled her close, his mouth claimed hers as his tongue did a rainbow dance with hers, demanding a response she couldn't deny and igniting a passion either was powerless to control.

And the train left the station. The ticket agent slammed a door and sanity slowly returned. "Darling, I think we should leave."

"Sweetheart, let me finish. I want to adopt Lee, be the father he never had, and, God willing, maybe you and I will have a son or daughter with this red hair." He curled a strand around his finger. "And together we will rebuild Trailwood, You can set up a trust in Lee's name so that it will always be a Macaulay heritage farm."

"Oh Rand, I do love you and I want to marry you." Her heart was so full of happiness she thought it would burst. She picked up his crutches.

"Lindsay, I'm going to leave the college, something I've wanted to do for some time. I'm going to open a private school for horsemen. I'm going to stress safety ahead of profit and teach drivers how to react when an accident happens, and unfortunately they will happen."

"If you can prevent just one...." Lindsay opened the station door.

There were only two vehicles in the parking lot, a Lincoln with Mac Townsend asleep behind the wheel and an old rattletrap that had seen better days.

For the two lovers, it was just a horseman's delight.

Epilogue

Ten years later
Riverton Racing News:

Lee Macaulay of the Trailwood Stable, a recent graduate of the Dyson School of Harness Racing, won his first race at the Riverton Raceway, driving Dreamstar, as his mother, Lindsay Macaulay Dyson and Lee's eight-year-old twin brothers Jeff and Jeb, cheered him on.

Meet

Irene Crawford-Siano

Irene Crawford-Siano began to write as an escape from the hectic hours of being a wife, mother and office supervisor of her husband's trucking business. Her first efforts were all regrets, but she jumped for joy when she received a check for $5 for a birthday story. From then on Irene went on to write bigger and better stories. Then a major newspaper offered her the opportunity of writing a weekly column, *"Senior Side of Living"*, and it became the main focus of her career for the next ten years. In between she managed to write 9 non-fiction books and several short articles.

In 2013 Irene was honored with the Queen Elizabeth 2 Silver Jubilee Medal for her writing. Now a widow with grandchildren, she has returned to her first love, writing fiction romances, which she says "keeps her young at heart:"

VISIT OUR WEBSITE
FOR THE FULL INVENTORY
OF QUALITY BOOKS:

http://www.wings-press.com

Quality trade paperbacks and downloads
in multiple formats,
in genres ranging from light romantic comedy to general fiction
and horror. Wings has something
for every reader's taste.
Visit the website, then bookmark it.
We add new titles each month!

83工 KV W

45103373R00123